LOST AT THE EARTH'S CORE

When the great dirigible, the O-220, sailed away from
the inner world of Pellucidar, it left behind one member
of its crew, a brave man they thought lost forever amid
the unexplored terrors of that primeval land.

That man was Lieutenant von Horst, and BACK TO
THE STONE AGE is the story of the strange adventures
that befell him as he wandered, friendless and alone,
from one danger to another. Here also is the story of the
love of this cultured man for a barbarian slave girl who
discouraged him and ran away from him for a strange
purpose that keeps the reader guessing to the very end.

Here is a thrilling novel of mighty beasts, savage men,
weird monsters, and human courage that rivals anything
you have ever read before.

EDGAR RICE BURROUGHS
1875-1950

One of Chicago's most famous sons was Edgar Rice Burroughs. Young Burroughs tried his hand at many businesses without success, until, at the age of thirty-five, he turned to writing. With the publication of *Tarzan of the Apes* and *A Princess of Mars,* his career was assured. The gratitude of a multitude of readers who found in his imagination exactly the kind of escape reading they loved assured him of a large fortune.

Edgar Rice Burroughs died at home in a town bearing the name of his brain child, Tarzana, California. But, to the countless millions who have enjoyed his works, he will live forever.

EDGAR RICE BURROUGHS

BACK TO THE STONE AGE

Original Title: Seven Worlds to Conquer

SF
ace books
A Division of Charter Communications Inc.
A GROSSET & DUNLAP COMPANY
51 Madison Avenue
New York, New York 10010

COVER PAINTING BY FRANK FRAZETTA

This Ace printing: January 1982

A SPECIAL ANNOUNCEMENT TO ALL
ERB ENTHUSIASTS

Because of the widespread, continuing interest in the books of Edgar Rice Burroughs, we are listing below the names and addresses of various ERB fan club magazines. Additional information may be obtained from the editors of the magazines themselves.

—THE EDITORS

ERB-DOM
Rt. 2, Box 119
Clinton, LA 70722

THE BURROUGHS BIBLIOPHILES
6657 Locust Street
Kansas City, Missouri 64131

THE JASOOMIAN
P. O. Box 1305
Yuba City, California 95991

TBN (THE BURROUGHS NEWSBEAT)
110 South Shore Drive
Clear Lake, Iowa 50428

ERBANIA
8001 Fernview Lane
Tampa, Florida 33615

I

LIVING DEATH

THE ETERNAL noonday sun of Pellucidar looked down upon such a scene as the outer crust of earth may not have witnessed for countless ages past, such a scene as only the inner world of the earth's core may produce today.

Hundreds of saber-toothed tigers were driving countless herbivorous animals into a clearing in a giant forest; and two white men from the outer crust were there to see, two white men and a handful of black warriors from far distant Africa.

The men had come in a giant dirigible with others of their kind through the north polar opening at the top of the world at the urgent behest of Jason Gridley, but that is a story that has been once told.

This is the story of the one who was lost.

"It doesn't seem possible," exclaimed Gridley, "that five hundred miles below our feet automobiles are dashing through crowded streets lined by enormous buildings; that there the telegraph, the telephone, and the radio are so commonplace as to excite no comment; that countless thousands live out their entire lives without ever having to use a weapon in self-defense, and yet at the same instant we stand here facing saber-toothed tigers in surroundings that may not have existed upon the outer crust since a million years."

"Look at them!" exclaimed von Horst. "Look at what

they've driven into this clearing already, and more coming."

There were great ox-like creatures with shaggy coats and wide-spreading horns. There were red deer and sloths of gigantic size. There were mastodons and mammoths, and a huge, elephantine creature that resembled an elephant and yet did not seem to be an elephant at all. Its great head was four feet long and three feet broad. It had a short, powerful trunk and from its lower jaw mighty tusks curved downward, their points bending inward toward the body. At the shoulder it stood at least ten feet above the ground, and in length it must have been fully twenty feet. But what resemblance it bore to an elephant was lessened by its small, pig-like ears.

The two white men, momentarily forgetting the tigers behind them in their amazement at the sight ahead, halted and looked with wonder upon the huge gathering of creatures within the clearing. But it soon became apparent that if they were to escape with their lives they must reach the safety of the trees before they were either dragged down by the sabertooths or trampled to death by the frightened herbivores which were already milling around looking for an avenue of escape.

"There is still one opening ahead of us, bwana," said Muviro, the black chief of the Waziri.

"We shall have to run for it," said Gridley. "The beasts are all headed in our direction now. Give them a volley, and then beat it for the trees. If they charge, it will be every man for himself."

The volley turned them back for an instant; but when they saw the great cats behind them, they wheeled about once more in the direction of the men.

"Here they come!" cried von Horst. Then the men broke into a run as they sought to reach the trees that offered the only sanctuary.

Gridley was bowled over by a huge sloth; then he scrambled to his feet just in time to leap from the path of a fleeing mastodon and reach a tree just as the main body of the stampeding herd closed about it. A moment later, temporarily safe among the branches, he looked about for his companions; but none was in sight, nor could any living thing so puny as man have remained alive beneath that solid mass of leaping, plunging, terrified beasts. Some of his fellows, he felt sure, might have reached the forest in safety; but he feared for von Horst, who had been some little distance in rear of the Waziri. But Lieutenant Wilhelm von Horst had escaped. In fact, he had succeeded in running some little distance into the forest without having to take to the trees. He had borne off to the right away from the escaping animals, which had veered to the left after they entered the forest. He could hear them thundering away in the distance, squealing and trumpeting, grunting and bellowing.

Winded and almost exhausted, he sat down at the foot of a tree to catch his breath and rest. He was very tired, and just for a moment he closed his eyes. The sun was directly overhead. When he opened his eyes again the sun was still directly overhead. He realized that he had dozed, but he thought that it had been for but an instant. He did not know that he had slept for a long time. How long, who may say? For how may time be measured in this timeless world whose stationary sun hangs eternally motionless at zenith?

The forest was strangely silent. No longer did he hear the trumpeting and squealing of the herbivores or the growls and snarls of the cats. He called aloud to attract the attention of his friends, but there was no response; then he set out in search of them, taking what he thought was a direct route back toward the main camp where the dirigible was moored and toward which he knew they would be sure to go. But instead of going north, as he should have done, he went west.

Perhaps it was just as well that he did, for presently he heard voices. He stopped and listened. Men were approaching. He heard them distinctly, but he could not recognize their language. They might be friendly; but, in this savage world, he doubted it. He stepped from the trail he had been following and concealed himself behind a clump of bushes, and a moment later the men that he had heard came into view. They were Muviro and his warriors. They were speaking the dialect of their own African tribe. At sight of them von Horst stepped into the trail. They were as glad to see him as he was to see them. Now if they could but find Gridley they would be happy; but they did not find him, though they searched for a long time.

Muviro knew no better than von Horst where they were or the direction of camp; and he and his warriors were much chagrined to think that they, the Waziri, could be lost in any forest. As they compared notes it seemed evident that each had made a large circle in opposite directions after they had separated. Only thus could they account for their coming together face to face as they had, since each insisted that he had not at any time retraced his steps.

The Waziri had not slept, and they were very tired. Von Horst, on the contrary had slept and was rested; so, when they found a cave that would give them all shelter, the Waziri went in where it was dark and slept while von Horst sat on the ground at the mouth of the cave and tried to plan for the future. As he sat there quietly a large boar passed; and, knowing that they would require meat, the man rose and stalked it. It had disappeared around a curve in the trail; but though he thought that he was close behind it he never seemed to be able to catch sight of it again, and there was such a patchwork of trails crossing and crisscrossing that he was soon confused and started back toward the cave.

He had walked a considerable distance before he realized that he was lost. He called Muviro's name aloud, but there was no response; then he stopped and tried very carefully to figure out in what direction the cave must be. He looked up at the sun mechanically, as though it might help him. It hung at zenith. How could he plot a course where there were no stars but only a sun that hung perpetually straight above one's head? He swore under his breath and set out again. He could only do his best.

For what seemed a very long time he plodded on, but it was still noon. Often, mechanically, he glanced up at the sun, the sun that gave him no bearings nor any hint of the lapse of time, until he came to hate the shining orb that seemed to mock him. The forest and the jungle teemed with life. Fruits and flowers and nuts grew in profusion. He never need lack for a variety of food if he but knew which he might safely eat and which he might not. He was very hungry and thirsty, and it was the latter that worried him most. He had a pistol and plenty of ammunition. In this lush game country he could always provide himself with meat, but he must have water. He pushed on. It was water that he was looking for now more than for his companions or for camp. He commenced to suffer from thirst, and he became very tired again and sleepy. He shot a large rodent and drank its blood; then he made a fire and cooked the carcass. It was only half cooked beneath the surface which was charred in places. Lieutenant Wilhelm von Horst was a man accustomed to excellent food properly prepared and served, but he tore at the carcass of his unsavory kill like a famished wolf and thought that no meal had ever

11

tasted more delicious. He did not know how long he had been without food. Now he slept again, this time in a tree; for he had caught a glimpse of a great beast through the foliage of the jungle, a beast with enormous fangs and blazing eyes.

Again, when he awoke, he did not know how long he had slept; but the fact that he was entirely rested suggested that it had been a long time. He felt that it was entirely possible in a world where there was no time that a man might sleep a day or a week. How was one to know? The thought intrigued him. He commenced to wonder how long he had been away from the dirigible. Only the fact that he had not quenched his thirst since he had been separated from his comrades suggested that it could not have been but a day or two, though now he was actually suffering for water. It was all that he could think of. He started off in search of it. He must have water! If he didn't he would die—die here alone in this terrible forest, his last resting place forever unknown to any human being. Von Horst was a social animal; and, as such, this idea was repugnant to him. He was not afraid to die; but this seemed such an entirely futile end—and he was very young, still in his twenties.

He was following a game trail. There were many of them; they crossed and crisscrossed all through the forest. Some of them must lead to water; but which one? He had chosen the one he was following because it was broader and more plainly marked than the others. Many beasts had passed along it and, perhaps, for an incalculable time, for it was worn deep; and von Horst reasoned that more animals would follow a trail that led to water than would follow any other trail. He was right. When he came to a little river, he gave a cry of delight and ran to it and threw himself face down upon the bank. He drank in great gulps. Perhaps it should have harmed him, but it did not. It was a clean little river that ran among boulders over a gravelly bottom, a gem of a river that carried on its bosom to the forest and the lowlands the freshness and the coolness and the beauty of the mountains that gave it birth. Von Horst buried his face in the water, he let it purl over his bare arms, he cupped his hands and dipped it up and poured it over his head, he revelled in it. He felt that he had never known a luxury so rare, so desirable. His troubles vanished. Everything would be all right now—he had water! Now he was safe!

He looked up. Upon the opposite bank of the little river squatted such a creature as was never in any book, the bones of which were never in any museum. It resembled a gigantic winged kangaroo with the head of a reptile, pterodactyl-like in its long, heavily fanged jaws. It was watching von Horst intently, its cold, reptilian, lidless eyes staring at him expressionlessly. There was something terribly menacing in its fixed gaze. The man started to rise slowly; then the hideous thing came to sudden life. With a hissing scream it cleared the little river in a single mighty bound. Von Horst turned to run, meanwhile tugging at the pistol in his holster; but before he could draw it, before he could escape, the thing pounced upon him and bore him to earth; then it picked him up in claw-like hands and held him out and surveyed him. Sitting erect upon its broad tail it towered fifteen feet in height, and at close range its jaws seemed almost large enough to engulf the puny man-thing that gazed in awe upon them. Von Horst thought that his end had come. He was helpless in the powerful grip of those mighty talons, beneath one of which his pistol hand was pinned to his side. The creature seemed to be gloating over him, debating, apparently, where to take the first bite; or at least so it seemed to von Horst.

At the point where the stream crossed the trail there

was an opening in the leafy canopy of the forest, through which the eternal noonday sun cast its brilliant rays upon the rippling water, the green sward, the monstrous creature, and its relatively puny captive. The reptile, if such it were, turned its cold eyes upward toward the opening; then it leaped high into the air, and as it did so it spread its wings and flapped dismally upward.

Von Horst was cold with apprehension. He recalled stories he had read of some great bird of the outer crust that carried its prey aloft and then killed it by letting it fall to the ground. He wondered if this were to be his fate, and he thanked his Maker that there would be so few to mourn him—no wife nor children to be left without protector and provider, no sweetheart to mourn his loss, pining for the lover who would never return.

They were above the forest now. The strange, horizonless landscape stretched away in all directions, fading gradually into nothingness as it passed from the range of human vision. Beyond the forest, in the direction of the creature's flight, lay open country, rolling hills, and mountains. Von Horst could see rivers and lakes and, in the far, hazy distance, what appeared to be a great body of water—an inland sea, perhaps, or a vast, uncharted ocean; but in whatever direction he might look lay mystery.

His situation was not one that rendered the contemplation of scenery a factor of vital interest, but presently whatever interest he had in it was definitely wiped out. The thing that carried him suddenly relinquished its hold with one paw. Von Horst thought that it was going to drop him, that the end had come. He breathed a little prayer. The creature raised him a few feet and then lowered him into a dark, odorous pocket which it held open with its other paw. When it released its hold upon him, von Horst was in utter darkness. For an instant he was at a loss to explain his situation; then it dawned upon him that he was in the belly pouch of a marsupial. It was hot and stifling. He thought he would suffocate, and the reptilian stench was almost overpowering. When he could endure it no longer he pushed himself upward until his head protruded from the mouth of the pouch.

The creature was flying horizontally by now, and the man's view was restricted to what lay almost directly beneath. They were still over the forest. The foliage, lying like billowed clouds of emerald, looked soft and inviting. Von Horst wondered why he was being carried away alive and whither. Doubtless to some nest or lair to serve as food, perhaps for a brood of hideous young. He fingered his pistol. How easy it would be to fire into that hot, pulsing body; but what would it profit him? It would mean almost certain death—possibly a lingering death if he were not instantly killed, for the only alternative to that would be fatal injuries. He abandoned the thought.

The creature was flying at surprising speed, considering its size. The forest passed from view; and they sped out over a tree-dotted plain where the man saw countless animals grazing or resting. There were great red deer, sloths, enormous primitive cattle with shaggy coats; and near clumps of bamboo that bordered a river was a herd of mammoths. There were other animals, too, that von Horst was unable to classify. Presently they flew above low hills, leaving the plain behind, and then over a rough, volcanic country of barren, black, cone-shaped hills. Between the cones and part way up their sides rioted the inevitable tropical verdure of Pellucidar. Only where no root could find a foothold was there no growth. One peculiar feature of these cones attracted von Horst's attention; there was an opening in the top of many of them, giving them the appearance of miniature extinct volcanoes. They ranged in size from a hundred feet to

several hundred in height. As he was contemplating
them, his captor commenced to circle directly above one
of the larger cones; then it dropped rapidly directly into
the yawning crater, alighting on the floor in the shaft of
light from the sun hanging perpetually at zenith.

As the creature dragged him from its pouch, von Horst
could, at first, see little of the interior of the crater; but
as his eyes quickly became accustomed to the surrounding gloom he saw what appeared to be the dead bodies
of many animals and men laid in a great circle around
the periphery of the hollow cone, their heads outward
from the center. The circle was not entirely completed,
there being a single gap of several yards. Between the
heads of the bodies and the wall of the cone was stacked
a quantity of ivory colored spheres about two feet in
diameter.

These things von Horst observed in a brief glance;
then he was interrupted by being lifted into the air. The
creature raised him, faced out, until his head was about
on a level with its own; then the man felt a sharp,
sickening pain in the back of his neck at the base of the
brain. There was just an instant of pain and momentary
nausea; then a sudden fading of all feeling. It was as
though he had died from the neck down. Now he was
aware of being carried toward the wall of the cone and
of being deposited upon the floor. He could still see;
and when he tried to turn his head, he found that he
could do so. He watched the creature that had brought
him here leap into the air, spread its wings, and flap
dismally away through the mouth of the crater.

II

THE PIT OF HORROR

As VON HORST, lying there in that gloomy cavern of death, contemplated his situation, he wished that he had died when he had had the opportunity and the power for self-destruction. Now he was helpless. The horror of his situation grew on him until he feared that he should go mad. He tried to move a hand, but it was as though he had no hands. He could not feel them, nor any other part of his body below his neck. He seemed just a head lying in the dirt, conscious but helpless. He rolled his head to one side. He had been placed at the end of the row of bodies at one side of the gap that had been left in the circle. Across the gap from him lay the body of a man. He turned his head in the other direction and saw that he was lying close to the body of another man; then his attention was attracted by a cracking and pounding in the opposite direction. Again he rolled his head so that he could see what lived in this hall of the dead.

His eyes were attracted to one of the ivory colored spheres that lay almost directly behind the body at the far side of the gap. The sphere was jerking to and fro. The sounds seemed to be coming from its interior. They became louder, more insistent. The sphere bobbed and rolled about; then a crack appeared in it, a jagged hole was torn in its surface, and a head protruded. It was a miniature of the hideous head of the creature that had brought him here. Now the mystery of the spheres was solved—they were the eggs of the great marsupial reptile; but what of the bodies?

Von Horst, fascinated, watched the terrible little creature burst its way from its egg. At last, successful, it rolled out upon the floor of the crater, where it lay inert for some time, as though resting after its exertions. Then it commenced to move its limbs, tenatively trying them. Presently it rose to its four feet; then it sat upright upon its tail and spread its wings. It flapped them at first weakly, then vigorously for a moment. This done, it fell upon its discarded shell and devoured it. The shell gone, it turned without hesitation toward the body of the man at the far side of the gap. As it approached it, von Horst was horrified to see the head turn toward the creature, the eyes wide with terror. With a hissing roar the foul little creature leaped upon the body, and simultaneously a piercing scream of terror burst from the lips of the man von Horst had thought was dead. The horror-filled eyes, the contorted muscles of the face reflected the mad efforts of the brain to direct the paralyzed nerve centers, to force them to react to the will to escape. So obvious was the effort to burst the invisible bonds that held him that it seemed inevitable that he must succeed, but the paralysis was too complete to be overcome.

The hideous fledgling fell upon the body and commenced to devour it; and though the victim may have felt no pain, his screams and groans continued to reverberate within the hollow cone of horror until, presently, the other creatures awaiting, doubtless, a similar fate raised their voices in a blood-curdling cacophony of terror. Now, for the first time, von Horst realized that all of these creatures were alive, paralyzed as he was. He closed his eyes to shut out the gruesome sight, but he could not close his ears to the abominable, soul-searing din.

Presently he turned his head away from the feeding reptile, toward the man lying upon his right, and opened his eyes. He saw that the man had not joined in the frightful chorus and that he was regarding him through steady, appraising eyes. He was a young man with a shock of coal-black hair, fine eyes, and regular features. He had an air about him, an air of strength and quiet dignity, that attracted von Horst; and he was favorably impressed, too, because the man had not succumbed to the hysteria of terror that had seized the other inmates of the chamber. The young lieutenant smiled at him and nodded. For an instant a faint expression of surprise tinged the other's countenance; then he, too, smiled. He spoke then, addressing von Horst in a language that was not understandable to the European.

"I'm sorry," said von Horst, "but I cannot understand you." Then it was the other's turn to shake his head in denial of comprehension.

Neither could understand the speech of the other; but they had smiled at one another, and they had a common bond in their expectancy of a common fate. Von Horst felt that he was no longer so much alone, almost that he had found a friend. It made a great difference, that slender contact of fellowship, even in the hopelessness of his situation. By comparison with what he had felt previously he was almost contented.

The next time he looked in the direction of the newly hatched reptile the body of its victim had been entirely devoured; there was not even a bone left, and with distended stomach the thing crawled into the round patch of brilliant sunlight beneath the crater opening and curled up for sleep.

The victims had relapsed into silence and again lay as though dead. Time passed; but how much time, von Horst could not even guess. He felt neither hunger nor thirst, a fact which he attributed to his paralysis; but occasionally he slept. Once he was awakened by the flapping of wings, and looked up to see the foul fledgling fly through the crater opening from the nest of horror in which it had been hatched.

After awhile the adult came with another victim, an antelope; and then von Horst saw how he and the other creatures had been paralyzed. Holding the antelope level with its great mouth, the reptile pierced the neck at the base of the brain with the needle-sharp point of its tongue; then it deposited the helpless creature at von Horst's left.

In this timeless void of living death there was no means of determining if there was any regularity of recurring events. Fledglings emerged from their shells, ate them, devoured their prey (always at the far edge of the gap to von Horst's left), slept in the sunlight, and flew away, apparently never to return; the adult came with new victims, paralyzed them, laid them at the edge of the gap nearest von Horst, and departed. The gap crept steadily around to the left; and as it crept, von Horst realized that his inevitable doom was creeping that much nearer.

He and the man at his right occasionally exchanged smiles, and sometimes each spoke in his own tongue. Just the sound of their voices expressing thoughts that the other could not understand was friendly and comforting. Von Horst wished that they might converse; how many eternities of loneliness it would have relieved! The same thought must often have been in the mind of the other, and it was he who first sought to express it and to overcome the obstacle that separated them from full enjoyment of their forced companionship. Once, when von Horst turned his eyes toward him, he said, "Dangar," and tried to indicate himself by bending his eyes toward himself and inclining his chin toward his chest. He repeated this several times.

Finally von Horst thought that he grasped his meaning.

"Dangar?" he asked, and nodded toward the other.

The man smiled and nodded and then spoke a word that was evidently an affirmative in his language. Then von Horst pronounced his own name several times, indicating himself in the same way that Dangar had. This was the beginning. After that it became a game of intense and absorbing interest. They did nothing else, and neither seemed to tire. Occasionally they slept; but now, instead of sleeping when the mood happened to seize one of them, each waited until the other wished to sleep; thus they could spend all their waking hours in the new and fascinating occupation of learning how to exchange thoughts.

Dangar was teaching von Horst his language; and since the latter had already mastered four or five languages of the outer crust, his aptitude for learning another was greatly increased, even though there was no similarity between it and any of the others that he had acquired.

Under ordinary circumstances the procedure would have been slow or seemingly hopeless; but with the compelling incentive of companionship and the absence of disturbing elements, other than when a fledgling hatched and fed, they progressed with amazing rapidity; or so it seemed to von Horst until he realized that in this timeless world weeks, months, or even years of outer terrestrial time might have elapsed since his incarceration.

At last the time arrived when he and Dangar could carry on a conversation with comparative ease and fluency, but as they had progressed so had the fateful gap of doom crept around the circle of the living dead closer and closer to them. Dangar would go first; then von Horst.

The latter dreaded the former event even more than he did the latter, for with Dangar gone he would be alone again with nothing to occupy his time or mind but the inevitable fate that awaited him as he listened for the cracking of the shell that would release death in its most horrible form upon him.

At last there were only three victims between Dangar and the gap. It would not be long now.

"I shall be sorry to leave you," said the Pellucidarian.

"I shall not be alone long," von Horst reminded him.

"No. Well, it is better to die than to remain here far from one's own country. I wish that we might have lived; then I could have taken you back to the land of Sari. It is a beautiful land of hills and trees and fertile valleys; there is much game there, and not far away is the great Lural Az. I have been there to the island of Anoroc, where Ja is king.

"You would like Sari. The girls are very beautiful. There is one there waiting for me now, but I shall never return to her. She will grieve; but—" (he sighed) "—she will get over it, and another will take her for his mate."

"I should like to go to Sari," said von Horst. Suddenly his eyes widened in surprise. "Dangar! Dangar!" he exclaimed.

"What is it?" demanded the Pellucidarian. "What has happened?"

"I can feel my fingers! I can move them!" cried von Horst. "And my toes, too."

"It does not seem possible, Von," exclaimed Dangar incredulously.

"But it is; it is! Just a little, but I can move them."

"How do you explain it? I cannot feel anything below my neck."

"The effects of the poison must be wearing off. Perhaps the paralysis will leave me entirely."

Dangar shook his head. "Since I have been here I have never seen it leave a victim that the Trodon stung with its poison tongue. And what if it does? Will you be any better off?"

"I think I shall," replied von Horst slowly. "I have had much leisure in which to dream and plan and imagine situations since I have been imprisoned here. I have often dreamed of being released from this paralysis and what I should do in the event that I were. I have it all planned out."

"There are only three between you and death," Dangar reminded him.

"Yes, I know that. All depends upon how quickly release comes."

"I wish you luck, Von, even though, if it comes to you, I shall not be here to know—there are only two between me and the end. The gap is creeping closer."

From that moment von Horst concentrated all his faculties upon overcoming the paralysis. He felt the glow of life creep gradually up his limbs, yet still he could move only his extremities, and these but slightly.

Another Trodon hatched, leaving but one between Dangar and death; and after Dangar, it would be his turn. As the horrid creature awoke from its sleep in the sunlight and winged away through the opening in the peak of the cone, von Horst succeeded in moving his hands and flexing his wrists; his feet, too, were free now; but oh, how slow, how hideously slow were his powers returning. Could Fate be so cruel as to hold out this great hope and then snatch it from him at the moment of fruition? Cold sweat broke out upon him as he weighed his chances—the odds were so terribly against him.

If only he could measure time that he might know the intervals of the hatching of the eggs and thus gain an approximate idea of the time that remained to him. He was quite certain that the eggs must hatch at reasonably regular intervals, though he could not actually know. He wore a wrist watch; but it had long since stopped, nor could he have consulted it in any event, since he could not raise his arm.

Slowly the paralysis disappeared as far as his knees and elbows. He could bend these now, and below them his limbs felt perfectly normal. He knew that if sufficient time were vouchsafed him he would eventually be in full command of all his muscles once again.

As he strained to break the invisible bonds that held him another egg broke, and shortly thereafter Dangar lay with no creature at his right—he would be next.

"And after you, Dangar, come I. I think I shall be free before that, but I wished to save you."

"Thank you, my friend," replied the Pellucidarian, "but I am resigned to death. I prefer it to living on as I now am—a head attached to a dead body."

"You wouldn't have to live like that for long, I'm sure," said von Horst. "My own experience convinces me that eventually the effects of the poison must wear off. Ordinarily there is enough to keep the victim paralyzed long beyond the time that he would be required to serve as food for the fledglings. If I could only free myself, I could save you, I am sure."

"Let us talk of other things," said Dangar. "I would not be a living dead man, and to entertain other hopes can serve but to tantalize and to make the inevitable end more bitter."

"As you will," said von Horst, with a shrug, "but you can't keep me from thinking and trying."

And so they talked of Sari and the land of Amoz, from whence Dian the Beautiful had come, and The Land of Awful Shadow, and the Unfriendly Islands in the Sojar Az; for von Horst saw that it pleased Dangar to recall these, to him, pleasant places; though when the Sarian described the savage beasts and wild men that roamed them, von Horst felt that as places of residence they left much to be desired.

As they talked, von Horst discovered that he could move his shoulders and his hips. A pleasant glow of life suffused his entire body. He was about to break the news to Dangar when the fateful sound of breaking shell came simultaneously to the ears of both men.

"Good-bye, my friend," said Dangar. "We of Pellucidar make few friends outside our own tribes. All other men are enemies to kill or be killed. I am glad to call you friend. See, the end comes!"

Already the newly hatched Trodon had gobbled its own shell and was eyeing Dangar. In a moment it would rush upon him. Von Horst struggled to rise, but something seemed to hold him yet. Then, with gaping jaws, the reptile started toward its prey.

III

THE ONLY HOPE

ONCE AGAIN von Horst struggled to rise; again he sank back defeated. Perspiration stood out in cold beads over his entire body. He wanted to curse and scream, but he remained silent. Silent, too, was Dangar. He did not cry out as had the others when death crept upon them. It was creeping upon him now—closer and closer. Von Horst raised himself to his left elbow; then he sank back, but as he did so he tried to reach for the gun at his hip—the gun he had tried unsuccessfully to reach before. This time he succeeded. His fingers closed upon the grip. He dragged the gun from its holster. Again he partially raised himself upon an elbow.

The Trodon was almost upon Dangar when von Horst fired. Voicing a piercing scream, it leaped high in air, fluttered its wings futilely for an instant, and then fell heavily to the floor of the pit—dead.

Dangar looked at von Horst in amazement and in gratitude. "You have done it," he said; "and I thank you, but what good will it do. How can we ever escape from this pit? Even if there were a way I could not take advantage of it—I who cannot move even a finger."

"That remains to be seen," replied von Horst. "When the paralysis has left you we shall find a way for that even as I have for this. But a moment since what would you have given for your chance of escaping the Trodon? Nothing, absolutely nothing; yet you are alive and the Trodon is dead. Who are you to say that the impossible cannot be accomplished?"

"You are right," replied Dangar. "I shall never doubt you again."

"Now to gain time," exclaimed von Horst. He picked up Dangar, then, and carried him across the gap and laid him down beside the last victim that the adult Trodon had brought in. As he lay down beside him, he remarked, "The next one to hatch will get neither of us, for it will go to the other side of the gap."

"But what about the old one when it brings in the next victim?" asked Dangar. "Won't it see that our positions have been changed? And there is the body of one of its young, too; what do you suppose it will do about that?"

"I doubt that the Trodon will notice us at all," replied von Horst, "but if it does, I shall be ready for it. I still have my pistol and plenty of ammunition; and as for the dead chicken, I'll dispose of that immediately. I think we can use it."

26

He rose then and dragged the carcass to one side of the pit, hiding it behind several eggs. Then he examined it closely, feeling of its skin. Apparently satisfied, he drew his hunting knife and fell to work to remove the skin from the carcass.

He worked rapidly but carefully, his whole attention rivetted upon his task, so that it came somewhat in the nature of a surprise when the sunlight beating in through the mouth of the crater was momentarily disturbed.

Glancing up, he saw the Trodon returning with another victim; and instantly he flattened himself prone against the wall of the pit behind some eggs that he had arranged for this purpose, at the same time drawing his pistol.

Just the top of his head and his eyes protruded above one of the eggs, these and the cold, black muzzle of his weapon, as he watched the unsuspecting reptile deposit its victim beside Dangar. As he had anticipated, the creature paid no attention to the Pellucidarian; and a moment later it had vanished through the opening in search of other prey.

Without further interruption, von Horst completed the skinning of the fledgling; then he dragged the body to the spot that Dangar had previously occupied.

The Sarian laughed. "A clever way to dispose of the carcass," he said, "if it works."

"I think it will," replied von Horst. "These brainless little devils are guided by instinct at first. They always go to the same spot for their first meal, and I'll wager they'll eat anything they find there."

"But what are you going to do with the skin?"

"Wait and see. It constitutes the most important part of my plan for escape. I'll admit that it's a rather harebrained scheme; but it's the only one that I have been able to formulate, and it has some chance for success.

Now I must go back and get busy at it again."

Von Horst returned to his work; and now he cut the skin into a continuous strip, starting from the outside. It took him a long time, and when he had completed the work it was necessary to trim the rough edges of the outside cut and scrape the inside surface of the long, flat strap that had resulted from his labors. While von Horst was measuring the strap by the crude tip-of-nose-to-tip-of-the-fingers method, his attention was attracted by the hatching of another Trodon.

"Sixty-six, sixty-seven, sixty-eight," counted von Horst as he watched the fledgling devour the shell of its egg. "That's over two hundred feet. Should be more than enough."

The other preliminaries having been gone through, the Trodon approached the skinned carcass of its brother. Both von Horst and Dangar watched with interest, as, without an instant's hesitation, the reptile fell upon the body and devoured it.

After it had flown away, von Horst crossed over and lay down beside Dangar. "You were right," admitted the latter, "it never knew the difference."

"I think they are so low in the scale of intelligence that they are guided almost exclusively by instinct, even the adults. That is why the old one did not notice that I was missing and that you were in a different place. If I am right, my plan will have a better chance of success.

"Do you feel any different, Dangar? Do you feel any life returning to your limbs?"

The Sarian shook his head. "No," he replied, rather dejectedly. "I'm afraid that will never happen, but I can't understand how you recovered. That still gives me hope. Can you explain it?"

"I don't know. I have a theory. You can see that all the victims of the Trodon are thin-skinned animals. That might indicate that the needle point of its tongue, by means of which the poison is injected, can either break only thin skin or can penetrate only to a shallow depth. While I was skinning the chicken I took off my leather jacket, and in examining it I discovered that the tongue of the Trodon ran through two thicknesses of leather and canvass lining at the back of the collar before entering my flesh. Look; see the round, green stain encircling the puncture. Perhaps some of the poison was wiped off, or perhaps the sting didn't puncture me deeply enough to have full effect.

"Anyhow, I am more than ever convinced that no matter how much poison a victim receives, short of a lethal dose, he will recover eventually. You unquestionably received a larger dose than I, but you have been here longer than I; so it may not be long now before you will note signs of recovery."

"I am commencing to have hope," replied Dangar.

"Something will have to be done soon," said the other. "Now that the paralysis has left me and my body is functioning normally, I am commencing to feel both hunger and thirst. I shall have to put my plan to the test at the first opportunity before I become too weak to carry through with it."

"Yes," said Dangar. "Get out if you can. Don't think of me."

"I'll take you with me."

"But that will be impossible—even if you can get out of this hole yourself, which I doubt."

"Nevertheless, I shall take you; or I will not go myself."

"No," demurred Dangar. "That would be foolish. I won't permit it."

"How are you going to prevent it?" laughed von Horst. "Leave it all to me. The plan may fail anyway. But I'm going to start putting it into effect at once."

He crossed the pit and took his long strap of reptile hide from behind the eggs where he had concealed it. Then he made a running noose in one end. This he spread on the floor at a point near where the adult Trodon would deposit its next victim. Carefully he ran the strap to his hiding place behind the eggs, left a coil there, and then took the remainder to a point beneath the mouth of the crater but just outside the circle of brilliant sunlight. Here he neatly coiled most of what remained of the strap, so that it might pay out smoothly. He took great pains with this. The remaining loose end he carried to his hiding place; then he settled himself comfortably to wait.

How long he waited, of course he never knew; but it seemed an eternity. Hunger and thirst assailed him, as did doubts and fears of the effectiveness of his plan. He tried not to sleep, for to sleep now might prove fatal; but he must have dozed.

He awakened with a start to see the great Trodon squatting in the shaft of sunlight injecting its paralyzing poison into the neck of a new victim. Von Horst felt suddenly very weak. It had been a close call. Another moment, perhaps, and it would have been too late to test his plan. He doubted that he could hold out until the reptile returned again. Everything, therefore, depended upon success at the first cast of the die—his life and Dangar's. Quickly he gathered his nervous forces under control. Again he was cool, collected. He loosened his pistol in its holster and took a new grip on the strap.

The Trodon crossed the pit, bearing the paralyzed victim to its place in the lethal circle. It placed one great hind paw in the open noose. Von Horst sent a running wave of the rope across the floor that lifted the noose up the creature's leg above the ankle; then he gave a quick jerk. The noose tightened a little. Was it enough?

Would it hold? As he had expected, the creature paid no attention to the strap. It appeared not to feel it, and von Horst was quite sure that it did not. So low was its nervous organization, he believed, that only a sharp blow on the leg would have carried any sensation to the brain.

After it had deposited the latest victim, the reptile turned toward the center of the pit, leaped into the air and fluttered aloft. Von Horst held his breath. Would the noose be shaken loose? Heaven forbid. It held. Von Horst leaped to his feet and ran toward the center of the pit, his pistol cocked and ready in his hand; and as the Trodon rose through the mouth of the crater and cleared the top of the hill, the man fired three shots in rapid succession.

He did not need the horrid screams of the wounded creature to tell him that his aim had been true, for he saw the great reptile career in air and plunge from sight beyond the rim of the crater; then von Horst leaped for the end of the strap, seized it, braced himself, and waited.

There was danger that the body of the creature, tumbling down the steep side of the cone-shaped hill, might not come to rest before it jerked the strap from his hands; so he quickly wound it around his body and hurriedly made it fast. He might be killed; but he wouldn't loose his strap or jeopardize this, his last chance of escape from the pit. For a moment the strap payed out rapidly from the coil; then it stopped. Either the body of the Trodon had come to rest or the noose had slipped from the hind leg. Which?

Von Horst pulled on the strap fearfully. Soon it tautened; then he knew that it was still attached to the creature. A vague doubt assailed him as to whether the Trodon had been killed or not. He knew how tenacious of life such creatures might be. Suppose it were not dead? What dire possibilites such an event might entail!

The man tugged on the strap. It did not give. Then he swung on it with all his weight. It remained as before. Still, clinging to the loose end, he crossed the pit to Dangar, who was gazing at him wide-eyed with astonishment.

"You should have been a Sarian," said Dangar with admiration.

Von Horst smiled. "Come," he said. "Now for you." He stooped and lifted the Pellucidarian from the ground and carried him to the center of the pit beneath the crater mouth; then he made the loose end of the strap secure about his body beneath the arms.

"What are you going to do?" asked Dangar.

"Just now I am going to make the inner world a little safer for thin-skinned animals," replied Von Horst.

He went to the side of the pit, commenced breaking the eggs with the butt of his pistol. In two eggs, those most closely approaching the end of the period of incubation, he discovered quite active young. These he destroyed; then he returned to Dangar.

"I hate to leave these other creatures here," he said, gesturing toward the unhappy victims; "but there is no other way. I cannot get them all out."

"You'll still be lucky if you get yourself out," commented Dangar.

Von Horst grinned. "We'll both be lucky," he replied, "but this is our lucky day." There was no word for day in the language of the inner world, where there is neither day nor night; so von Horst substituted a word from one of the languages of the outer world. "Be patient and you'll soon be out."

He grasped the strap and started up hand-over-hand. Dangar lay on his back watching him, renewed admiration shining in his eyes. It was a long, dangerous climb; but at length von Horst reached the mouth of the crater.

As he topped the summit and looked down, he saw the carcass of the Trodon lodged on a slight ledge a short distance beneath him. The creature was quite evidently dead. That was the only interest that the man had in it; so he turned at once to his next task, which was to haul Dangar to the mouth of the crater.

Von Horst was a powerful man; but his strength had already been tested to its limit, and perhaps it had been partially sapped by the long period of paralysis he had endured. Added to this was the precarious footing that the steep edge of the crater mouth afforded; yet he never for a moment lost hope of eventual success; and though it was slow work, he was finally rewarded by seeing the inert form of the Pellucidarian lying at the summit of the hill beside him.

He would have been glad to rest now, but his brief experience of Pellucidar warned him that this exposed hilltop was no place to seek sanctuary. He must descend to the bottom, where he could see a few trees and a little stream of water, take Dangar with him, and search for a hiding place. The hillside was very steep, but fortunately it was broken by rudimentary ledges that offered at least a foothold. In any event, there was no other way to descend; and so von Horst lifted Dangar across one of his broad shoulders and started the perilous descent. Slipping and stumbling, he made his slow way down the steep hillside; and constantly he kept his eyes alert for danger. Occasionally he fell, but always managed to catch himself before being precipitated to the bottom.

He was fairly spent when he finally staggered into the shade of a clump of trees growing beside the little stream that he had seen from the summit of the hill. Laying Dangar on the sward, he slaked his thirst with the clear water of the brook. It was the second time that he had drunk since he had left the camp where the great dirigible, O-220, had been moored. How much time had elapsed he could not even guess; days it must have been, perhaps weeks or even months; yet for most of that time the peculiar venom of the Trodon had not only paralyzed him but preserved the moisture in his body, keeping it always fresh and fit for food for the unhatched fledgling by which it was destined to be devoured.

Refreshed and strengthened, he rose and looked about. He must find a place in which to make a more or less permanent camp, for it was quite obvious that he could not continue to carry Dangar in his wanderings. He felt rather helpless, practically alone in this unknown world. In what direction might he go if he were free to go? How could he ever hope to locate the O-220 and his companions in a land where there were no points of compass? when, even if there had been, he had only a vague idea of the direction of his previous wanderings and less of the route along which the Trodon had carried him?

As soon as the effects of the poison should have worn off and Dangar was free from the bonds of paralysis, he would have not only an active friend and companion but one who could guide him to a country where he might be assured of a friendly welcome and an opportunity to make a place for himself in this savage world, where, he was inclined to believe, he must spend the rest of his natural life. It was by far not this consideration alone that prompted him to remain with the Sarian but, rather, sentiments of loyalty and friendship.

A careful inspection of the little grove of trees and the area contiguous to it convinced him that this might be as good a place as any to make a camp. There was fresh water, and he had seen that game was plentiful in the vicinity. Fruits and nuts grew upon several of the trees; and to his question as to their edibility, Dangar assured him that they were safe.

"You are going to stay here?" asked the Sarian.

"Yes, until you recover from the effects of the poison."

"I may never recover. What then?"

Von Horst shrugged. "Then I shall be here a long while," he laughed.

"I could not expect that even of a brother," objected Dangar. "You must go in search of your own people."

"I could not find them. If I could, I would not leave you here alone and helpless."

"You would not have to leave me helpless."

"I don't understand you," said von Horst.

"You would kill me, of course; that would be an act of mercy."

"Forget it," snapped von Horst. The very idea revolted him.

"Neither one of us may forget it," insisted Dangar. "After a reasonable number of sleeps, if I am not recovered, you must destroy me." He used the only measure of time that he knew—sleeps. How much time elapsed between sleeps or how long each sleep endured, he had no means of telling.

"That is for the future," replied von Horst shortly. "Right now I'm interested only in the matter of making camp. Have you any suggestions?"

"There is greatest safety in caves in cliffsides," replied Dangar. "Holes in the ground are often next best; after that, a platform or a shelter built among the branches of a tree."

"There are no cliffs here," said von Horst, "nor do I see any holes in the ground; but there are trees."

"You'd better start building, then," advised the Pellucidarian, "for there are many flesh eaters in Pellucidar; and they are always hungry."

With suggestions and advice from Dangar, von Horst constructed a platform in one of the larger trees, using reeds that resembled bamboo, which grew in places along the margin of the stream. These he cut with his hunting knife and lashed into place with a long, tough grass that Dangar had seen growing in clumps close to the foot of the hill.

At the latter's suggestion, he added walls and a roof as further protection against the smaller arboreal carnivora, birds of prey, and carnivorous flying reptiles.

He never knew how long it took him to complete the shelter; for the work was absorbing, and time flew rapidly. He ate nuts and fruit at intervals and drank several times, but until the place was almost completed he felt no desire to sleep.

It was with considerable difficulty, and not without danger of falling, that he carried Dangar up the rickety ladder that he had built to gain access to their primitive abode; but at length he had him safely deposited on the floor of the little hut; then he stretched out beside him and was asleep almost instantly.

IV

SKRUF OF BASTI

WHEN von Horst awoke he was ravenously hungry. As he raised himself to an elbow, Dangar looked at him and smiled.

"You have had a long sleep," he said, "but you needed it."

"Was it very long?" asked von Horst.

"I have slept twice while you slept once," replied Dangar, "and I am now sleepy again."

"And I am hungry," said von Horst, "ravenously hungry; but I am sick of nuts and fruit. I want meat; I need it."

"I think you will find plenty of game down stream," said Dangar. "I noticed a little valley not far below here while you were carrying me down the hill. There were many animals there."

Von Horst rose to his feet. "I'll go and get one."

"Be careful," cautioned the Pellucidarian. "You are a stranger in this world. You do not know all the animals that are dangerous. There are some that look quite harmless but are not. The red deer and the thag will often charge and toss you on their horns or trample your life out, though they eat no meat. Look out for the bucks and the bulls of all species and the shes when they have young. Watch above, always, for birds and reptiles. It is well to walk where there are trees to give you shelter from these and a place into which to climb to escape the others."

"At least I am safe from one peril," commented von Horst.

"What is that?" asked Dangar.

"In Pellucidar, I shall never die of ennui."

"I do not know what you mean. I do not know what *ennui* is."

"No Pellucidarian ever could," laughed von Horst, as he quit the shelter and descended to the ground.

Following Dangar's suggestion, he followed the stream down toward the valley that the Sarian had noticed, being careful to remain as close to trees as possible and keeping always on the alert for the predatory beasts, birds, and reptiles that are always preying upon lesser creatures.

He had not gone far when he came in sight of the upper end of the valley and saw a splendid buck antelope standing alone as though on guard. He offered a splendid shot for a rifle, but the distance was too great to chance a pistol shot; so von Horst crept closer, taking advantage of the cover afforded by clumps of tall grasses, the bamboo-like reeds, and the trees. Cautiously he wormed his way nearer and nearer to his quarry that he might be sure to bring it down with the first shot. He still had a full belt of cartridges, but he knew that when these were gone the supply could never be replenished—every one of them must count.

His whole attention centered upon the buck, he neglected for the moment to be on the watch for danger. Slowly he crept on until he reached a point just behind some tall grasses that grew but a few paces from the still unsuspecting animal. He raised his pistol to take careful aim, and as he did so a shadow passed across him. It was but a fleeting shadow, but in the brillant glare of the Pellucidarian sun it seemed to have substance. It was almost as though a hand had been laid upon his shoulder. He looked up, and as he did so he saw a hideous thing diving like a bullet out of the blue apparently straight for him—a mighty reptile that he subconsciously recognized as a pteranodon of the Cretaceous. With a roaring hiss, as of a steam locomotive's exhaust, the thing dropped at amazing speed. Mechanically, von Horst raised his pistol although he knew that nothing short of a miracle could stop or turn that frightful engine of destruction before it reached its goal; and then he saw that he was not its target. It was the buck. The antelope stood for a moment as though paralyzed by terror; then it sprang away—but too late. The pteranodon swooped upon it, seized it in its mighty talons, and rose again into the air.

Von Horst breathed a sigh of relief as he wiped the perspiration from his forehead. "What a world!" he muttered, wondering how man had survived amidst such savage surroundings.

Farther down the little valley he now saw many animals grazing. There were deer and antelope and the great, shaggy bos so long extinct upon the outer crust. Among them were little, horse-like creatures, no larger than a fox terrier, resembling the Hyracotherium of the Eocene, early progeniators of the horse, which but added to the amazing confusion of birds, mammals, and reptiles of various eras of the evolution of life on the outer crust.

The sudden attack of the pteranodon upon one of their number frightened the other animals in the immediate vicinity; and they were galloping off down the valley, snorting, squealing, and bucking leaving von Horst to contemplate the flying hoofs of many a fine dinner. There was nothing to do but follow them if he would have meat; and so he set off after them, keeping close to the fringe of trees along the stream which wound along one side of the valley. But to add to his discomfiture, those that had initiated the stampede bore down upon the herds grazing below them, imparting their terror to these others, with the result that the latter joined them; and in a short time all were out of sight.

Most of them kept on down the valley, disappearing from the man's view where the valley turned behind the hills; but he saw a few large sheep run into a canyon between two nearby cones, and these he decided to pursue. As he entered the canyon he saw that it narrowed rapidly, evidently having been formed by the erosion of water which had uncovered the broken lava rocks of a previous flow. Only a narrow trail ran between some of the hugh blocks, hundreds of which were scattered about in the wildest confusion.

The sheep had been running rapidly; and as they had started considerably ahead of him, he knew that they must be out of earshot by now; so he made no effort to hide his pursuit, but moved at a quick walk along the winding trail between the rocks. He came at last to a point where the trail debouched upon a wider portion of the canyon, and as he was about to enter it he heard plainly the sound of running feet coming toward him from the upper portion of the canyon, which he could not see. And then he heard a disconcerting series of growls and snarls from the same direction. He had already seen enough of Pellucidar and its bloodthirsty fauna to take it for granted that practically everything that had life might be considered a potential menace; so he leaped quickly behind a large lava rock and waited.

He had scarcely concealed himself, when a man came running from the upper end of the gorge. It seemed to von Horst that the newcomer was as fleet as a deer. And it was well for him that he was fleet, for behind him came the author of the savage snarls and growls that von Horst had heard—a great, dog-like beast as large and savage as a leopard. As fleet as the man was, however, the beast was gaining on him; and it was apparent to von Horst that it would overtake its quarry and drag him down before he had crossed the open space.

The fellow was armed only with a crude stone knife, which he now carried in one hand, as though determined to make what fight for his life he might when he could no longer outdistance his pursuer; but he must have realized, as did von Horst, how futile his weapon would be against the powerful beast bearing down upon him.

There was no question in von Horst's mind as to what he should do. He could not stand idly by and see a human being torn to pieces by the cruel fangs of the Hyaenodon, and so he stepped from behind the rock that had concealed him from both the man and the beast; and, jumping quickly to one side where he might obtain an unobstructed shot at the creature, raised his pistol, took careful aim, and fired. It was not a lucky shot; it was a good shot, perfect. It bored straight through the left side of the brute's chest and buried itself in his heart. With a howl of pain and rage, the carnivore bounded forward almost to von Horst; then it crumpled at his feet, dead.

The man it had been pursuing, winded and almost spent, came to a halt. He was wide-eyed and trembling as he stood staring at von Horst in wonder and amazement. As the latter turned toward him he backed away, gripping his knife more tightly.

"Go away!" he growled. "I kill!"

He spoke the same language that Dangar had taught von Horst, which, he had explained, was the common language of all Pellucidar; a statement that the man from the outer crust had doubted possible.

"You kill what?" demanded von Horst.

"You."

"Why do you wish to kill me?"

"So that I shall not be killed by you."

"Why should I kill you?" asked von Horst. "I just saved your life. If I had wished you to die, I could have just left you to that beast."

The man scratched his head. "That is so," he admitted after some reflection; "but still I do not understand it. I am not of your tribe; therefore there is no reason why you should not wish to kill me. I have never seen a man like you before. All other strangers that I have met have tried to kill me. Then, too, you cover your body with strange skins. You must come from a far country."

"I do," von Horst assured him; "but the question now is, are we to be friends or enemies?"

Again the man ran his nails through his shock of black hair meditatively. "It is very peculiar," he said. "It is something that I have never before heard of. Why should we be friends?"

"Why should we be enemies?" countered von Horst. "Neither one of us has ever harmed the other. I am from a very far country, a stranger in yours. Were you to come to my country, you would be treated well. No one would wish to kill you. You would be given shelter and fed. People would be kindly toward you, just because they are kindly by nature and not because you could be of any service to them. Here, it is far more practical that we be friends; because we are surrounded by dangerous beasts, and two men can protect themselves better than one.

"However, if you wish to be my enemy, that is up to you. I may go my way, and you yours; or, if you wish to try to kill me, that, too, is a matter for you to decide; but do not forget how easily I killed this beast here. Just as easily could I kill you."

"Your words are true words," said the man. "We shall be friends. I am Skruf. Who are you?"

In his conversations with Dangar, von Horst had noticed that no Pellucidarians that the other had mentioned had more than one name, to which was sometimes added a descriptive title such as the Hairy One, the Sly One, the Killer, or the like; and as Dangar usually called him von, he had come to accept this as the name he would use in the inner world; so this was the name that he gave to Skruf.

"What are you doing here?" asked the man. "This is a bad country because of the Trodons."

"I have found it so," replied von Horst. "I was brought here by a Trodon."

The other eyed him skeptically. "You would be dead now if a Trodon had ever seized you."

"One did, and took me to its nest to feed its young.

42

I and another man escaped."

"Where is he?"

"Back by the river in our camp. I was hunting for food when I met you. I was following some sheep up this canyon. What were you doing here?"

"I was escaping from the Mammoth Men," replied Skruf. "Some of them captured me. They were taking me back to their country to make a slave of me, but I escaped from them. They were pursuing me, but when I reached this canyon I was safe. In places it is too narrow to admit a mammoth."

"What are you going to do now?"

"Wait until I think they have given up the chase and then return to my own country."

Von Horst suggested that Skruf come to his camp and wait and that then the three of them could go together as far as their trails were identical, but first he wished to bag some game. Skruf offered to help him, and with the latter's knowledge of the quarry it was not long before they had found the sheep and von Horst had killed a young buck. Skruf was greatly impressed and not a little frightened by the report of the pistol and the, to him, miraculous results that von Horst achieved with it.

After skinning the buck and dividing the weight of the carcass between them, they set off for camp, which they reached without serious interruption. Once a bull thag charged them, but they climbed trees and waited until it had gone away, and another time a sabertooth crossed their path; but his belly was full, and he did not molest them. Thus, through the primitive savagery of Pellucidar, they made their way to the camp.

Dangar was delighted that von Horst had returned safely, for he knew the many dangers that beset a hunter in this fierce world. He was much surprised when he saw Skruf; but when the circumstances were explained to him he agreed to accept the other as a friend, though this relationship with a stranger was as foreign to his code as to Skruf's.

Skruf came from a land called Basti which lay in the same general direction as Sari, though much closer; so it was decided that they would travel together to Skruf's country as soon as Dangar recovered.

Von Horst could not understand how these men knew in what direction their countries lay when there were no means of determining the points of the compass, nor could they explain the phenomenon to him. They merely pointed to their respective countries, and they pointed in the same general direction. How far they were from home neither knew; but by comparing notes, they were able to assume that Sari lay very much farther away than Basti. What von Horst had not yet discovered was that each possessed, in common with all other inhabitants of Pellucidar, a well developed homing instinct identical with that of most birds and which is particularly apparent in carrier pigeons.

As sleeps came and went and hunting excursions were made necessary to replenish their larder, Skruf grew more and more impatient of the delay. He was anxious to return to his own country, but he realized the greater safety of numbers and especially that of the protection of von Horst's miraculous weapon that killed so easily at considerable distances. He often questioned Dangar in an effort to ascertain if there was any change in his condition, and he was never at any pains to conceal his disappointment when the Sarian admitted that he still had no feeling below his neck.

On one occasion when von Horst and Skruf had gone farther afield than usual to hunt, the latter broached the subject of his desire to return to his own country; and the man of the outer crust learned for the first time the urge that prompted the other's impatience.

"I have chosen my mate," explained Skruf, "but she demanded the head of a tarag to prove that I am a brave man and a great hunter. It was while I was hunting the tarag that the Mammoth Men captured me. The girl has slept many times since I went away. If I do not return soon some other warrior may bring the head of a tarag and place it before the entrance to her cave; then, when I return, I shall have to find another who will mate with me."

"There is nothing to prevent your returning to your own country whenever you see fit," von Horst assured him.

"Could you kill a tarag with that little thing that makes such a sharp noise?" inquired Skruf.

"I might." Von Horst was not so certain of this; at least he was not certain that he could kill one of the mighty tigers quickly enough to escape death from its formidable fangs and powerful talons before it succumbed.

"The way we have come today," remarked Skruf, tentatively, "is in the direction of my country. Let us continue on."

"And leave Dangar?" asked von Horst.

Skruf shrugged. "He will never recover. We cannot remain with him forever. If you will come with me, you can easily kill a tarag with the thing you call pistol; then I will place it before the entrance to the girl's cave, and she will think that I killed it. In return, I will see that the tribe accepts you. They will not kill you. You may live with us and be a Bastian. You can take a mate, too; and there are many beautiful girls in Basti."

"Thanks," replied von Horst; "but I shall remain with Dangar. It will not be long now before he recovers. I am sure that the effects of the poison will disappear as they did in my case. The reason that they have persisted so much longer is that he must have received a much larger dose than I."

"If he dies, will you come with me?" demanded Skruf.

Von Horst did not like the expression in the man's eyes as he asked the question. He had never found Skruf as companionable as Dangar. His manner was not as frank and open. Now he was vaguely suspicious of his intentions and his honesty, although he realized that he had nothing tangible upon which to base such a judgment and might be doing the man an injustice. However, he phrased his reply to Skruf's question so that he would be on the safe side and not be placing a premium on Dangar's life. "If he lives," he said, "we will both go with you when he recovers." Then he turned back toward the camp.

Time passed. How much, von Horst could not even guess. He had attempted to measure it once, keeping his watch wound and checking off the lapse of days on a notched stick; but where it is always noon it is not always easy to remember either to wind or consult a watch. Often he found that it had run down; and then, of course, he never knew how long it had been stopped before he discovered that it was not running; nor, when he slept, did he ever know for how long a time. So presently he became discouraged; or, rather, he lost interest. What difference did the duration of time make, anyway? Had not the inhabitants of Pellucidar evidently existed quite as contentedly without it as they would have with? Doubtless they had been more contented. As he recalled his world of the outer crust he realized that time was a hard task master that had whipped him through life a veritable slave to clocks, watches, bugles, and whistles.

Skruf often voiced his impatience to be gone, and Dangar urged them not to consider him but to leave him where he was if they would not kill him. And so the two men slept or ate or hunted through the timeless noon of the eternal Pellucidarian day; but whether it was for hours or for years, von Horst could not tell.

He tried to accustom himself to all this and to the motionless sun hanging forever in the exact center of the hollow sphere, the interior surface of which is Pellucidar and the outer, the world that we know and that he had always known; but he was too new to his environment to be able to accept it as did Skruf and Dangar who never had known aught else.

And then he was suddenly awakened from a sound sleep by the excited cries of Dangar. "I can move!" exclaimed the Sarian. "Look! I can move my fingers."

The paralysis receded rapidly, and as Dangar rose unsteadily to his feet the three men experienced a feeling of elation such as might condemned men who had just received their reprieves. To von Horst it was the dawning of a new day, but Dangar and Skruf knew nothing of dawns. However, they were just as happy.

"And now," cried Skruf, "we start for Basti. Come with me, and you shall be treated as my brothers. The people will welcome you, and you shall live in Basti forever."

V

INTO SLAVERY

THE ROUTE that Skruf took from the country of the black craters to the land of Basti was bewilderingly circuitous, since it followed the windings of rivers along the banks of which grew the trees and thickets that offered the oft needed sanctuary in this world of constant menace, or led through gloomy forests, or narrow, rocky gorges. Occasionally, considerable excursions from the more direct route were necessitated when periods of sleep were required, for then it became imperative that hiding places be discovered where the three might be reasonably safe from attack while they slept.

Von Horst became so confused and bewildered during the early stages of the long journey that he had not the remotest conception of even the general direction in which they were travelling, and often doubted Skruf's ability to find his way back to his own country; but neither the Bastian nor Dangar appeared to entertain the slightest misgiving.

Game was plenty—usually far too plenty and too menacing—and von Horst had no difficulty in keeping them well supplied; but the steady drain upon his store of ammunition made him apprehensive for the future, and he determined to find some means of conserving his precious cartridges that he might have them for occasions of real emergency when his pistol might mean a matter of life and death to him.

His companions were, culturally, still in the stone age, having no knowledge of any weapon more advanced than clubs, stone knives, and stone tipped spears; so, having witnessed the miraculous ease and comparative safety with which von Horst brought down even large beasts with his strange weapon, they were all for letting him do the killing.

For reasons of his own, largely prompted by his suspicions concerning Skruf's loyalty, von Horst did not wish the others to know that his weapon would be harmless when his supply of ammunition was exhausted; and they were too ignorant of all matters concerning firearms to deduce as much for themselves. It was necessary, therefore, to find some plausible excuse for insisting that their hunting be done with other weapons.

Skruf was armed with a knife and a spear when they set out upon their journey; and as rapidly as he could find the materials and fashion them, Dangar had fabricated similar weapons for himself. With his help, von Horst finally achieved a spear; and shortly thereafter commenced to make a bow and arrows. But long before they were completed he insisted that they must kill their game with the primitive weapons they possessed because the report of the pistol would be certain to attract the attention of enemies to them. As they were going through a country in which Skruf assured them they might meet hunting and raiding parties from hostile tribes, both he and Dangar appreciated the wisdom of von Horst's suggestion; and thereafter the three lay in wait for their prey with stone-shod spears.

The ease with which von Horst adapted himself to the primitive life of his cave-men companions was a source of no little wonder even to himself. How long a time had elapsed since he left the outer crust, he could not know; but he was convinced that it could not have been more than a matter of months; yet in that time he had sloughed practically the entire veneer of civilization that it had taken generations to develop, and had slipped back perhaps a hundred thousand years until he stood upon a common footing with men of the old stone age. He hunted as they hunted, ate as they ate, and often found himself thinking in terms of the stone age.

Gradually his apparel of the civilized outer crust had given way to that of a long dead era. His boots had gone first. They had been replaced by sandals of mammoth hide. Little by little his outer clothing, torn and rotten, fell apart until he no longer covered his nakedness; then he had been forced to discard it and adopt the skin loin cloth of his companions. Now, indeed, except for the belt of cartridges, the hunting knife, and the pistol, was he a veritable man of the Pleistocene.

With the completion of his bow and a quantity of arrows, he felt that he had taken a definite step forward. The thought amused him. Perhaps now he was ten or twenty thousand years more advanced than his fellows. But he was not to remain so long. As soon as he had perfected himself in the use of the new weapons, both Dangar and Skruf were anxious to possess similar ones. They were as delighted with them as children with new toys; and soon learned to use them, Dangar, especially, showing marked aptitude. Yet the pistol still intrigued them. Skruf had constantly importuned von Horst to permit him to fire it, but the European would not let him even touch it.

"No one can safely handle it but myself," he explained. "It might easily kill you if you did."

"I am not afraid of it," replied Skruf. "I have watched you use it. I could do the same. Let me show you."

But von Horst was determined to maintain the ascendancy that his sole knowledge of the use of the pistol gave him, and it was later to develop that his decision was a wise one. But the best corroborating evidence of his assurance to Skruf that the weapon would be dangerous to anyone but von Horst was furnished by Skruf himself.

All during the journey Skruf kept referring to his desire to take home the head of a tarag that he might win the consent of his lady-love. He was constantly suggesting that von Horst shoot one of the great brutes for him, until it became evident to both von Horst and Dangar that the fellow was terrified at the thought of attempting to kill one by himself. Von Horst had no intention of tempting fate by seeking an encounter with this savage monster, a creature of such enormous proportions, great strength, and awful ferocity that it has been known to drag down and kill a bull mastodon singlehanded.

They had not chanced to cross the path of one of the monsters; and von Horst was hopeful that they would not, but the law of chance was against him. No one may blame von Horst for a disinclination to pit himself against this monster of a bygone age with the puny weapons that he carried. Even his pistol could do little more than enrage the creature. Could he reach its heart with any weapon it would die eventually, but probably not quickly enough to save him from a terrible mauling and almost certain death. Yet, of course, there was always a chance that he might conquer the great brute.

Then it happened, and so suddenly and unexpectedly that there was no opportunity for preparation. The three men were walking single file along a forest trail. Von Horst was in the lead, followed by Skruf. Suddenly, without warning, a tarag leaped from the underbrush directly in their path not three paces from von Horst. To the eyes of the European it appeared as large as a buffalo, and perhaps it was. Certainly it was a monstrous creature with gaping jaws and flaming eyes.

The instant that it struck the ground in front of the men it leaped for von Horst. Skruf turned and fled, knocking Dangar down in his precipitate retreat. Von Horst had not even time to draw his pistol, so quickly was the thing upon him. He happened to be carrying his spear in his right hand with the tip forward. He never knew whether the thing he did was wholly a mechanical reaction or whether by intent. He dropped to one knee, placed the butt of the spear on the ground and pointed the head at the beast's throat; and in the same instant the tarag impaled itself upon the weapon. Von Horst held his ground; the shaft of the spear did not break; and notwithstanding all its strength and size, the beast could not quite reach the man with its talons.

It screamed and roared and threshed about, tearing

at the spear in an agony of pain and rage; and every instant von Horst expected that the shaft must break and let the beast fall upon him. Then Dangar ran in and, braving the dangers of those clawing talons, thrust his spear into the tarag's side—not once, but twice, three times the sharp stone point sank into the heart and lungs of the great tiger until, with a final scream, it sank lifeless to the ground. And when it was all over, Skruf descended from a tree in which he had taken refuge and fell upon the carcass with his crude knife. He paid no attention to either von Horst or Dangar as he hacked away until he finally severed the head. Then he wove a basket of long grasses and strapped the trophy to his back. All this he did without even a by-your-leave, nor did he thank the men who had furnished the trophy with which he hoped to win a mate.

Both von Horst and Dangar were disgusted with him, but perhaps the European was more amused than angry; however, the remainder of that march was made in silence, nor did one of them refer to the subject again in any way, though the stench from the rotting head waxed more and more unbearable as they proceeded on their way to the country of the Bastians.

The three men had hidden themselves away in a deserted cave high in a cliffside to sleep, shortly following the encounter with the tarag which had occurred after Skruf had made his final appeal for a chance to show what he could do with a pistol, when von Horst and Dangar were awakened by a shot. As they leaped to their feet, they saw Skruf toppling to the floor of the cave as he hurled the pistol from him. Von Horst rushed to the man's side where he lay writhing and moaning, but a brief examination convinced the European that the fellow was more terrified than hurt. His face was powder marked, and there was a red welt across one cheek where the bullet had grazed it. Otherwise, the only damage done was to his nervous system; and that had received a shock from which it did not soon recover. Von Horst turned away and picked up his pistol. Slipping it into its holster, he lay down again to sleep. "The next time it will kill you, Skruf," he said. That was all. He was confident that the man had learned his lesson. For some time after the incident in the cave, Skruf was taciturn and surly; and on several occasions von Horst detected the man eyeing him with an ugly expression on his dark countenance; but eventually this mood either passed or was suppressed, for as they neared Basti he grew almost jovial.

"We'll soon be there," he announced after a long sleep. "You're going to see a tribe of fine people, and you're going to be surprised by the reception you'll get. Basti is a fine country; you'll never leave it."

On that march, they left the low country and the river they had been following and entered low hills beyond which loomed mountains of considerable height. Eventually Skruf led them into a narrow gorge between chalk cliffs. It was a winding gorge along which they could see but a short distance either ahead or behind. A little stream of clear water leaped and played in the sunlight on its way down to some mysterious, distant sea. Waving grasses grew upon thin topsoil at the summit of the cliffs; and there was some growth at the edges of the stream where soil, washing down from above, had lodged—some flowering shrubs and a few stunted trees.

Skruf was in the lead. He appeared quite excited, and kept repeating that they were almost at the village of the Bastians. "Around the next turn," he said presently, "the lookout will see us and give the alarm."

The prophesy proved correct, for as they turned a sharp corner of the cliff upon their left, a voice boomed out from above them in a warning that reverberated up and down the gorge. "Some one comes!" it shouted, and then to those below him, "Stop! or I kill. Who are you who come to the land of the Bastians?"

Von Horst looked up to see a man standing upon a ledge cut from the face of the chalk cliff. Beside him were a number of large boulders that he could easily shove off onto anyone beneath.

Skruf looked up at the man and replied, "We are friends. I am Skruf."

"I know you," said the lookout, "but I do not know the others. Who are they?"

"I am taking them to Frug, the chief," replied Skruf. "One is Dangar, who comes from a country he calls Sari; the other comes from another country very far away."

"Are there more than three?" asked the lookout.

"No," replied Skruf; "there are only three."

"Take them to Frug, the chief," directed the lookout.

The three continued along the gorge, coming at length to a large, circular basin in the surrounding walls of which von Horst saw many caves. Before each cave was a ledge, and from one ledge to the next ladders connected the different levels. Groups of women and children clustered on the ledges before the mouths of the caves, staring down at them questioningly, evidently having been warned by the cry of the lookout. A row of warriors stretched across the basin between them and the cliffs where the caves lay. They, too, appeared to have been expecting the party, and were ready to receive them in whatever guise they appeared, whether as friends or foes.

"I am Skruf," cried that worthy. "I wish to see Frug. You all know Skruf."

"Skruf has been gone for many sleeps," replied one. "We thought he was dead and would come no more."

"But I am Skruf," insisted the man.

"Come forward then, but first throw down your weapons."

They did as they were bid; but Skruf, who was in the lead, did not observe that von Horst retained his pistol. The three men advanced, and as they did so they were completely surrounded by the warriors of Basti who were now pressing forward.

"Yes, he is Skruf," remarked several as they drew nearer; but there was no cordiality in their tones, no slightest coloring of friendship. They halted presently before a huge man, a hairy man. He wore a necklace of the talons of bears and tigers. It was Frug.

"You are Skruf," he announced. "I see that you are Skruf, but who are these?"

"They are prisoners," replied Skruf, "that I have brought back to be slaves to the Basti. I have also brought the head of a tarag that I killed. I shall place it before the cave of the woman I would mate with. Now I am a great warrior."

Von Horst and Dangar looked at Skruf in amazement. "You have lied to us, Skruf," said the Sarian. "We trusted you. You said that your people would be our friends."

"We are not the friends of our enemies," growled Frug, "and all men who are not Bastians are our enemies."

"We are not enemies," said von Horst. "We have hunted and slept with Skruf as friends for many sleeps. Are the men of Basti all liars and cheats?"

"Skruf is a liar and a cheat," said Frug; "but I did not promise that I would be your friend, and I am chief. Skruf does not speak for Frug."

"Let us go our way to my country," said Dangar. "You have no quarrel with me or my people."

Frug laughed. "I do not quarrel with slaves," he said. "They work, or I kill them. Take them away and put them to work," he ordered, addressing the surrounding warriors.

Immediately several Bastians closed in on them and seized them. Von Horst saw that resistance would be futile. He might kill several of them before he emptied his pistol; but they would almost certainly overpower him in the end; or, more probably, run a half dozen spears through him. Even though they did not, and he escaped temporarily, the lookout in the gorge below would but have to topple a couple of boulders from his ledge to finish him as effectually.

"I guess we're in for it," he remarked to Dangar.

"Yes," replied the Sarian. "I see now what Skruf meant when he said that we would be surprised by the reception we got and that we would never leave Bəsti."

The guards hustled them to the foot of the cliff and herded them up ladders to the highest ledge. Here were a number of men and women working with crude stone instruments chipping and scraping away at the face of the chalk cliff, scooping out a new ledge and additional caves. These were the slaves. A Bastian warrior squatting upon his heels in the shadow of the entrance to a new cave that was being excavated directed the work. Those who had brought Dangar and von Horst to the ledge turned them over to this man.

"Was it Skruf who took these men prisoners?" asked the guard. "It looked like him from here, but it doesn't seem possible that such a coward could have done it."

"He tricked them," explained the other. "He told them they would be received here as friends and be well treated. He brought back the head of a tarag, too; he is going to put it at the entrance to the cave where the slave girl, La-ja, sleeps. He asked Frug for her, and the chief told him he could have her if he brought back the head of a tarag. Frug thought that was a good joke—the same as saying no."

"Men of Basti do not mate with slaves," said the guard.

"They have," the other reminded him; "and Frug has given his word, and he will keep it—only I'd have to see Skruf kill a tarag before I'd believe it."

"He didn't kill it," said Dangar.

The two men looked at him in surprise. "How do you know?" asked the guard.

"I was there," replied Dangar, "when this man killed the tarag. He killed it with a spear while Skruf climbed a tree. After it was dead he came down and cut off its head."

"That sounds like Skruf," said the warrior who had accompanied them to the ledge; then the two turned their attention to von Horst.

"So you killed a tarag with a spear?" one demanded, not without signs of respect.

Von Horst shook his head. "Dangar and I killed it together," he explained. "It was really he who killed it."

Then Dangar told them how von Horst had faced the beast alone and impaled it on his spear. It was evident during the recital that their respect for von Horst was increasing.

"I hope that I am lucky enough to get your heart," said the guard; then he found tools for them and set them to work with the other slaves.

"What do you suppose he meant when he said that he hoped he would be lucky enough to get my heart," asked von Horst after the guard had left them.

"There are men who eat men," replied Dangar. "I have heard of them."

VI

LA-JA

THE SHADOWY coolness of the cave in which von Horst and Dangar were put to work was a relief from the glare and heat of the sun in the open. At first the men were only dimly aware of the presence of others in the cave; but when their eyes became accustomed to the subdued light, they saw a number of slaves chipping at the walls. Some of them were on crude ladders, slowly extending the cave upward. Most of the slaves were men; but there were a few women among them, and one of the latter was working next to von Horst.

A Bastian warrior who was directing the work in the cave watched von Horst for a few moments; then he stopped him. "Don't you know anything?" he demanded. "You are doing this all wrong. Here!" He turned to the woman next to the European. "You show him the way, and see that he does it properly."

Von Horst turned toward the woman, his eyes now accustomed to the subdued light of the cave. She had stopped work and was looking at him. The man saw that she was young and very good looking. Unlike the Bastian women he had seen, she was a blond.

"Watch me," she said. "Do as I do. They will not ill treat you if you are slow, but they will if you make a poor job of what you are doing."

Von Horst watched her for awhile. He noted her regular features, the long lashes that shaded her large, intelligent eyes, the alluring contours of her cheek, her neck, and her small, firm breasts. He decided that she was very much better looking than his first glance had suggested.

Suddenly she turned upon him. "If you watch my hands and the tools you will learn more quickly," she said.

Von Horst laughed. "But nothing half so pleasant," he assured her.

"If you wish to do poor work and get beaten, that is your own affair."

"Watch me," he invited. "See if I have not improved already just from watching your profile."

With his stone chisel and mallet he commenced to chip away at the soft chalk; then, after a moment, he turned to her again. "How is that?" he demanded.

"Well," she admitted reluctantly, "it is better; but it will have to be *much* better. When you have been here as long as I have, you will have learned that it is best to do good work."

"You have been here long?" he asked.

"For so many sleeps that I have lost count. And you?"

"I just came."

The girl smiled. "Came! You mean that you were just brought."

Von Horst shook his head. "Like a fool, I came. Skruf told us that we would be well received, that his people would treat us as friends. He lied to us."

"Skruf!" The girl shuddered. "Skruf is a coward and a liar; but it is well for me that he is a coward. Otherwise he might bring the head of a tarag and place it before the entrance to the cave where I sleep."

Von Horst opened his eyes in astonishment. "You are La-ja, then?" he demanded.

"I am La-ja, but how did you know?" In her musical tones her name was very lovely—the broad a's, the soft j, and the accent on the last syllable.

"A guard said that Frug had told Skruf that he might have you if he brought the head of a tarag. I recalled the name; perhaps because it is so lovely a name."

She ignored the compliment. "I am still safe, then," she said, "for that great coward would run from a tarag."

"He did," said von Horst, "but he brought the head of the beast back to Basti with him."

The girl looked horrified and then skeptical. "You are trying to tell me that Skruf killed a tarag?" she demanded.

"I am trying to tell you nothing of the sort. Dangar and I killed it; but Skruf cut off its head and brought it with him, taking the credit."

"He'll never have me!" exclaimed La-ja tensely. "Before that, I'll destroy myself."

"Isn't there something else you can do? Can't you refuse to accept him?"

"If I were not a slave, I could; but Frug has promised me to him; and, being a slave, I have nothing to say in the matter."

Von Horst suddenly felt a keen personal interest—just why, it would have been difficult for him to explain. Perhaps it was the man's natural reaction to the plight of a defenseless girl; perhaps her great beauty had something to do with it. But whatever the cause, he wanted to help her.

"Isn't there any possibility of escape?" he asked. "Can't we get out of here after dark? Dangar and I would help you and go with you."

"After dark?" she asked. "After what is dark?"

Von Horst grinned ruefully. "I keep forgetting," he said.

"Forgetting what?"

"That it is never dark here."

"It is dark in the caves," she said.

"In my country it is dark half the time. While it is

dark, we sleep; it is light between sleeps."

"How strange!" she exclaimed. "Where is your country, and how can it ever be dark? The sun shines always. No one ever heard of such a thing as the sun's ceasing to shine."

"My country is very far away, in a different world. We do not have the same sun that you have. Some time I will try to explain it to you."

"I thought you were not like any man I had ever seen before. What is your name?"

"Von," he said.

"Von—yes, that is a strange name, too."

"Stranger than Skruf or Frug?" he asked, grinning.

"Why, yes; there is nothing strange about those names."

"If you heard all of my name, that might sound strange to you."

"Is there more than Von?"

"Very much more."

"Tell it to me."

"My name is Frederich Wilhelm Eric von Mendeldorf und von Horst."

"Oh, I could never say all that. I think I like Von."

He wondered why he had told her that Frederich Wilhelm Eric von Mendeldorf und von Horst was his name. Of course he had used it for so long that it seemed quite natural to him; but now that he was no longer in Germany, perhaps it was senseless to continue with it. Yet what difference did it make in the inner world? Von was an easy name to pronounce, an easy one to remember— Von he would continue to be, then.

Presently the girl yawned. "I am sleepy," she said. "I shall go to my cave and sleep. Why do you not sleep at the same time; then we shall be awake at the same time, and—why, I can show you about your work."

"That's a good idea," he exclaimed, "but will they let

me sleep now? I just started to work."

"They let us sleep whenever we wish to, but when we awaken we have to come right back to work. The women sleep in a cave by themselves, and there is a Basti woman to watch them and see that they get to work as soon as they are awake. She is a terrible old thing."

"Where do I sleep?" he asked.

"Come, I'll show you. It is the cave next to the women's."

She led the way out onto the ledge and along it to the mouth of another cave. "Here is where the men sleep," she said. "The next cave is where I sleep."

"What are you doing out here?" demanded a guard.

"We are going to sleep," replied La-ja.

The man nodded; and the girl went on to her cave, while von Horst entered that reserved for the men slaves. He found a number of them asleep on the hard floor, and was soon stretched out beside Dangar, who had accompanied them.

How long he slept, von Horst did not know. He was awakened suddenly by loud shouting apparently directly outside the entrance to the cave. At first he did not grasp the meaning of the words he heard; but presently, after a couple of repetions, he was thoroughly awake; and then he grasped their full import and recognized the voice of the speaker.

It was Skruf; and he was shouting, over and over, "Come out, La-ja! Skruf has brought you the head of a tarag. Now you belong to Skruf."

Von Horst leaped to his feet and stepped out onto the ledge. There, before the entrance to the adjoining cave, lay the rotting head of the tarag; but Skruf was nowhere in sight.

At first von Horst thought that he had entered the cave in search of La-ja; but presently he realized that the voice was coming from below. Looking over the edge of the ledge, he saw Skruf standing on a ladder a few feet below. Then he saw La-ja run from the cave, her countenance a picture of tragic despair.

He had stepped to the head of the ladder, beside which lay the tarag's head, and so was directly in front of the mouth of the cave as La-ja emerged. Something about her manner, her expression, frightened him. She did not seem to see him as she ran past him toward the edge of the cliff. Intuitively, he knew what was in her mind; and as she passed him, he threw an arm about her and drew her back.

"Not that, La-ja," he said quietly.

She came to herself with a start, as though from a trance. Then she clung to him and commenced to sob. "There is no other way," she cried. "He must not get me."

"He shall not," said the man; then he looked down upon Skruf. "Get out of here," he said, "and take your rotten head with you." With his foot, he pushed the mass of corruption over the edge of the ledge so that it fell full upon Skruf. For an instant it seemed that it had toppled him from the ladder, but with agility of a monkey he regained his hold.

"Go on down," directed von Horst, "and don't come up here again. This girl is not for you."

"She belongs to me; Frug said I could have her. I'll have you killed for this." The man was almost frothing at the mouth, so angry was he.

"Go down, or I'll come down there and throw you down," threatened von Horst.

A hand was laid on his shoulder. He swung around. It was Dangar who stood beside him. "Here comes the guard," he said. "You are in for it now. I am with you. What shall we do?"

The guard was coming along the ledge, the same big

fellow that had received them. There were other guards in the several caves that were being excavated, but so far the attention of only this one seemed to have been attracted.

"What are you doing, slave?" he bellowed. "Get to work! What you need is a little of this." He swung a club in his hairy right fist.

"You're not going to hit me with that," said von Horst. "If you come any closer, I'll kill you."

"Your pistol, Von," whispered Dangar.

"I can't waste ammunition," he replied.

The guard had paused. He seemed to be attempting to discover just how the slave intended killing him and with what. To all appearances the man was unarmed; and while he was tall, he was far from being as heavy a man as the guard. Finally the fellow must have concluded that von Horst's words were pure bluff, for he came on again.

"You'll kill me, will you?" he roared; then he rushed forward with club upraised.

He was not very fast on his feet, and his brain was even slower—his reactions were pitifully retarded. So when von Horst leaped forward to meet him, he was not quick enough to change his method of attack in time to meet the emergency. Von Horst stepped quickly to one side as the fellow lunged abreast of him; then he swung a terrific blow to the Bastian's chin, a blow that threw him off balance on the very brink of the ledge. As he tottered there, von Horst struck him again; and this time he toppled out into space; and, with a scream of fright, plunged down toward the bottom of the cliff a hundred feet below.

Dangar and the girl stood there wide-eyed in consternation. "What have you done, Von!" cried the latter. "They will kill you now—and all on my account."

Even as she spoke, another guard emerged from one of the caves farther along the ledge; and then the remaining two came from the other caves in which they had been directing the work of the slaves. The scream of the fellow that von Horst had knocked from the ledge had attracted their attention.

"Get behind me," von Horst directed La-ja and Dangar, "and fall back to the far end of the ledge. They can't take us if they can't get behind us."

"They'll have us cornered then, and there will be no hope for us," objected the girl. "If we go into one of the caves where it is not so light and where there are loose bits of rock to throw at them we may be able to hold them off. But even so, what good will that do? They will get us anyway, no matter what we do."

"Do as I tell you," snapped von Horst, "and be quick about it."

"Who are you to give me orders?" demanded La-ja. "I am the daughter of a chief."

Von Horst wheeled and pushed her back into Dangar's arms. "Take her to the far end of the ledge," he ordered; then he fell back with them, as Dangar dragged the furious La-ja along the ledge. The guards were advancing toward the three. They did not know exactly what had happened, but they knew that something was wrong.

"Where is Julp?" demanded one.

"Where you will be if you don't do as I tell you," replied von Horst.

"What do you mean by that, slave? Where is he?"

"I knocked him off the ledge. Look down."

The three paused and peered over the edge. Below them they saw the body of Julp, and now the angry voices of those who had gathered about it rose to them. Skruf was there. He alone could surmise what had befallen Julp, and he was telling the others about it in a loud tone of voice as Frug joined the group.

"Bring that slave down to me," Frug shouted to the guards on the ledge.

The three started forward again to seize von Horst. The man whipped his pistol from its holster. "Wait!" he commanded. "If you don't wish to die, listen to me. There is the ladder. Go down."

The three eyed the pistol, but they did not know what it was. To them it was nothing more than a bit of black stone. Perhaps they thought that von Horst purposed throwing it at them or using it as a club. The idea made them grin; so they came on, contemptuously.

Now, the woman who guarded the women slaves came from their cave, attracted by all the commotion outside, and joined the men. She was an unprepossessing slattern of indeterminate age with a vicious countenance. Von Horst guessed that she might be even more formidable than the men, but he shrank from the necessity of shooting down a woman. In fact, he did not wish to shoot any of them—poor ignorant cave dwellers of the stone age— but it was their lives or his and Dangar's and La-ja's.

"Go back!" he cried. "Go down the ladder. I don't wish to kill you."

For answer, the men laughed at him and came on. Then von Horst fired. One of the men was directly behind the leader, and at the shot they both collapsed, screaming, and rolled from the ledge. The other man and the woman stopped. The report of the pistol would alone have been sufficient to give them pause, so terrifying was it to them; but when they saw their comrades pitch from the ledge their simple minds were overwhelmed.

"Go down," von Horst commanded them, "before I kill you, too. I shall not give you another chance."

The woman snarled and hesitated, but the man did not wait. He had seen enough. He sprang toward the ladder and hastened to descend, and a moment later the woman gave up and followed him. Von Horst watched them; and when they had reached the next ledge below, he motioned Dangar to him. "Give me a hand with this ladder," he said, and the two dragged it up to the ledge on which they stood. "This will stop them for awhile," he remarked.

"Until they bring another ladder," suggested Dangar.

"That will take a little time," replied von Horst, "—a long time if I take a shot at them while they are doing it."

"Now, what are we to do next?" inquired Dangar.

La-ja was eyeing von Horst from beneath lowering brows, her eyes twin pits of smoldering anger; but she did not speak. Von Horst looked at her and was glad that she did not. He saw trouble ahead in that beautiful, angry face—beautiful even in anger.

The other slaves were now coming fearfully from the caves. They looked about for the guards and saw none; then they saw that the ladder had been drawn up.

"What has happened?" one asked.

"This fool has killed three guards and driven the others away," snapped La-ja. "Now we must either remain here and starve to death or let them come up and kill us."

Von Horst paid no attention to them. He was looking up, scanning the face of the cliff that inclined slightly inward to the summit about thirty feet above him.

"He killed three guards and drove the others off the ledge?" demanded one of the slaves, incredulously.

"Yes," said Dangar; "alone, he did it."

"He is a great warrior," said the slave, admiringly.

"You are right, Thorek," agreed another. "But La-ja is right, too; it is death for us now no matter what happens."

"Death but comes a little sooner; that is all," replied Thorek. "It is worth it to know that three of these eaters of men have been killed. I wish that I had done it."

"Are you going to wait up here until you starve to death or they come up and kill you?" demanded von Horst.

"What else is there to do?" demanded a slave from Amdar.

"There are nearly fifty of us," said von Horst. "It would be better to go down and fight for our lives than wait here to die of thirst or be killed like rats, if there were no other way; but I think there is."

"Your words are the words of a man," exclaimed Thorek. "I will go down with you and fight."

"What is the other way?" asked the man from Amdar.

"We have this ladder," explained von Horst, "and there are other ladders in the caves. By fastening some of them together we can reach the top of the cliff. We could be a long way off before the Bastians could overtake us, for they would have to go far down the gorge before they came to a place where they could climb out of it."

"He is right," said another slave.

"But they might overtake us," suggested another who was timid.

"Let them!" cried Thorek. "I am a mammoth man. Should I fear to fight with my enemies? Never. All my life I have fought them. It was for this that my mother bore me and my father trained me."

"We talk too much," said von Horst. "Talk will not save us. Let those who wish to, come with me; let the others remain here. Fetch the other ladders. See what you can find with which to fasten them together."

"Here comes Frug!" shouted a slave. "He is coming up with many warriors."

Von Horst looked down to see the hairy chief climbing upward toward the ledge; behind him came many warriors. The man from the outer crust grinned, for he knew that his position was impregnable.

"Thorek," he said, "take men into the caves to gather fragments of rock, but do not throw them down upon the Bastians until I give you the word."

"I am a mammoth man," replied Thorek, haughtily. "I do not take orders from any but my chief."

"Right now I am your chief," snapped von Horst. "Do as I tell you. If each of us tries to be chief, if no one will do as I order, we may stay here until we rot."

"I take orders from no man who is not a better man than I," insisted Thorek.

"What does he mean, Dangar?" asked von Horst.

"He means you'll have to fight him—and win—before he'll obey you," explained the Sarian.

"Are all the rest of you fools too?" demanded von Horst. "Do I have to fight each one of you before you will help me to help you escape?"

"If you defeat Thorek, I will obey you," said the man from Amdar.

"Very well, then," agreed von Horst. "Dangar, if any of these idiots will help you, go in and get rocks to hold off Frug until the matter is settled. Just try to keep them from setting up another ladder to this ledge. Thorek, you and I will go into one of the caves and see who is head man. If we tried to decide the matter out here, we'd probably both wind up at the bottom of the cliff."

"All right," agreed the mammoth man. "I like your talk. You will make a great chief—if you win; but you won't. I am Thorek, and I am a mammoth man."

Von Horst was almost amused by the evidences of haughty pride that these primitive people revealed. He had seen it in La-ja in an exaggerated form and now, again, in Thorek. Perhaps he admired them a little for it —he had no patience with spineless worms—but he felt that they might have mixed a little common sense with it. He realized, however, that it reflected a tremendous ego, such as the human race must have possessed in its earliest stages to have permitted it to cope with the forces that must constantly have threatened it with extinction.

He turned to Thorek. "Come," he said; "let's get it over, so that something worth while can be done." As he spoke, he entered one of the caves; and Thorek followed him.

"With bare hands?" asked von Horst.

"With bare hands," agreed the mammoth man.

"Come on, then."

Von Horst, from boyhood, had been a keen devotee of all modes of defense and offense with various weapons and with none at all. He had excelled as an amateur boxer and wrestler. Heretofore it had availed him little of practical value, other than a certain prideful satisfaction in his ability; but now it was to mean very much indeed. It was to establish his position in the stone age among a rugged people who admitted no superiority that was not physical.

At his invitation, Thorek charged down upon him like a wild bull. In height they were quite evenly matched, but Thorek was stockier and outweighed von Horst by ten or fifteen pounds. Their strength was, perhaps, about equal, though the Pellucidarian looked far more powerful because of his bulging muscles. It was skill that would count, and Thorek had no skill. His strategy consisted in overwhelming an antagonist by impetus and weight, crushing him to earth, and pommelling him into insensibility. If he killed him in the process—well, that was just the other fellow's tough luck.

But when he threw himself at von Horst, von Horst was not there. He had ducked beneath the flailing arms and sidestepped the heavy body; then he had landed a heavy blow at Thorek's jaw that had snapped his head and dazed him. But the fellow still kept his feet, turned, and came lumbering in again for more; and he got it. This time he went down. He tried to stagger to his feet, and another blow sent him sprawling. He didn't have a chance. Every time he got part way to his feet, he was knocked flat again. At last he gave up and lay where he had fallen.

"Who is chief?" demanded von Horst.

"You are," said Thorek.

VII

FLIGHT OF THE SLAVES

As von Horst turned and ran out of the cave, Thorek rose groggily to his feet and followed him. On the ledge a number of the slaves were lined up with Dangar ready to hurl rocks on the ascending Bastians, whom von Horst saw had reached the second ledge below that was occupied by the slaves.

He looked about and saw Thorek emerging from the cave. "Take some men and get the ladders," von Horst directed his late antagonist.

The other slaves looked quickly at the mammoth man to see how he would accept this command. What they saw astonished them. Thorek's face was already badly swollen, there was a cut above one eye and his nose was bleeding. His whole face and much of his body were covered with blood, which made his injuries appear graver than they really were.

Thorek turned toward the other slaves. "Some of you go into each cave and bring out the ladders," he said.

"Let the women find thongs with which to bind them together."

"Who is chief?" asked one of the men so addressed.

"He is chief," replied Thorek, pointing at von Horst.

"He is not my chief, and neither are you," retorted the man, belligerently.

Von Horst was suddenly hopeless. How could he get anywhere, how could he accomplish anything, with such stupid egotists to contend with? Thorek, however, was not at all discouraged. He suddenly leaped upon the fellow; and before the man had time to gather his slow wits, lifted him above his head and hurled him from the cliff. Then he turned to the others. "Get the ladders," he said, and as one man they set about doing his bidding.

Now von Horst turned his attention again to Frug and the other warriors below. They offered an excellent target; and he could easily have driven them back had he cared to, but he had another plan. In low tones he issued instructions to his companions, having them line up along the ledge while the Bastians climbed to that directly below. In the meantime the ladders had been carried out; and the women were busy lashing several of them together, making two long ladders.

La-ja stood sullenly apart, glaring at von Horst, and making no pretense of helping the other women with their work; but the man paid no attention to her, which probably added to her resentment and her wrath. Frug was bellowing threats and commands from the ledge below, and from the bottom of the cliff the women and children were shouting encouragement to their men.

"Bring me the man called Von," shouted Frug, "and none of the rest of you shall be punished."

"Come up and get him," challenged Thorek.

"If the men of Basti were better than old women they would do something more than stand down there and shout," taunted von Horst. He threw a small fragment of rock that struck Frug on the shoulder. "See," he exclaimed, "how easily we could drive away the old women who are not strong enough to hurl their spears up here!"

That insult was too much for the Bastians. Instantly spears began to fly; but the slaves were ready, and as the weapons rose to their level they reached out and seized many of them. As the others dropped back to the Bastians, they were hurled again; and soon the slaves were armed, as von Horst had hoped.

"Now, the rocks," he directed; and the slaves commenced to pelt their antagonists with small missiles until they took refuge in the caves on the level below. "Don't let them come out," ordered von Horst. "Dangar, you take five men and let every Bastian that shows his head get a rock on it; the rest of you men raise the ladders."

When the ladders, rickety and sagging, were leaned against the cliff they just topped its summit; and von Horst breathed a sigh of relief as he saw the success of his plan thus more nearly assured. He turned to Thorek. "Take three men and go to the top of the cliff. If the way is clear, tell me; and I will send up the women and the rest of the men."

As Thorek and the three climbed aloft, the ladders creaked and bent; but they held, and presently the mammoth man called down that all was well.

"Now, the women," said von Horst; and all the women but one started up the ladders. That one was La-ja. She ignored the ladders as she had ignored von Horst, and again the man paid no attention to her. Soon all but Dangar and his five men, von Horst, and La-ja had climbed safely to the cliff top. One by one, von Horst sent the five up; and he and Dangar kept the Bastians below confined in the caves where they might not know what was going on upon the ledge above; for he knew that they could bring other ladders from the caves in which they were hiding and enough of them reach the ledge that he and Dangar were defending to overcome them easily.

La-ja, now, was his greatest problem. Had she been a man, he would have left her; and his better judgment told him that he should leave her anyway, but he could not. Perhaps she was a stubborn little fool; but he realized that he could not know what strange standards of pride, custom, environment, and heredity had bequeathed her. How might he judge her? Her attitude might seem right and proper to her, no matter how indefensible it appeared to him.

"I wish you would go up with the others, La-ja," he said. "We three may be recaptured if you don't."

"Go yourself, if you wish," she retorted. "La-ja will remain here."

"Do not forget Skruf," he reminded her.

"Skruf will never have me. I can always die," she replied.

"You will not come, then?" he asked.

"I would rather stay with Skruf than go with you."

Von Horst shrugged and turned away. The girl was watching him intently to see what effects her insult had upon him, and she flushed with anger when he showed no resentment.

"Give them a few more rocks, Dangar," directed von Horst; "then get to the cliff top as fast as you can."

"And you?" asked the Sarian.

"I shall follow you."

"And leave the girl?"

"She refuses to come," replied von Horst.

Dangar shrugged. "She needs a beating," he said.

"I would kill any man that laid a hand on me," said La-ja, belligerently.

"Nevertheless, you need a beating," insisted Dangar; "then you would have more sense." He gathered up several rocks and hurled them at a head that appeared from one of the caves below; then he turned and swarmed up one of the ladders.

Von Horst walked toward the other ladder. It took him close to La-ja. Suddenly he seized her. "I am going to take you with me," he said.

"You are not," she cried, and commenced to strike and kick him.

Without great difficulty he carried her as far as the ladder; but when he tried to ascend it, she clung to it. He struggled upward and gained a couple of rounds, but she fought so viciously and clung so desperately that he soon saw they must be overtaken if the Bastians reached this ledge.

Already he heard their voices raised more loudly from below, indicating that they had come from the caves. He heard Frug directing the raising of a ladder. In a moment they would be upon them. He looked down at the beautiful face of the angry girl. He could drop her and leave her to the tender mercies of the Bastians. There was still time for him to gain the summit of the cliff alone. But there was another way, a way he shrank from; yet he saw no alternative if he were to save them both. He drew back a clenched fist and struck her heavily on the side of the head, and instantly she went limp in his arms; then he climbed upward as rapidly as he could with the dead weight of the unconscious girl hampering his every movement. He had almost reached the top when he heard a shout of triumph below him. Glancing downward, he saw a Bastian just clambering onto the ledge upon which the ladder rested. If the fellow could lay hands upon the ladder he could drag them down to death or recapture. Von Horst shifted the weight of the girl so that her body hung balanced over his left shoulder. This freed his left hand so that he could cling to the ladder as he drew his pistol with his right. He had to swing out and backward to get a bead on the Bastian; and he had to do all this in a fraction of the time it takes to tell it; for if the first man reached the ledge, there would be another directly behind him; and one shot would not stop them both.

He fired just as the Bastian was about to step from the ladder to the ledge. The fellow toppled backward. There were yells and curses from below; and though von Horst could not see what happened, he was certain that the falling body had knocked others from the ladder. Once again he hastened upward, and a moment later Dangar and Thorek reached down and dragged him and the girl to the summit of the cliff.

"Your luck is with you," said Thorek. "Look; they are right behind you."

Von Horst looked down. The Bastians had raised other ladders and were clambering rapidly onto the ledge below. Some of them were already climbing the ladders that the slaves had raised to the cliff top. Others of the slaves were standing near von Horst looking down at the Bastians. "We had better run," said one. "They will soon be up here."

"Why run?" demanded Thorek. "Are we not armed even better than they? We have most of their spears."

"I have a better plan," said von Horst. "Wait until the ladders are full."

He called other slaves to him then, and waited. It was but a matter of seconds when the ladders were both filled with climbing Bastians; then von Horst gave the word, and a score of hands pushed the ladders outward from the face of the cliff. Screams of terror broke from the lips of the doomed Bastians as the slaves toppled the ladders over backward, and a dozen bodies hurtled down the face of the cliff to fall at the feet of the women and children.

"Now," said von Horst, "let's get out of here." He looked down at the girl still lying on the sward where they had placed her, and he was suddenly stunned by the realization that she might be dead—that the blow he had struck her had killed her. He dropped to his knees beside her and placed an ear over her heart. It was beating, and beating strongly. With a sigh of relief, he lifted the inanimate form to his shoulder again.

"Where to now?" he asked, addressing the entire gathering of escaped slaves.

"At first we'd better get out of the Bastian country," counselled Thorek. "After that, we can plan."

The way led through hills and mountain gorges, and finally out into a lovely valley teeming with wild life; but though they often encountered fierce beasts they were not attacked.

"There are too many of us," explained Dangar when von Horst commented upon their apparent immunity. "Occasionally you'll find a beast that will attack a whole tribe of men, but ordinarily they are afraid of us when we are in numbers."

Long before they reached the valley, La-ja regained consciousness. "Where am I?" she demanded. "What has happened?"

Von Horst lowered her from his shoulder and steadied her until he saw that she could stand. "I brought you away from Basti," he explained. "We are free now."

She looked at him, knitting her brows as though trying to recall a fleeting memory that eluded her. "You brought me!" she said. "I said I would not come with you. How did you do it?"

"I—er—I put you to sleep," he fumbled hesitatingly.

The thought that he had struck her humiliated him.

"Oh, I remember," she said; "you struck me."

"I had to," he replied. "I am very sorry, but there was no other way. I could not leave you there among those beasts."

"But you did strike me."

"Yes, I struck you."

"Why did you wish to bring me? Why did you care whether or not I was left to Skruf?"

"Well, you see—I—but how could I leave you there?"

"If you think I am going to be your mate now, you are mistaken," she said with emphasis.

Von Horst flushed. The young lady seemed to be jumping to embarrassing conclusions. She was certainly candid. Perhaps that was a characteristic of the stone age. "No," he replied; "after the things that you said to me and did to me, I had no reason either to believe that you would be my mate or that I would wish you to be."

"Well," she snapped, "I wouldn't be—I should prefer Skruf."

"Thanks," said von Horst. "Now we understand one another."

"And hereafter," said La-ja, "you can attend to your own affairs and leave me alone."

"Certainly," he replied stiffly, "just so long as you obey me."

"I obey no one."

"You'll obey me," he said determinedly, "or I'll punch your head again." The words surprised him much more than they seemed to surprise the girl. How could he have said such a thing to a woman? Was he reverting to some primordial type? Was he becoming, indeed, a man of the old stone age? She walked away from him then and joined the women. On her lips was a strange little melody, such perhaps as women of the outer crust hummed to the singing stars when the world was young.

When they reached the valley, some of the men made a kill; and they all ate. Then they held a council, discussing plans for the future.

Each individual wished to go his way to his own country, and while there was safety in numbers there was also danger to each in going into the country of another. There were some, like Dangar, who could promise a friendly reception to those who wished to accompany them to their land; but there were few who dared take the chance. Both von Horst and Dangar recalled the fair promises of Skruf and the manner in which they had been belied.

To von Horst, it was a strange world; but then, he realized, it might be anywhere from fifty thousand to half a million years younger than the world with which he was familiar, with a corresponding different philosophy and code of ethics. Yet these people were quite similar to types of the outer crust. They were more naive, perhaps; less artificial, and they certainly had fewer inhibitions; but they revealed, usually in a slightly exaggerated form, all the characteristics of present day men and women of a much older humanity.

He considered La-ja. Envisioning her frocked in the latest mode, he realized that she might pass unnoticed, except for her great beauty, in any capital of Europe. No one would dream, to look at her, that she had stepped from the Pleistocene. He was not so certain, however, as to what one might think who crossed her.

The result of the council was a decision of each to return to his own country. There were several from Amdar, and they would go together. There were others from Go-hal. Thorek came from Ja-ru, the country of the mammoth-men; La-ja from Lo-har; Dangar, from Sari. These three, with von Horst, could proceed together for awhile, as their paths lay in the same general direction.

After the council, they sought and found a place to sleep—a place of caves in cliffs. As they awoke, each individual or each party set out in the direction of his own country with only instinct as his guide. The countries of most of them were not far distant. Sari was the farthest. From what von Horst could gather, it might be half way around this savage world; but what was a matter of distance when there was no time by which to measure the duration of a journey?

There were no good-byes. A group or an individual walked out of the lives of those others with whom they had suffered long imprisonment, with whom they had fought and won to freedom; and there was no sign of regret at parting—just the knowledge that when next they met, they would meet as mortal enemies, each eager to slay the other. This was true of most of them, but not of all. There was a real friendship existing between von Horst and Dangar, and something that approached it between these two and Thorek. Where La-ja stood, who might know? She was very aloof. Perhaps because she was the daughter of a chief; perhaps because she was a very beautiful young woman whose pride had been hurt, or who was nursing a knowledge that her woman's intuition had vouchsafed her, or because she was by nature reserved. Whatever her reason, she kept her own counsel.

Several sleeps after the party of slaves had broken up, Thorek announced that his path now diverged from theirs. "I wish that you were coming to Ja-ru with me," he said to von Horst. "You should have been a mammoth man; we are all great warriors. If we ever meet again, let us meet as friends."

"That suits me," replied von Horst. "May it hold for all of us." He looked at Dangar and La-ja.

"A Sarian may be friends with any brave warrior," said the former. "I would be friends always with you."

"I would be friends with Thorek and Dangar," said La-ja.

"And not with Von?" asked the Sarian.

"I would not be friends with Von," she replied.

Von Horst shrugged and smiled. "But I am your friend, always, La-ja," he said.

"I do not wish you for a friend," she replied. "Did I not say so?"

"I'm afraid you can't help yourself."

"We'll see about that," she said, enigmatically.

So Thorek left them, and the three continued on their way. It seemed a hopeless, aimless journey to von Horst. In the bottom of his consciousness, he did not believe that either Dangar or La-ja had the slightest conception of where they were going. He did not possess the homing instinct himself, and so he could not conceive that such a sense existed in man or woman.

When they were confronted by high mountains they circled them. They followed mysterious rivers until they found a ford, and then they crossed in constant danger from weird reptiles that had been long extinct upon the outer crust. The fords were quite bad enough; they never dared swim a river. Never did they know what lay ahead of them, for this country was as strange to the two Pellucidarians as it was to von Horst.

They came through low hills to a narrow valley upon the far side of which grew a dense forest, such a forest as von Horst had never seen before in this world or his own. Even at a distance it looked grim and forbidding. As they passed down the valley, von Horst was glad that their way did not lead through the forest; for he knew how depressing the long gloom of a broad forest might become.

Presently La-ja stopped. "Which way is your country, Dangar?" she asked.

He pointed down the valley. "That way," he said, "until we reach the end of these high hills; then I turn to the right."

"It is not my way," said La-ja. "Lo-har lies this way," and she pointed straight toward the forest. "Now I must leave you and go to my own country."

"The forest does not look good to me," said Dangar. "Perhaps you would never get through it alive. Come to Sari with Von and me. You will be well treated."

The girl shook her head. "I am the daughter of a chief," she said. "I must return to Lo-har and bear sons, for my father has none; otherwise there will be no good chief to rule over my father's people after he is dead."

"But you cannot go alone," said von Horst. "You could never come through alive. You would merely be throwing away your life, and then you would never have any sons at all."

"I must go," she insisted, "or for what purpose am I the daughter of a chief?"

"Aren't you afraid?" asked von Horst.

"I am the daughter of a chief," she said, with her chin in the air, defiantly; but von Horst thought that her square little chin trembled. Perhaps it was just a shadow.

"Good-by, Dangar," she said presently, and turned away from them toward the forest. She did not say good-bye to von Horst; she did not even look at him.

The man from the outer crust watched the trim, clean cut figure of the girl as she made her way toward the wood. He noted for the thousandth time the poise of that blond head, the almost regal carriage, the soft and graceful tread of the panther.

The man did not know what motivated him, he could not interpret the urges that seemed to possess him; something quite beyond reason, something that exhilarated one as might an inspiration, prompted him. He did not wish to reason it out; he wished merely to obey.

He turned to Dangar. "Good-by," he said.

"Good-by?" exclaimed Dangar. "Where are you going?"

"I am going to Lo-har with La-ja," replied von Horst.

VIII

THE FOREST OF DEATH

DANGAR LOOKED at von Horst with surprise as the latter announced that he was going with La-ja. "Why?" he asked.

Von Horst shook his head. "I do not know," he replied. "I have one excellent reason, and that is that I could not see a girl go alone through this savage country, into that beastly looking forest; but I know that there is something else, much deeper, that impels me; something as inexplicable and inescapable as instinct."

"I will come with you," said Dangar.

Von Horst shook his head. "No. Go on to Sari. If I live, I'll follow you later."

"You could never find Sari."

"With your help, I can."

"How can I help you if I am not with you?" demanded Dangar.

"You can blaze the trail. Put marks on trees. Place stones upon the ground, like this, showing the direction you are going." He placed some stones in a row pointing in the direction they had been going, forming an arrow. "Mostly you follow animal trails; so you will have only to indicate the places that you branch off from the main trails. If you will do these things, I can follow you. I shall blaze my trail from here to wherever I go; so that I can find my way back."

"I do not like to leave you," said Dangar.

"It is best," replied von Horst. "There is a girl waiting for you in Sari. There is no one waiting for me anywhere. We do not know how far it is to La-ja's country. We might never reach it; we might never return if we did. It is best that you go on to Sari."

"Very well," said Dangar. "I shall be expecting you there. Good-by." He turned and started off down the little valley.

Von Horst watched him for a moment, thinking of the strange circumstances that had brought them together across five hundred thousand years; thinking also of the even more remarkable fact that they had found so much in common upon which to build an enduring friendship. He sighed and turned in the direction that La-ja had gone.

The girl was half way to the forest, swinging along easily with her chin up and never looking back. She looked so little against the background of that mighty forest, and so brave. Something very much like tears momentarily dimmed the man's eyes as he watched her; then he set out after her.

Something of what he was doing he realized, but not all. He knew that it was quite likely that he was following the girl into an untracked wilderness from which neither of them would ever emerge; and that he was cutting himself off, doubtlessly forever, from his only friend in all this savage world, from the chance to go to a country where he might live in comparative security and make new friends—and all this for a girl who shunned and snubbed him. But what he did not know was that Jason Gridley would eventually decide to remain in the inner world, when the rest of the expedition sailed for the north polar opening and the outer crust, and proceed to Sari, there to form an expedition to search for him. He did not know that he was quite probably throwing away this one chance for succor; but if he had known it, there is little likelihood that it would have altered his decision.

He overtook La-ja just at the edge of the forest. She had heard his footsteps behind her and had turned to see who or what was following her. She did not seem greatly surprised. In fact, it seemed to von Horst that nothing could surprise La-ja.

"What do you want?" she inquired.

"I am going with you to Lo-har," he replied.

"The warriors of Lo-har will probably kill you when you get there," she prophesied cheerfully.

"I am going with you just the same," insisted von Horst.

"I did not ask you to come. You had better go back and go to Sari with Dangar."

"Listen to me, La-ja," he begged. "I cannot let you go alone, knowing the dangers you may have to face—wild beasts and savage men. I must go with you as long as there is no one else to go; so why can't we be friends? Why do you dislike me so? What have I done?"

"If you come with me it will have to be as though we were friends—just friends—whether we are friends or not," she replied, ignoring his last two queries. "Do you understand that—just as friends?"

"I understand," he said. "Have I ever asked more of you?"

"No." She rather snapped the word.

"Nor shall I. My only thought is for your safety. When you are among your own people, I shall leave you."

"If they don't kill you before you can escape," she reminded him.

"Why should they wish to kill me?" he demanded.

"You are a stranger; and we always kill strangers, so that they will not kill us—or nearly always. Sometimes, if we have reason to like them very much we let them live; but Gaz will not like you. He will kill you if the others don't."

"Who is Gaz? Why should he wish to kill me?"

"Gaz is a great warrior, a mighty hunter; single-handed he has killed a ryth."

"I am not a ryth; so I still don't see why he should wish to kill me," insisted von Horst.

"He will not like it when he learns that we have been together for so many sleeps. He is a very jealous man."

"What is he to you?" demanded von Horst.

"He hoped to mate with me before I was captured by the Bastian. If he has not taken another mate, he will still wish to. Gaz has a very quick temper and a very bad one. He has killed many men. Often he kills them first and then inquires about them later. Thus has he killed many men whom he would not have killed had he taken the time to discover that they had not harmed him."

"Do you wish to mate with him?" asked von Horst.

She shrugged her shapely shoulders. "I must mate with some one, for I must bear sons that Lo-har may have a chief when my father dies; and La-ja would mate only with a mighty man. Gaz is a mighty man."

"I asked you if you wished to mate with him—do you love him, La-ja?"

"I do not love any one," she replied; "and, furthermore, it is none of your affair. You are always meddling and asking questions that do not concern you. Come, if you are coming with me. We cannot get to Lo-har by standing still talking nonsense."

"You will have to lead the way," he said. "I do not know where Lo-har lies."

They started on. "Where is your country?" she asked. "Perhaps it lies beyond Lo-har in the same direction. That would be fine for you, provided, of course, that you got out of Lo-har alive."

"I do not know where my country is," he admitted.

She knitted her brows and looked at him in astonishment. "You mean that you could not find your way home?" she demanded.

"Just that. I wouldn't have the faintest idea even in which direction to start."

"How strange," she commented. "I have never heard of any so stupid as that, other than the poor creatures whose heads are sick. They know nothing at all. I have seen a few such. They get that way from blows on the head. Once a boy I knew fell out of a tree and landed on his head. He was never right again. He used to think he was a tarag and go roaring and growling about on his hands and knees, but one day his father got tired of listening to him and killed him."

"Do you think I am like that boy?" asked von Horst.

"I have never seen you act like a tarag," she admitted; "but you do have very peculiar ways, and in many things you are very stupid."

Von Horst could not repress a smile, and the girl saw him. She appeared nettled. "Do you think it anything to laugh about?" she demanded. "Say, what are you doing? Why do you chop at so many trees with your knife? That is enough to make one think that there may be something the matter with your head."

"I am marking the trail that we pass," he explained, "so that I can find my way back after I leave you."

She seemed very interested. "Perhaps your head is not

so sick after all," she said. "Even my father never thought of anything like that."

"He wouldn't have to if he can find his way about as easily as you Pellucidarians can," von Horst reminded her.

"Oh, it is not always so easy to find our way any place except to our own countries," she explained. "Take us anywhere in Pellucidar and we can find our way home, but we might not be able to find our way back again to the place we had been taken. With your method, we could. I shall have to tell this to my father."

As they penetrated more deeply into the forest, von Horst was impressed by its strangely somber and gloomy atmosphere. The dense foliage of the tree tops formed an unbroken roof above their heads, shutting out all direct rays of the sun. The result was a perpetual twilight, with a temperature considerably lower than any he had experienced in the open—the two combining to retard the growth of underbrush, so that the ground between the boles of the trees was almost bare of anything other than a carpet of dead leaves. What few plants had had the hardihood to withstand these conditions were almost colorless—unhealthy, grotesque appearing forms that but added to the melancholy aspect of the repellent wood.

From the moment that they entered the forest the ground rose rapidly until they were climbing a very considerable ascent; then they suddenly topped a ridge and descended into a ravine, but the forest continued unbroken as far as they could see.

As La-ja crossed the ravine and started up the farther ascent, von Horst asked her why she didn't try to find an easier way by following the ravine down until they reached the end of the hills.

"I am following a straight line to Lo-har," she replied.

"But suppose you came to a sea?" he asked.

"I would go around it, of course," she replied; "but where I can go at all, I go in a straight line."

"I hope there are no Alps on our route," he remarked, half aloud.

"I do not know what Alps are," said La-ja, "but there will be plenty of other animals."

"There will have to be more animals than we have seen since we got into this wood," remarked von Horst, "if we are to eat. I haven't seen even so much as a bird."

"I have noticed that," replied La-ja. "I have also noticed that there are no fruits or nuts, nor any other edible thing. I do not like this forest. Perhaps it is the Forest of Death."

"What is the Forest of Death?"

"I have heard of it. My people speak of it. It lies down some distance from Lo-har. In it live a race of horrible people who are not like any other people. Perhaps this is it."

"Well, we haven't seen anything so far that could harm us," von Horst reassured her.

They had climbed out of the ravine and were on more level ground. The forest seemed even denser than it had been farther back. Only a dim, diffused light relieved the darkness.

Suddenly La-ja stopped. "What was that?" she asked in a whisper. "Did you see it?"

"I saw something move, but I did not see what it was," replied the man. "It disappeared among the trees ahead of us and to the right. Is that what you saw?"

"Yes. It was right over there." She pointed. "I do not like this forest. I do not know why, but it is as though it were vile—unclean."

Von Horst nodded. "It is eerie. I shall be glad when we are well out of it."

"There!" exclaimed La-ja. "There it is again. It is all white. What could it be?"

"I don't know. I just had the briefest glimpse of it; but I thought—I thought it was something almost human. It is so dark in here that it is difficult to discern objects clearly unless one is very close to them."

They walked on in silence, keeping a sharp lookout in all directions; and von Horst noticed that the girl remained very close to him. Often her shoulder touched his breast as though she sought the reassurance of personal contact. He was doubly glad now that he had insisted upon coming with her. He knew that she would not admit that she was frightened; and he would not suggest it, but he knew that she was frightened. For some inexplicable reason—inexplicable to him—he was glad that she was. Perhaps it satisfied the protective instinct in him. Perhaps it made her seem more feminine, and von Horst liked feminine women.

They had gone some little distance from the point at which they had seen the mysterious creature moving among the trees, without seeing any other suggestion of life in the forest, when they were startled by a series of shrieks, mingled with which were roars and a strange hissing sound. They both stopped, and La-ja pressed close to von Horst. He felt her tremble ever so slightly; and threw an arm about her, reassuringly. The sounds were coming rapidly closer. The screams, sounding strangely human, were filled with terror and despair, rising to a piercing crescendo of fright. Then the author of them burst into view—a naked man, his face distorted by terror. And such a man! His skin was a dead white, without life or beauty; and his hair was white. Two great canine tusks curved downward to his chin, the pink irises of his eyes surrounded blood-red pupils to make an already repellent countenance still further hideous.

Behind him, hissing and roaring, galloped a small dinosaur. It was not much larger than a Shetland pony; but its appearance might easily have caused even the bravest of men misgivings, so similar was it in everything but size to the mighty Tyrannosaurus Rex, the king of the tyrant reptiles of the Cretaceous.

At sight of La-ja and von Horst, the dinosaur veered suddenly in their direction and came hissing and roaring down upon them like a steam locomotive gone amuck. So close was it that there was not even time to seek safety behind a tree; and von Horst's reaction was the natural and almost mechanical one of a man of his training. He whipped his revolver from its holster and fired; then he leaped quickly out of the path of the charging brute, dragging La-ja with him.

The dinosaur, badly hit, roared with rage, nearly going down. As it stumbled past him, the man fired again, placing a heavy .45 slug just behind the left shoulder. This time the beast fell; but knowing the remarkable life tenacity of the reptilia, von Horst was not over confident that all danger was past. Grasping La-ja by a hand, he ran quickly to the nearest tree, behind the bole of which they sought concealment. Above them and out of reach were the lowest branches—a perfect sanctuary that they could not gain. If the two bullets had not permanently stopped the dinosaur, their principal hope lay in the possibility that after it regained its feet, if it did not immediately see them it would go blundering off in the wrong direction.

From behind the tree, von Horst watched the beast pawing up the matted vegetation as it sought to regain its feet. He could see that it was far from dead, although badly hit. La-ja pressed close to him. He could feel her heart beating against his side. It was a tense moment as the dinosaur finally staggered up. For a moment it swayed as though about to fall again; then it swung slowly about in a circle, its muzzle raised, sniffing the air. Presently it started in their direction—slowly, cautiously. Its appearance now seemed far more menacing to von Horst than had its mad charge. It gave the impression of being a cold, calculating, efficient engine of destruction, an animated instrument of revenge that would demand an eye for an eye and not give up the ghost until vengeance had been achieved. It was coming straight toward the tree behind which they were hiding. Whether it had discovered the small portion of von Horst's head that was revealed beyond the edge of the bole, the man did not know; but it was certainly coming toward them guided either by sight or by scent.

It was a tense moment for von Horst. For the instant he was uncertain as to what he should do. Then he decided. Leaning close to La-ja, he whispered, "The beast is coming. Run for that tree behind us, keeping this tree between you and the beast, so that it does not see you; then keep going from one tree to another until you are safely away. When it is dead I will call to you."

"And what will you do? Will you come with me?"

"I'll wait here to make sure that it dies," he replied. "I can give it a few more shots if necessary."

She shook her head. "No."

"Hurry!" he urged. "It is quite close. It is looking for us."

"I shall remain here with you," said La-ja with finality.

From her tone of voice he knew that there was nothing more to be said. From past experience he knew his La-ja. With a shrug, he gave up the argument; then he looked out once more to see the dinosaur within a few paces of the tree.

Suddenly he leaped from behind the tree and started on a run across the front of the beast. He had acted so quickly that La-ja was stunned to inaction by surprise. But not the dinosaur. It did just what von Horst had hoped and believed it would. With a bellow of rage, it took after him. Thus he drew it away from the girl. This accomplished, he turned and faced the brute. Standing his ground, he fired rapidly from his automatic, placing his bullets in the broad chest. Yet the thing came on.

Von Horst emptied his weapon; the dinosaur was almost upon him; he saw La-ja running rapidly toward him, as though in an effort to divert the charge of the infuriated reptile with the comparatively puny spear that she carried. He tried to leap aside from the path of the charging beast, but it was too close. It rose upon its hind feet and struck at his head with a taloned fore paw, felling him, unconscious, to the ground.

IX

THE CHARNEL CAVES

VON HORST experienced a sensation of peace and well being. He was vaguely aware that he was awakening from a long and refreshing sleep. He did not open his eyes. He was so comfortable that there seemed no reason to do so, but rather to court a continuance of the carefree bliss he was enjoying.

This passive rapture was rudely interrupted by a growing realization that his head ached. With returning consciousness his nervous system awoke to the fact that he was far from comfortable. The sensation of peace and well being faded as the dream it was. He opened his eyes and looked up into the face of La-ja, bending solicitously close above his own. His head was pillowed in her lap. She was stroking his forehead with a soft palm.

"You are all right, Von?" she whispered. "You will not die?"

He smiled up at her, wryly. " 'O Death! Where is thy sting?' " he apostrophized.

"It didn't sting you," La-ja assured him; "it hit you with its paw."

Von Horst grinned. "My head feels as though it had hit me with a sledge hammer. Where is it? What became of it?" He turned his head painfully to one side and saw the dinosaur laying motionless near them.

"It died just as it struck you," explained the girl. "You are a very brave man, Von."

"You are a very brave girl," he retorted. "I saw you running in to help me. You should not have done that."

"Could I have stood and watched you being killed when you had deliberately drawn the charge of the zarith upon yourself to save me?"

"So that is a zarith?"

"Yes, a baby zarith," replied the girl. "It is well for us that it was not a fullgrown one, but of course one would never meet a fullgrown zarith in a forest."

"No? Why not?"

"For one reason they are too big; and, then, they couldn't find any food here. A fullgrown zarith is eight times as long as a man is tall. It couldn't move around easily among all these trees; and when it stood up on its hind feet, it'd bump its head on the branches. They kill thags and tandors and other large game that seldom enters the forests—at least not forests like this one."

Von Horst whistled softly to himself as he tried to visualize a reptile nearly fifty feet in length that fed on the great Bos, the progenitors of modern cattle, and upon the giant mammoth. "Yes," he soliloquized, "I imagine it's just as well that we ran into Junior instead of papa. But, say, La-ja, what became of that man-thing the zarith was chasing?"

"He never stopped running. I saw him looking back after you made the loud noise with that thing you call peestol, but he did not stop. He should have come back to help you, I think; though he must have thought that you were sick in the head not to run. It takes a very brave man not to run from a zarith."

"There wasn't any place to run. If there had been, I'd still be running."

"I do not believe that," said La-ja. "Gaz would have run, but not you."

"You like me a little better, La-ja?" he asked. He was starved for friendship—for even the friendship of this savage little girl of the stone age.

"No," said La-ja, emphatically. "I do not like you at all, but I know a brave man when I see one."

"Why don't you like me, La-ja?" he asked a little wistfully. "I like you. I like you—a lot." He hesitated. How much did he like her?

"I don't like you because you are sick in the head, for one thing; for another, you are not of my tribe; furthermore, you try to order me around as though I belonged to you."

"I'm sure sick in the head now," he admitted; "but that doesn't effect my good disposition or my other sterling qualities, and I can't help not being a member of your tribe. You can't hold that against me. It was just a mistake on the part of my father and mother in not having been born in Pellucidar; and really you can't blame them for that, especially when you consider that they never even heard of the place. And, La-ja, as for ordering you around; I never do it except for your own good."

"And I don't like the way you talk sometimes, with a silent laugh behind your words. I know that you are laughing at me—making fun of me because you think that the world you came from is so much better than Pellucidar—that its people have more brains."

"Don't you think that you will ever learn to like me?" he asked, quite solemn now.

"No," she said; "you will be dead before I could have time."

"Gaz, I suppose, will attend to that?" he inquired.

"Gaz, or some other of my people. Do you think you could stand now?"

"I am very comfortable," he said. "I have never had such a nice pillow."

She took his head, quite gently, and laid it on the ground; then she stood up. "You are always laughing at me with words," she said.

He rose to his feet. "*With* you, La-ja; never *at* you," he said.

She looked at him steadily as though meditating his words. She was attempting, he was sure, to conjure some uncomplimentary double meaning from them; but she made no comment.

"Do you think you can walk?" was all that she said.

"I don't feel much like dancing even a saraband," he replied, "but I think I can walk all right. Come on, lead the way to Lo-har and the lightsome Gaz."

They resumed their journey deeper into the gloomy wood, speaking seldom as they toiled up the steep ascents that constantly confronted them. At length they came to a sheer cliff that definitely blocked their further progress in a straight line. La-ja turned to the left and followed along its foot. As she did not hesitate or seem in the slightest doubt, von Horst asked her why she turned to the left instead of to the right. "Do you know the shortest way when you cannot go in a straight line?" he asked.

"No," she admitted; "but when one does not know and cannot follow one's head, then one should always turn to the left and follow one's heart."

He nodded, comprehendingly. "Not a bad idea," he said. "At least it saves one from useless speculation." He glanced up the face of the cliff, casually measuring its height with his eyes. He saw the same great trees of the forest growing close to the edge, indicating that the forest continued on beyond; and he saw something else—just a fleeting glimpse of something moving, but he was sure that he recognized it. "We are being watched," he said.

La-ja glanced up. "You saw something?" she asked.

He nodded. "It looked like our white-haired friend, or another just like him."

"He was not our friend," remonstrated the literal La-ja.

"I was laughing with words, as you say," he explained.

"I wish that I liked you," said La-ja.

He looked at her in surprise. "I wish that you did, but why do *you* wish it?"

"I would like to like a man who can laugh in the face of danger," she replied.

"Well, please try; but do you really think that fellow is dangerous? He didn't look very dangerous when we saw him presenting the freedom of the forest to the zarith."

She knit her brows and looked at him with a puzzled expression. "Sometimes you seem quite like other people," she said; "and then you say something, and I realize that your head is very sick."

Von Horst laughed aloud. "I opine that the twentieth

century brand of humor doesn't go so well in the Pleistocene."

"There you go again!" she snapped. "Even my father, who is very wise, would not know what you were talking about half the time."

As they moved along the foot of the cliff, they kept constantly alert for any further sign that they were being watched or followed.

"What makes you think that this white-haired man is dangerous?" he asked.

"He alone might not be dangerous to us: but where there is one there must be a tribe, and any tribe of strange people would be dangerous to us. We are in their country. They know the places where they might most easily set upon us and kill us. We do not know what is just beyond the range of our vision.

"If this is the Forest of Death, the people who dwell here are dangerous because they are not as other men. I have heard it said. None of my people who are living has ever been here, but stories handed down from father to son tell of strange things that have happened in the Forest of Death. My people are brave people, but none of them would go to that forest. There are things in Pellucidar that warriors cannot fight with weapons. It is known that there are such things in the Forest of Death. If we are indeed in it, we shall never live to reach Lo-har."

"Poor Gaz!" exclaimed von Horst.

"What do you mean?"

"I am sorry for him because he will not have the pleasure of killing me or taking you for his mate."

She looked at him in disgust, continuing on in silence. They both watched for signs of the trailers they were sure were following them; but no sound broke the deathly silence of the wood, nor did they see aught to confirm their suspicions; so at length they decided that whatever it was they had seen at the cliff top had departed and would not molest them.

They came to the mouth of a cave in the cliff; and as they had not slept for some time, von Horst suggested that they go in and rest. His head still ached, and he felt the need of sleep. The mouth of the cave was quite small, making it necessary for von Horst to get down on his hands and knees and crawl in to investigate. He shoved his spear in ahead of him and felt around with it to assure himself that no animal was lairing in the darkness of the interior as well as to discover if the cave were large enough to accommodate them.

Having satisfied himself on both these points, he entered the cave; and a moment later La-ja joined him. A cursory exploration assured them that the cave ran back some little distance into the cliff, but as they were only interested in enough space wherein to sleep they lay down close to the entrance. Von Horst lay with his head to the opening, his spear ready to thrust at any intruder that might awaken him. La-ja lay a few feet from him farther back in the cave. It was very dark and quiet. A gentle draft of fresh air came through the entrance dispelling the damp and musty odors which von Horst had come to expect in caves. Soon they were asleep.

When von Horst awoke, his head no longer ached; and he felt much refreshed. He turned over on his back and stretched, yawning.

"You are awake?" asked La-ja.

"Yes. Are you rested?"

"Entirely. I just woke up."

"Hungry?"

"Yes, and thirsty, too," she admitted.

"Let's get started, then," he suggested. "It looks as

though we'd have to get out of this forest before we find food."

"All right," she said, "but what makes it so dark out?"

Von Horst got to his knees and faced the entrance to the cave. He could see nothing. Even the gloom of the forest had been blotted out. He thought it possible that he had become turned around in his sleep and was looking in the wrong direction, but no matter which way he turned he was confronted always by the same impenetrable blackness. Then he crawled forward, feeling with his hands. Where he had thought the entrance to be he found the rounded surface of a large boulder. He felt around its edges, discovering loose dirt.

"The entrance has been blocked up, La-ja," he said.

"But what could have done it without awakening us?" she demanded.

"I don't know," he admitted, "but in some way the mouth of the cave has been filled with a boulder and loose dirt. There isn't a breath of air coming in as there was when we entered."

He tried to push the boulder away, but he could not budge it. Then he started to scrape away the loose dirt, but what he scraped away was replaced by more sifting in from the outside. La-ja came to his side and they exerted their combined weight and strength in an effort to move the boulder, but to no avail.

"We are penned up here like rats in a trap," said von Horst in deep disgust.

"And with our air supply shut off we'll suffocate if we don't find some way to get out."

"There must be another opening," said von Horst.

"What makes you think so?" asked the girl.

"Don't you recall that when we came in there was a draft of air entering from the outside?" he asked.

"Yes, that's right; there was."

"Well, if the air came in this entrance in a draft, it must have gone out some other opening; and if we can find that opening, perhaps we can get out, too."

"Do you suppose the white-haired man and his people blocked the entrance?" asked La-ja.

"I imagine so," replied von Horst. "It must have been men of some kind; no animal could have done it so quietly as not to have awakened us; and, of course, for the same reason, an earthquake is out of the question."

"I wonder why they did it?" mused the girl.

"Probably an easy and safe way to kill strangers who come to their country," suggested von Horst.

"Just let us starve to death or suffocate," said the girl in disgust. "Only cowards would do that."

"I'll bet Gaz would never do anything like that," said von Horst.

"Gaz? He has killed many men with his bare hands. Sometimes he bites the great vein in their neck and they bleed to death, and once he pushed a man's head back until he broke his neck."

"What a nice little play fellow!"

"Gaz never plays. He loves to kill—that is his play."

"Well, if I'm going to meet him, I'll have to get out of here. Let's follow the cave back and see if we can find the other opening. Stay close behind me."

Von Horst rose slowly to gauge the height of the cave and found that they could stand erect; then he groped his way cautiously toward the rear, touching a wall with one hand. He moved very slowly, feeling ahead with each foot for solid ground before he planted it. They had not gone far when von Horst felt what appeared to be twigs and leaves beneath his feet. He stooped and felt of them. They were dry branches with dead leaves still clinging to them and long thick grasses. The floor of the cave here was strewn thickly with them.

"Must have been a sleeping place for some animal or perhaps for men," he suggested. "I wish we had a light; I don't like groping along in the dark like this."

"I have my fire stones," said La-ja. "If we had some tinder, I could light a bundle of these grasses."

"I'll make some," said von Horst.

He stooped and cleared a place on the floor, exposing the bare ground; then he gathered some of the dried leaves and powdered them between his palms, making a little pile of the tinder on the bare ground.

"Come and try it, now," he said. "Here," he guided her hand to the tinder.

La-ja knelt beside him and struck her fire stones together close above the little a single fragment, and it commenced to glow. La-ja bent low and blew gently upon it. Suddenly it burst into flame. Von Horst was ready with a bundle of the grasses he had gathered for the purpose, and a moment later he held a blazing torch in his hand.

In the light of the torch they looked about them. They were in a large chamber formed by the widening of the cave. The floor was littered with twigs and grasses among which were a number of gnawed bones. Whether it was the den of beasts or men, von Horst could not tell; but from the presence of the bedding he judged that it was the latter. Yet there was no article of cast-off clothing, no broken or discarded weapon or tool that he could find, no potsherds. If men had dwelt here they must have been of a very low order.

Before their torch burned low they gathered grasses and made a quantity of them, and thus supplied with the assurance of light for a considerable time they continued on through the large chamber into a narrow corridor that wound and twisted into the heart of the escarpment. Presently they came to another even larger chamber. This, too, bore evidence of having been inhabited; but the relics here were of a grisly nature. The floor was strewn with the bones and skulls of human beings. A foul odor of decaying flesh permeated the air of this subterranean charnel chamber.

"Let's get out of here," said von Horst.

"There are three openings beside the one we came in," said La-ja. "Which one shall we take?"

Von Horst shook his head. "We may have to try them all," he said. "Let's start with the one farthest on our right. It may be as good a guess as any; and at best it's only a guess, no matter which one we decide on."

As they approached the opening they were almost overpowered by the stench that came from it, but von Horst was determined to investigate every possible avenue of escape; so he stepped through the opening into a smaller chamber. The sight that met his eyes brought him to a sudden halt. A dozen human corpses were piled against the far wall of the chamber. A single glance showed von Horst that there was no outer opening leading from the room; so he beat a hasty retreat.

One of the two remaining openings from the large chamber was smoke blackened, and on the floor of the cave just in front of it were the ashes and charcoal of many wood fires. It's appearance gave von Horst an idea. He walked to the second opening and held his smoking torch close to it, but the smoke rose steadily; then he went to that before which fires had been built, and now the smoke from his torch was drawn steadily into the opening.

"This one must lead to the outer opening," he said, "and it also served as a chimney when they cooked their feasts. Nice lot, whoever they are that inhabit these caves. I think I prefer Gaz. We'll try this one, La-ja."

A narrow corridor rose steeply. It was blackened with

soot, and the draft that wafted continually up it was laden with the stench from the horror chambers below.

"It can't be far to the top," said von Horst. "The cliff didn't look more than fifty feet high, and we have been climbing a little all the time since we first entered the cave."

"It's getting light ahead," said La-ja.

"Yes, there's the opening!" exclaimed von Horst.

Ten feet from the surface they passed the openings to two corridors or chambers, one on either side of the shaft they were ascending; but so engrossed were they in escaping from the foul air that surrounded them that they scarce noticed them. Nor did they see the forms lurking in the darkness just within.

La-ja was just behind von Horst. It was she who discovered the danger first—but too late. She saw hands reach out of one of the openings just as von Horst passed it, seize him, and drag him in. She voiced a cry of warning, and at the same instant she was seized and drawn into the opening on the opposite side.

X

GORBUSES

Von Horst struggled and fought to free himself. He shouted aloud to La-ja to run to the opening they had seen ahead of them and make her escape. He did not know that she, too, had been captured. It seemed that a dozen hands clung to each of his arms, and though he was a powerful man he could neither escape nor wrench his arm free long enough to draw his pistol. His spear had been snatched from him at the moment of his seizure.

It was very dark in the corridor down which he was being dragged along a steep declivity; so that he could not see whether they were men or beasts that had captured him. Yet, though they did not speak, he was sure that they were men. Presently, at a sudden turning of the corridor, they came into a lighted chamber—a vast subterranean room illuminated by many torches. And here von Horst saw the nature of the creatures into whose hands he had fallen. They were of the same race as the man he had seen fleeing from the zarith. They were mostly men; but there were a few women among them and perhaps a dozen children. All had white skins, white hair, and the pink and red eyes of Albinos, which in themselves are not disgusting. It was the bestial, brutal faces of these creatures that made them appear so horrible.

Most of the assemblage, which must have numbered several hundred people, sat or squatted or lay near the wall of the roughly circular chamber, leaving a large open space in the center. To this space von Horst was dragged; then he was thrown to the ground, his hands tied behind his back, and his ankles secured.

As he lay on his side, taking in all that he could see of the repulsive concourse, his heart suddenly sank. From the mouth of a corridor opposite that through which he had been brought into the chamber he saw La-ja being dragged. They brought her to the open space where he lay and bound her as they had bound him. The two lay facing one another. Von Horst tried to smile, but there was not much heart in it. From what he had seen of these people and what he had guessed of their customs, he could draw no slightest ray of hope that they might escape a fate similar to that of those whose ghastly remains they had seen in those other two chambers of the cave.

"It looks like a hard winter," he said.

"Winter? What is winter?" she asked.

"It is the time of year—oh, but then you don't even know what a year is. What's the use? Let's talk about something else."

"Why do we have to talk?"

"I don't know why I have to, but I do. Ordinarily I'm not a very loquacious person, but right now I've got to talk or go crazy."

"Be careful what you say, then," she whispered, "if you are thinking of talking of a way to escape."

"Do you suppose these things can understand us?" he demanded.

"Yes, we can understand you," said one of the creatures standing near them, in hollow, sepulchral tones.

"Then tell us why you captured us. What are you going to do with us?"

The fellow bared his yellowed teeth in a soundless laugh. "He asks what we are going to do with them," he announced in loud tones that were none the less suggestive of the grave because of their loudness.

The audience rocked with silent mirth. "What are we going to do with them?" echoed several, and then they went off into gales of hideous, mirthless laughter that was as silent as the tomb.

"If they want to know, let's show them now," suggested one.

"Yes, Torp," said another, "now, now."

"No," said he who had been addressed as Torp, the same fellow who had originally spoken to von Horst. "We already have plenty, many of which have aged too long as it is." He stepped closer to the prisoners; and, stooping, pinched their flesh, digging a filthy forefinger between their ribs. "They need fattening," he announced. "We shall feed them for a while. Plenty of nuts and a little fruit will put a layer of juicy fat on their ribs." He rubbed his palms together and licked his flabby lips. "Some of you take them away and put them in that little room over there, get nuts and fruit for them; and keep them there until they get fat."

As he finished speaking, another of the creatures entered the room from one of the runways that led above. He was very much excited as he ran into the center of the cavern.

"What's the matter with you, Durg?" demanded Torp.

"I was chased by a zarith," exclaimed Durg, "but that is not all. A strange gilak with a woman made many loud noises with a little black stick, and the zarith fell down and died. The strange gilak saved Durg's life; but why, I do not know."

The men who had gathered about von Horst and La-ja to take them to the chamber in which they were to be fattened had removed the thongs from their ankles and dragged them to their feet just as Durg finished his story; so that he saw them now for the first time.

"There they are!" he exclaimed excitedly. "There is the same gilak that saved Durg's life. What are you going to do with them, Torp?"

"They are going to be fattened," replied Torp; "they are too thin."

"You should let them go, because they saved my life," urged Durg.

"Should I let them go because the man is a fool?" demanded Torp. "If he had any sense he would have killed and eaten you. Take them away."

"He saved a Gorbus!" cried Durg, addressing the assembled tribe. "Should we let him be killed for that? I say, let them go free."

"Let them go!" cried a few, but there were more who shrieked, "Fatten them! Fatten them!"

As the men were pushing them toward the entrance to the chamber in which they were to be confined, von Horst saw Durg facing Torp angrily.

"Some day I am going to kill you," threatened the former. "We need a good chief. You are no good."

"I am chief," screamed Torp. "It is I who will kill you."

"You?" demanded Durg with disgust. "You are only a killer of women. You murdered seven of them. You never murdered a man. I murdered four."

"You poisoned them," sneered Torp.

"I did not!" shrieked Durg. "I killed three of them with a cleaver and stabbed the other with a dagger."

"In the back?" asked Torp.

"No, not in the back, you woman killer."

As von Horst was pushed from the large cavern into the darkness of the small one that adjoined it the two Gorbuses were still quarrelling; and as the European meditated upon what he had heard, he was struck not so much by the gruesomeness of their words as by Durg's use of two English words—cleaver and dagger.

This was sufficiently remarkable in itself, and even more so coming from the lips of a member of a tribe that was apparently so low in the scale of evolution that they had no weapons of any description. How could Durg know what a dagger was? How could he ever have heard of a cleaver? And where did he learn the English words for them? Von Horst could discover no explanation of the mystery.

The Gorbuses left them in the smaller cave without bothering to secure their ankles again, though they left their hands tied behind them. There were leaves and grasses on the floor, and the two prisoners made themselves as comfortable as they could. The torch-light from the larger cave relieved the gloom of their prison cell, permitting them to see one another dimly as they sat on the musty bedding that littered the floor.

"What are we going to do now?" demanded La-ja.

"I don't know of anything that we can do right now," replied the man, "but it appears that later on we are going to be eaten—when we are fatter. If they feed us well we should do our best to get fat. We must certainly leave a good impression behind us when we go."

"That is stupid," snapped the girl. "Your head must be very sick indeed to think of anything so stupid."

"Perhaps 'thick' would be a better word," laughed von Horst. "Do you know, La-ja, it is just *too* bad."

"What is too bad?"

"That you have no sense of humor," he replied. "We could have a much better time if you had."

"I never know when you are serious and when you are laughing with words," she said. "If you will tell me when the things you say are supposed to be funny, perhaps I can laugh at them."

"You win, La-ja," the man assured her.

"Win what?" she demanded.

"My apology and my esteem—you have a sense of humor, even though you don't know it."

"You said a moment ago," said La-ja, "that you didn't know of anything that we could do right now. Don't you wish to escape, or would you rather stay here and get eaten?"

"Of course I'd prefer escaping," replied von Horst, "but I don't see any possibility of it at present while all those creatures are in the big cave."

"What have you got that thing you call peestol for?" demanded La-ja, not without a note of derision. "You killed a zarith with it. You could much more easily kill these Gorbuses; then we could escape easily."

"There are too many of them, La-ja," he replied. "If I fired away all my ammunition, I could not possibly kill enough of them to make escape certain; furthermore my hands are tied behind me. But even were they free, I'd wait to the very last moment before attempting it.

"You have no way of knowing it, La-ja; but when I have used up all these shiny little things tucked in my belt, the pistol will be of no more use to me; for I can never get any more of them. Therefore, I must be very careful not to waste them.

"However, you may rest assured that before I'll let 'em eat either one of us, I'll do a little shooting. My hope is that they will be so surprised and frightened by the reports that they'll fall over one another in their efforts to escape."

As he ceased speaking, a Gorbus entered their little cave. It was Durg. He carried a small torch which illuminated the interior, revealing the rough walls, the litter of leaves and grasses, the two figures lying uncomfortably with bound hands.

Durg looked them over in silence for a moment; then he squatted on the floor near them. "Torp is a stubborn fool," he said in his hollow voice. "He ought to set you free, but he won't. He's made up his mind that we're going to eat you, and I guess we shall.

"It's too bad though. No one ever saved a Gorbus's life before; it was unheard of. If I had been chief, I would have let you go."

"Maybe you can help us anyway," suggested von Horst.

"How?" asked Durg.

"Show us how we can escape."

"You can't escape," Durg assured him emphatically.

"Those people don't stay in that other cave all the time, do they?" demanded the European.

"If they go away, Torp will leave a guard here to see that you don't get away."

Von Horst mused for a moment. Finally he looked up at their grotesque visitor. "You'd like to be chief, wouldn't you?" he demanded.

"S-s-sh!" cautioned Durg. "Don't let anyone hear you say that. But how did you know?"

"I know many things," replied von Horst in a whisper, mysteriously.

Durg eyed him half fearfully. "I knew that you were not as other gilaks," he said. "You are different. Perhaps you are from that other life, that other world, of which Gorbuses get fleeting glimpses out of the dim background of almost forgotten memories. Yes, they are forgotten; and yet there are always reminders of them constantly tormenting us. Tell me—who are you? From whence came you?"

"I am called Von; and I come from the outer world— from a world very different from this one."

"I knew it!" exclaimed Durg. "It must be that there is another world. Once we Gorbuses lived in it. It was a happy world; but because of what we did we were sent away from it to live here in this dark forest, miserable and unhappy."

"I do not understand," said von Horst. "You didn't come from my world; there is no one like you there."

"We were different there," said Durg. "We all feel that we were different. To some the memories are more distinct than to others, but they are never wholly clear. We get fleeting glimpses that are blurred and dim and that fade quickly before we can decipher them or fix them definitely in our memories. It is only those that we murdered that we see clearly—we see them and the way that we murdered them; but we do not see ourselves as we were then, except rarely; and then the visions are only hazy suggestions. But we know that we were not as we are here. It is tantalizing; it drives us almost to mad-

111

ness—never quite to see, never quite to recall.

"I can see the three that I killed with the cleaver—my father and two older brothers—I did it that I might get something they had; I do not know what. They stood in my way. I murdered them. Now I am a naked Gorbus feeding on human bodies. Some of us think that thus we are punished."

"What do you know about cleavers?" asked von Horst, now much interested in the weird recital and its various implications.

"I know nothing of cleavers except that it was with a cleaver I killed my father and my two brothers. With a dagger, I stabbed a man. I do not know why. I can see him—his pain distorted features clearly, the rest of him very vaguely. He had on blue clothes with shiny buttons. Ah, now he has faded away—all but his face. He is glaring at me. I almost had something then—clothes, buttons! What are they? I almost knew—now they are gone. What were the words? What words did I just say? They have gone, too. It is ever thus. We are plagued by half pictures that are snatched away from us immediately."

"You all suffer thus?" asked von Horst.

"Yes," said Durg. "We all see those we have murdered; those are the only memories that we retain permanently."

"You are all murderers?"

"Yes. I am one of the best. Torp's seven women are nothing. Some he killed while they were embracing him with love—he smothered them or choked them. One he strangled with her own hair. He is always bragging about that one."

"Why did he kill them?" demanded La-ja.

"He wished something that they had. It was thus with all of us. I can't imagine what it was I wished when I killed my father and brothers, nor what any of the others wished. Whatever it was, we didn't get it; for we have nothing here. The only thing we ever crave is food, and we have plenty of that. Anyway, no one would kill for food. It gives no satisfaction. It is nauseating. We eat because if we didn't we believe that we would die and go to a worse place than this. We are afraid of that."

"You don't enjoy eating?" asked von Horst. "What do you enjoy?"

"Nothing. There is no happiness in the Forest of Death. There are cold and hopelessness and nausea and fear. Oh, yes; there is hate. We hate one another. Perhaps we get some satisfaction from that, but not a great deal. We are all hating, and you can't get a great deal of pleasure doing what every one else is doing.

"I derived a little pleasure from wishing to set you free—that was different; that was unique. It is the first pleasure I have ever had. Of course I am not certain just what pleasure is, but I thought I recognized the sensation as pleasure because while I was experiencing it I forgot all about cold and hopelessness and nausea and fear. Anything that makes one forget must be a pleasure."

"You are all murderers?" asked La-ja.

"We have each killed something," replied Durg. "Do you see that old woman sitting over there with her face in her hands? She killed the happiness of two people. She remembers it quite clearly. A man and a woman. They loved each other very much. All that they asked was to be left alone and allowed to be happy.

"And that man standing just beyond her. He killed something more beautiful than life. Love. He killed his wife's love.

"Yes, each of us has killed something; but I am glad that it was men that I killed and not happiness or love."

"Perhaps you are right," said von Horst. "There are far too many men in the world but not half enough happiness or love."

A sudden commotion in the outer cave interrupted further conversation. Durg jumped to his feet and left them; and von Horst and La-ja, looking out, saw two prisoners being dragged into the cavern.

"More food for the larder," remarked the man.

"And they don't even enjoy eating it," said La-ja. "I wonder if what Durg told us is true—about the murders, I mean, and the other life they half recall."

Von Horst shook his head. "I don't know; but if it is, it answers a question that has been bothering generations of men of the outer crust."

"Look," said La-ja. "They are bringing the prisoners this way."

"To the fattening pen," said von Horst with a grin.

"One of them is a very big man, is he not?" remarked La-ja. "It takes many Gorbuses to force him along."

"That fellow looks familiar to me," said von Horst. "Not the big one—the other. There are so many Gorbuses around them that I can't get a good look at either of them."

The new prisoners were brought to the smaller cave and thrust in roughly, so that they almost fell upon the two already there. The larger man was blustering and threatening; the other whined and complained. In the semi-darkness of the interior it was impossible to distinguish the features of either.

They paid no attention to von Horst or La-ja although they must have been aware of their presence; yet the former felt certain that the loud bragging of the larger man must be for the purpose of impressing them, as the Gorbuses had departed; and the fellow's companion did not appear to be the type that any one would wish to impress. He was quite evidently a coward and in a blue funk of terror. He was almost gibbering with fright as he bemoaned the fate that had ever brought him to the

Forest of Death; but the other man paid no attention to him, each rambling on quite independently of the other.

As von Horst, half amused, listened to them, several Gorbuses approached the cave, bearing fruits and nuts. One of them carried a torch, the light from which illuminated the interior of the cave as the fellow entered; and in the flickering light, the faces of the prisoners were revealed to each other.

"You?" fairly screamed the big fellow who had been blustering, as his eyes fell upon von Horst. It was Frug, and his companion was Skruf.

XI

FATTENED FOR SLAUGHTER

As THE FULL significance of the situation revealed itself to von Horst, he was of two minds as to whether he should laugh or curse. Their predicament had been bad enough before, but with the presence of these two it might be infinitely worse. Frug's reaction when he recognized them augured no good. However, if the situation was menacing it was also amusing; and von Horst smiled as he contemplated the excitement of the massive cave man.

"And the girl, too!" exclaimed Skruf.

"Yes," said von Horst, "it is indeed we. To what do we owe the pleasure of this unexpected visit? We had thought of you as being safely beside the home fires of Basti cooking your meat, and here you are waiting to be cooked as some one else's meat! Ah, but is not life filled with surprises? Some pleasurable, some—er—not so pleasurable."

"If I could break these bonds and get my hands on you!" shouted Frug.

"Yes? What would you do then, my man?" inquired von Horst.

"I'd break your neck; I'd pound your face to a pulp; I'd—"

"Wait," begged von Horst. "Permit me to suggest a different order of procedure. If you were to break my neck first, as you intimate is your intention, you would derive little pleasure from beating my face to a pulp, as I should be dead and therefore unable to appreciate what you were doing to me. Really, Frug, you are not very bright. I cannot conceive how a person of such limited intelligence ever came to be chosen chief of Basti, but perhaps you were chosen because of the circumference of your biceps rather than for that of your cranium."

The Gorbuses had dumped a quantity of fruit and nuts upon the floor of the cave and departed, leaving the cavern again in semi-darkness. Frug was still struggling with his bonds. Skruf was whimpering and moaning. Von Horst was contemplating the food. "We can negotiate the softer fruit with our hands tied behind us," he remarked to La-ja, "but how do they expect us to crack the shells of some of those nuts."

"Perhaps we can free our hands," suggested the girl. "Roll over close to me, with your back against mine; then try to untie the thongs that bind my wrists. If you can free me, I can easily free you."

She had spoken in a low whisper lest Frug or Skruf hear and act upon the suggestion before she and von Horst were free. The European wriggled his body into position behind that of the girl; then he fell to work upon the knots at her wrists. It was a slow process, partially because he could not see what he was doing and

partially because of the limited use he had of his hands;
but after what seemed an eternity he felt a knot loosening. With practice he became more adept, and soon the
second knot gave to his perseverance. There were several
more; but eventually the last one succumbed, and La-ja's
hands were free. Immediately she rolled over, facing his
back; and he could feel her nimble fingers searching out
the secret of the knots. When she touched his hands or
arms he experienced a strange thrill that was new to
him. He had felt the contact of her flesh before but
always then she had been angry and resentful, sometimes violently so; and he had experienced no pleasurable
reaction. Now it was different; because, for the first time,
she was ministering to him and of her own free will.

"What are you two doing?" demanded Frug. "You are
very quiet. If you think you are going to eat all the food
they brought, I'll tell you you'd better not. I'll kill you if
you try that."

"Before or after you break my neck?" asked von Horst.

"Before, of course," snapped Frug. "No, after. No—
what difference does it make? You talk like a fool."

"And after you have killed me and broken my neck,
or broken my neck and killed me, in whichever order you
finally decide to procede, you and Skruf will undoubtedly
eat the food. Am I right?"

"Of course you're right," growled Frug.

"And do you know the purpose for which the food is
intended?" inquired von Horst.

"For us to eat, of course."

"But why should they care whether or not we eat?"
asked the European. "Are you laboring under the delu-
sion that they are at all concerned about either our happiness or our comfort?"

"Then why did they bring it?" demanded Skruf.

"To fatten us," explained von Horst. "It seems that

they like their meat fat, or perhaps I should say that it tastes less nauseating to them fat and fresh."

"Fatten us? Eat us?" gasped Skruf.

Frug made no comment, but von Horst could see that he was redoubling his efforts to free himself of his bonds. A moment later La-ja succeeded in negotiating the last knot, and von Horst felt the thongs slip from his wrists. He sat up and gathered a handful of fruit, passing to to La-ja; then he turned to Frug.

"My hands are free," he said. "I am going to remove your bonds, and then you can liberate Skruf. You are not going to kill me. If you try to, I'll kill you. I still have the weapon with which Skruf has seen me kill many beasts and you have seen some of your own warriors killed. I am going to set you free for two reasons. One is, that you may eat. The other is not a very good reason unless you have more brains than I give you credit for. I hope for the best, but I am skeptical."

"My brains are all right," growled Frug. "What is your other reason for setting us free?"

"We are all in the same fix here," von Horst reminded him. "If we don't escape, we shall be killed and eaten. Working together, we may be able to escape. If we waste our time trying to kill one another or trying to keep from being killed, none of us will escape. Now what do you and Skruf intend to do about it? It is up to you. I shall free your hands in any event; and I shall kill you before you can lay your hands on me, if you try to."

Frug scratched his head. "I swore to kill you," he said. "You got me into this trouble. If you hadn't escaped from Basti, I wouldn't be here. It was while we were tracking you that we were captured. You killed some of my warriors. You liberated all of our slaves, and now you ask me not to kill you."

Von Horst shrugged. "You are mis-stating the facts,"

he said. "I am not asking you not to kill me; I am asking you not to make me kill you. Frug, while I have this weapon, you haven't a chance on earth to kill me. Perhaps I should have said a chance in the earth."

"Promise him, Frug," begged Skruf. "He is right. We can't escape if we fight among ourselves. At least you and I can't, for he can kill us both. I have seen him kill with the little black stick. He does not have to be near the thing he wishes to kill."

"Very well," Frug finally assented. "We will not try to kill one another until after we have escaped from these people."

Von Horst moved over to the chief of Basti and removed the bonds from his wrists; then Frug released Skruf. All but the latter immediately fell to eating. Skruf sat apart, his face resolutely turned away from the food.

"Why don't you eat?" demanded Frug.

"And get fat?" cried Skruf. "The rest of you can get fat and be eaten, but I shall remain so thin that no one will eat me."

Time passed, as it must even in a timeless world. They ate and slept, but von Horst and La-ja never slept at the same time—Frug and Skruf had indicated too great an interest in the pistol. When von Horst slept, La-ja watched. Durg came occasionally to talk with them. He always appeared friendly, but he could hold out no hope that they might eventually escape the fate that Torp had decreed for them.

Von Horst had often wondered where the nuts and fruits came from with which they were fed, as he had seen no sign of either in the grim forest he and La-ja had traversed. He had a theory that perhaps the end of the forest was not far distant, and this he wished to determine. He had by no means given up hope of escape. When he asked Durg where the Gorbuses got the food for them, he was told that it grew at no great distance, near the edge of the Forest of Death. This was what von Horst was most anxious to hear. He also learned the direction in which they went to gather the fruit. But when he attempted to persuade Durg to assist them in their attempt to escape, he met with flat refusal; and finally he desisted, being careful to give Durg the impression that he had wholly abandoned the idea.

The rich nuts, the lack of exercise soon began to show in added layers of fat. Only Skruf remained noticeably thin, steadfastly refusing to eat more than enough to sustain life. Frug put on fat far more rapidly than either von Horst or La-ja.

Finally Skruf called his attention to it. "They will eat you first," he prophesied. "You are very fat."

"Do you think so?" asked the chief, feeling of the fold of fat that encircled his waist. He seemed perturbed. "I thought we were going to try to escape," he said to von Horst.

"I have been hoping that the Gorbuses would leave for a while," replied the European, "but only a few of them go away at a time."

"Most of them are asleep now," remarked La-ja. "Many of their torches have gone out."

"That's right," said von Horst, looking out into the other chamber. "I've never seen so many of them asleep at one time."

"I think they have been feeding," said La-ja. "They have been going out in small parties constantly since I slept last. Perhaps that is why they are sleepy."

"There go some more torches," whispered von Horst. "There are only a few burning now."

"And all the rest of the Gorbuses are nodding." La-ja could not hide her excitement. "If they all fall asleep, we can get away."

But they did not all sleep. One remained awake, nursing his torch. It was Torp. Finally he arose and approached the cave where the prisoners were confined. When they saw him coming they lay down in such positions as to hide the fact that their hands were free, as they had in the past whenever a Gorbus came to their cave. Torp entered, carrying his torch. He looked them over carefully. Finally he poked Skruf with a foot. "There is no use waiting for you to get fat," he grumbled. "We will kill you after this sleep; then we won't have to feed you any more."

"Kill the other first," begged Skruf; "They are much fatter than I. Give me a chance, and I will get fat."

Torp yawned. "We'll kill you all at the same time," he said; then he turned to leave the cave.

Von Horst looked beyond him and saw that every torch in the outer room was extinguished—the place lay in utter darkness. Then he leaped silently to his feet, drawing his pistol as he did so. Raising the pistol, von Horst struck Torp a single heavy blow on the skull. Without a sound, the fellow dropped in his tracks. Von Horst seized his torch.

"Come!" he whispered.

Silently the four ran across the larger cavern to one of the exits and up the steeply inclined shaft to the corridor that led to the outer world. As they passed from the dim precincts of the cavern even the grim and gloomy wood looked fair and lovely by comparison.

How long they had been imprisoned von Horst could not even guess, but he felt that it must have been a long time. They had lost count of sleeps, there had been so many; and they had all, with the exception of Skruf, put on considerable weight, indicating that their imprisonment had been of long duration. At a trot they set off in the direction they believed led to the nearest edge of the Forest of Death, for they were determined to put as much distance as possible between themselves and the caves of the Gorbuses before their escape was discovered.

When in good condition, Pellucidarians can maintain a steady trot for great distances; but it was not long before all except Skruf were panting from the exertion—additonial proof that they had been long confined. At length they were forced to slacken their gait to a walk.

"When do we commence killing one another, Frug?" inquired von Horst. "The truce was to last only until we had escaped—and we have escaped."

Frug eyed the pistol in its holster and pulled on his beard, meditatively. "Let us wait until we have left the forest and separated," he suggested; "then, if we ever meet again, I shall kill you."

"For your sake let us hope that we never meet again," laughed von Horst, "but what assurance have I that in the meantime you and Skruf will honor the agreement? I certainly have no reason to trust Skruf."

"No one trusts Skruf," replied Frug; "but you have my word that I will not kill either one of you until after we separate, and I promise Skruf that I will kill him if he does."

With this loose understanding von Horst had to be satisfied; but he felt some confidence in Frug's word, because the very nature of the man seemed to preclude any possibility of duplicity on his part. He was brutal and savage, but he was also forthright and candid. If he intended killing you, he climbed to a house top and screamed it to the world. He was not the sort to sneak up on a man from behind and stab him in the back—that was more like Skruf.

And so they hurried on until, at last, much sooner

than they had expected, the forest thinned, the type of trees changed, and they came into what seemed a new world. Once again the noon-day sun beat down upon lush vegetation growing between the boles of an open forest. Flowers bloomed, birds sang. Presently they saw an open plain upon which they stood at the outer rim of the forest land. No sign of pursuit had developed, and the Pellucidarians were certain that the Gorbuses would never venture out into the sunlight beyond their gloomy wood.

"They won't follow us here," said Frug. "No man has ever seen a Gorbus outside the Forest of Death."

"Then let's find a place to sleep," suggested von Horst. "We need rest. Afterward we can go on until we are ready to separate."

"Which way do you go?" demanded Frug.

Von Horst looked questioningly at La-ja. "Which way?" he asked.

The girl pointed out across the plain.

"That is the way I go, too," said von Horst.

"We turn this way," said Frug, pointing to the left. "We shall skirt the forest until we can pass around it. I will never enter the Forest of Death again."

"Then after we have slept we separate," said von Horst.

"Yes," replied Frug. "I hope that we shall meet again soon, that I may kill you."

"When you get an idea into that thick skull of yours, you certainly stick to it," commented von Horst with a grin.

"We will look for a place to sleep," announced the Bastian. "There may be caves in this cliff."

They discovered a place where they could descend the escarpment, and on a natural ledge they found an out-jutting stratum beneath which erosion had worn a large niche in which a dozen men might have found shelter from the hot rays of the sun.

"You sleep first, La-ja," said von Horst, "and I will watch."

"I am not sleepy," she replied. "You sleep. I have slept since you."

It was a bare rock that von Horst stretched out upon, such a bed as some far distant forebear might have found good but it was a far cry from box springs and hair mattresses. Yet so quickly had the man sloughed the last veneer of civilization and reverted to some primordial type, he seemed quite content with the naked rock; and in a moment he was asleep.

When he awoke he felt that he must have slept for a long time, so thoroughly rested and refreshed was he. He stretched luxuriously before turning over to greet La-ja and see if the others were awake. When he did turn, he found himself alone. Frug and Skruf were gone and La-ja, too.

He stepped to the edge of the shelf before the cave and looked out across the plain and to the left and to the right. There was no one in sight. He thought at first that La-ja had run away from him, and then it occurred to him that Frug and Skruf had stolen her. Anger and resentment swelled in his bosom at the duplicity of the Bastian chief in whose word he had trusted, and then of a sudden a new thought came to him. After all, had Frug broken his pledge? He had only promised not to kill; he had not promised not to abduct!

XII

MAMMOTH MEN

FROM THE FOOT of the cliff where the cave lay, the plain stretched away knee deep in lush grasses; and from his position above, von Horst saw where a new trail had been recently trampled toward the left. That was the direction which Frug had said he and Skruf would take to avoid the Forest of Death on their return to Basti. The grass was not trampled out across the plain in the direction of Lo-har; there was just the one plain trail toward the left—a trail that would be easy to follow as long as it ran through the deep grass.

Von Horst wished that he knew how long he had slept, so that he might have some idea of the start the abductors had; for he was certain that they were abductors. It was inconceivable that La-ja would have accompanied them back to Basti voluntarily. The trail appeared quite plain from above, but when he reached the foot of the cliff he saw that it was not so apparent. A close examination showed that only the grasses that had been actually crushed and broken by the passage of the three remained down to mark the trail; all others had returned to their normal positions. It was this discovery that gave von Horst greatest concern, as it seemed to indicate that the two men and the girl were far ahead of him.

At the foot of the cliff there were some indications of a struggle. The grasses here had been crushed and broken over a considerable area. The man could visualize what had taken place. La-ja had tried to break away from her captors and had probably put up a good fight, but

125

finally she had been overcome and carried away.

He stood looking along that dim trail that led away into a new unknown. It led away from Sari, to what unknown dangers he could not even guess. Should he follow it? And for what? There was little likelihood that he could overtake the three; and if they reached Basti, none that he could rescue the girl. Why should he wish to risk his life in an attempt to save her—an attempt that was almost certain to fail? She disliked him. She had not taken even decent precautions to hide the fact. And if he did rescue her it would be only to be killed by her savage fellow tribesmen for his pains. He thought of Gaz, the terrible man who crushed lives out with his bare hands.

Were he to turn in the opposite direction he might skirt that end of the forest and pick up Dangar's trail. The thought of Dangar and the pleasurable anticipation of the friendly welcome awaiting him in Sari filled him with longing. He desired companionship; he longed to feel the warmth of a friend's hand again, to see the light of a friendly smile. He was tired of indifference, and enmity, and hatred. With a sigh, he turned back and followed the dim trail toward the left. Off there somewhere in the distance was a little figure with a wealth of golden hair, perhaps an *ignis fatuus* luring him to his doom.

"I wonder why I do it," he said half aloud; and then he shrugged his shoulders and swung on into the unknown.

Profiting by past experience and the schooling he had received from Dangar, he kept in mind constantly the necessity of directing his steps so that he would never be too far from some haven of safety were he threatened by any of the savage creatures that haunt the Pellucidarian scene. Trees were the prime factor in his defensive strategy. Never before had trees loomed so large in his consciousness, and all too often did he have to seek sanctuary among their branches. Now it would be a huge cave lion that drove him to shelter; again a mighty tarag, or some fearsome reptile of a forgotten age.

Along the route that he followed he found the places that Frug and Skruf and La-ja had slept; and here he slept, too. For food he had the eggs of birds and reptiles, fruits that grew upon some of the trees or bushes along his route, and various edible tubers that Dangar or La-ja had taught him to find and recognize. He made fire as had his primitive progenitors who trod the outer crust with the bos and the cave bear, and he took the time to fashion a new bow and arrows that he might have meat without wasting his precious ammunition. A sturdy spear he fashioned, too, its tip fire hardened as were the tips of his arrows.

He tried to make up for the time thus lost by pushing on throughout the endless day until utter exhaustion forced him to halt for sleep. Often, between his own sleeps, he passed one and sometimes two of the sleeping places of those he pursued; and this assurance that he was gaining on them heartened him and spurred him on, yet there were times when his quest seemed utterly hopeless and discouragement sat heavily upon him. The great forest seemed to run on interminably, but at last it ended at the foot of a transverse range of rough hills. Here he had difficulty in following the trail, for the ground was no longer carpeted with tall grass but was oftentimes hard and stony.

Beyond the hills stretched another rolling plain through which wound a large river. He viewed it first from the summit of the pass that he had followed through the hills along an ancient trail worn deep by the feet of men and beasts through countless ages. There was a fringe of forest along the river and little patches of wood scattered about the plain which stretched away to his right to merge in the distance with what seemed the blue of an ocean. Ahead of him, far away, another forest bounded the plain upon that side, while to his left the hills curved around to meet the forest in the distance. Game dotted the landscape as far as the eye could reach. In the nearer foreground he could distinguish bos and red deer, antelopes, tapirs, sheep, and several species of herbivorous dinosaurs; while at the edge of the forest skirting the river he made out the huge forms of mammoths and giant sloths. It was a scene of such primitive beauty and interest that von Horst stood spellbound for several minutes, fascinated by its loveliness. For the moment he forgot everything but the scene below him; but presently his empty belly recalled him to the realities of life; so that it was no aesthete that crept silently down toward the plain, but a primitive hunter of the stone age. He followed the stream when he reached the foot of the hills, taking advantage of the cover offered by the trees that bordered it. He thought that he might get a sheep, several of which were grazing close to the fringing trees; but he knew how wary they were and how difficult to stalk.

The river wound in great loops, and to save time he took short cuts across the low hillocks which the river skirted in its wide bends like a great serpent gliding smoothly toward the sea. While he was below the summits of the hillocks he could not see the sheep, nor they him; yet he moved always cautiously since he never knew what dangers might confront him upon the hillocks' opposite slopes, for the country was game filled; and where the herbivores are, there also are the flesh eaters.

As he topped one little hill he saw that which brought

him to a sudden halt—a great, hairy mammoth lying upon its side moaning. It lay upon a small level flat beside the river at which was evidently a watering place or a ford, and not its moaning alone proclaimed that it was suffering but the agonized trembling of its huge bulk as well. Notwithstanding the fact that von Horst knew that these mighty beasts might be highly dangerous, there was ordinarily such a sweet placidity in their appearance and such a suggestion of dependability and intelligence in their great bulk and dignified mien that he was wont to be lulled into a feeling of security in their presence; and there had been aroused within him a considerable fondness and respect for these shaggy progenitors of the modern elephant.

To see one suffering thus filled him with compassion; and though his better judgment warned him against it, he could not resist the urge to approach more closely and investigate; though what he might accomplish was doubtless scarcely more than a nebulous conjecture in his mind. As he came closer the small eyes of the pachyderm discovered him; and it raised its head and trumpeted angrily, but it made no effort to rise. Thus assured that it was helpless, von Horst came close and examined it; and as he did so he discovered numerous sharp pointed splinters of bamboo protruding an inch or so above the surface of the mud in which the beast lay at the river's edge; so that he had to move with great care to avoid stepping on them.

Almost immediately he saw the cause of the beast's helplessness and suffering—several of these splinters were imbedded in the sole of each great pad; so that the creature could not stand without suffering extreme agony. It was evident that the sharp stakes had been planted by men; and the purpose of them was quite apparent; for how more easily could men of the old stone age, with their primitive weapons, bring down the giant mammoth and render it helpless that they might dispatch it in safety?

The presence of the stakes suggested the proximity of men, and von Horst had already had sufficient evidence to convince him that all men in this savage world were enemies; yet, though he looked carefully in all directions, he saw no sign that any were about; then he turned his attention once more to the beast and its predicament. If he could remove the splinters and permit the mammoth to arise what might he expect from the pain racked creature? Von Horst ran his fingers through his hair dubiously; then the beast moaned again and so piteously that the man, casting discretion to the winds, decided to do what he could to assuage its suffering.

As he started to pick his way among the splinters closer to those huge pads, he realized that the beast would only be impaled upon others the moment it arose after he had removed those that it had already collected; so he set to work to pick the sharpened stakes from the ground over the entire area that they covered, a strip about twenty feet wide across the trail leading to the river; and as he worked, the eyes of the mammoth were on him constantly, watching his every move.

As he worked near the great beast's head he noticed a patch of white hair the width of a man's hand growing down the side of the animal's cheek. He had seen many mammoths, but he had never seen one similarly marked. It gave the beast a strange, patriarchal expression, as though he wore an enormous white burnside. Von Horst noted the strange marking casually as he went about his work, but his principal interest was centered on speculation as to what the gigantic beast would do when it was able to rise. Some of the stakes were planted within reach of the mighty trunk; but the man gathered these, as he did the others, apparently unconcerned by the risk he took. And always the little eyes watched his every move, but whether in sullen hate or wary curiosity he could not guess.

At length came the time when all the stakes that he could locate had been removed, and the next were those embedded in the great pads. Without a moment's hesitation von Horst walked to the hind feet of the pachyderm and, one by one, drew out the torturing slivers. Then he moved to the front feet, well within reach of the sinuous trunk and the great, curving tusks. Methodically, he commenced to remove the slivers from the fore pads, the powerful trunk weaving above him like a huge serpent. He felt it touch him, the moist tip of it gliding over his naked body. It encircled him, but he paid no attention to it. He had invited death by a humane gesture, and he was game. The trunk wrapped about his torso—gently, almost caressingly. It did not tighten; it did not interfere with his work; yet he sensed it might close instantly at the slighest false move on his part. Death seemed very close.

When he had removed the last sliver he stood slowly erect. For a moment he waited; then, very gently, he laid hold of the trunk and sought to push it from him. There was no resistance. He moved unhurriedly, with great deliberation; yet he was under high nervous strain. At last he stood free and moved slowly away. He did not stop, but continued on along the river in the direction he had been going when he discovered the mammoth. For a moment he was obsessed by a powerful urge to run—to put as much distance between himself and the beast as he could before it regained its feet; but he did not. Instead, he moved on slowly, nonchalantly, casting an occasional glance behind him.

The beast lay quiet for a moment; then slowly it commenced to raise its bulk from the ground. Tentatively, it tried bearing its weight on its front feet; and it stood thus for a moment; then it rose and stood with all four feet on the ground. It took a few steps. Evidently its feet did not pain it greatly. It raised its trunk and trumpeted; then it moved off on the trail of the man.

At first von Horst argued to himself that it was not following him and that presently it would turn aside and go about its own affairs, but it did not—it came steadily after him at a speed considerably in excess of that at which von Horst was walking. The man shrugged resignedly. What a sentimental fool he had been! He might have known that this savage beast could not feel gratitude. He should have left it alone or put it out of its misery with a single well placed bullet. Now it was too late. Presently it would overtake him and toss him. Such were his thoughts as he walked slowly along the trail. Overtake him it did. The sinuous trunk wrapped suddenly about him and he was lifted from the ground. "This," thought von Horst, "is the end."

The mammoth stopped and passed him back to its right side where it placed him on the ground; but it still let its trunk rest lightly about him, holding him facing its side; and what von Horst saw there awoke within him a realization of the sagacity of the animal, for this side, upon which it had lain, was thickly studded with bamboo slivers such as he had plucked from his feet. It wished the man to remove them as he had removed those others.

Von Horst breathed a sigh of relief as he set about his work, and when it was completed he once again moved on along the trail he had been following. From the tail of an eye he saw the mammoth swing about in its tracks and depart in the opposite direction. In a few moments it was lost to sight. The man felt that he was well out of a nasty situation that what he described to himself as maudlin sentimentality had gotten him into. But now that it was well over and he had seen the last of the great beast he was glad that he had gone to its aid.

His hunger, momentarily forgotten, manifested itself once more as he started to stalk the sheep again. From the summit of a rise he saw them, and again he was the primitive huntsman of the Pleistocene. Only a cartridge belt and a forty-five differentiated him in appearance from his progenitors of the stone age. From the next rise of ground that he mounted he saw the sheep again, much closer now; but he saw something else, far to the right across the river. At first glance he thought it only a herd of mammoths moving down a gently sloping plain from the foot-hills, coming toward the river; but instantly he recognized the truth—astride the neck of each of the great beasts rode a man.

The sight recalled to his memory Thorek, the mammothman of Ja-ru. These, indeed, must be mammothmen; perhaps the country to which he had wandered was Ja-ru. However, the fact that he had been on friendly terms with Thorek induced no illusions as to the reception he might expect from the savage tribesmen of his erstwhile companion in slavery. Discretion counselled him to keep out of sight; and so he moved cautiously down the hill toward a clump of trees that grew beside the river, where, concealed from their view, he could still watch the approach of the company.

As he reached the trees he saw the embers of a camp fire still glowing; and his heart leaped in his bosom, for he knew that he was now close on the trail of La-ja and her abductors. Which way had they gone from here? They could not be far, for no matter how much the timelessness of Pellucidar might deceive the mind of man it could not befuddle the laws of combustion—fire would consume wood as quickly and embers would remain hot as long here as upon the outer crust and no longer.

He hastily examined the ground about the camp site. For the moment the mammoth-men were forgotten in contemplation of the nearness of La-ja and the surge of rage against Frug and Skruf, now almost within reach of his vengeance. He loosened the gun in its holster. He would give no quarter, but would shoot them down as he would a couple of mad dogs; nor was there a question of doubt as to the rightness of his contemplated act, so easily does man slough the thin veneer of inhibitions with which civilization conceals but does not eradicate primal instincts and characteristics of mankind. There were no laws here for him other than those he made himself.

His search revealed the footsteps of those he sought in the soft earth at the river's edge. He recognized them all—the imprints of the great, splay feet of the men, those of La-ja, small and perfect. They led to the river and did not return. By that he knew that they had crossed. He looked in that direction and saw the mammoth-men steadily approaching. They were much nearer now, the long, swinging strides of the mammoths covering ground rapidly.

Trees and bushes grew upon the far bank of the river, grew in isolated clumps as though planted by the hand of some master landscape gardener. Between two such clusters of bushes he could still see the mammoth-men, but he could see to no great distance either to the right or left. He wished to cross the river in pursuit of those he sought, but he did not wish to attract the attention of the mammoth-men to him, Cautiously he moved down stream until a clump of bushes on the opposite bank hid him from the view of the approaching warriors;

then, careless of the possible presence of dangerous reptiles, he plunged into the stream, which was neither wide nor swift. A few powerful strokes carried him to the opposite bank, where he again sought the trail of the trio. Nor did he have far to search, for he found it almost immediately leading out toward the plain where the mammoth-men rode.

To follow immediately would be to reveal his presence to the approaching warriors, who could not fail to see him should he expose himself now, as they were not over a quarter of a mile away. They had changed their course slightly and were moving up stream more nearly parallel with the course of the river. Presently they would pass him, and he would be free to continue his search for La-ja. As he waited, he stood partially concealed behind a bush, only a little of his face showing. Thus he watched the mammoth-men. They were moving steadily upon their course, like soldiers of any age upon the march, the monotony of which lulls even exuberant spirits into quiescence. But suddenly there was a change. A rider looking toward the river suddenly halted his mount and shouted to his fellows, pointing back down stream at something evidently some distance below the point where von Horst was hiding. Simultaneously he started in the direction he had pointed, urging his lumbering mount into a swifter gait; and after him trooped the remainder of the company.

Savage, primitive to the degree was the sight of that war-like company to von Horst—extinct men upon extinct mounts; animated monuments of savage might. The European was thrilled; and, too, his curiosity was aroused. What had the warrior seen? What were they approaching or pursuing? Risking discovery, von Horst, moved stealthily around the end of the bush that had concealed him, until he could look down the valley in the direction the mammoth-men were riding.

At first he saw nothing. A tiny hillock, scarcely more than a mound, shut off his view. Assured that the attention of the riders was riveted upon whatever quarry lay ahead of them and that they would not notice him, von Horst crept forward to the mound and up its side until he could see beyond its summit. What he saw brought his heart into his mouth.

XIII

CAPTURED

Von Horst sprang from his concealment and ran out into the open; and as he did so he reached for his gun, but his holster was empty. There was no time to go back and search for the weapon. He recalled loosening it in its holster before he plunged into the river, and now he assumed that it had fallen out at that time. It was a tragic loss; but there was nothing that he could do about it, and that which he saw before him tended to crowd all other considerations into the background. Running toward the river from out upon the plain and pursued now by the mammoth-men were three figures which he instantly recognized as La-ja and her abductors.

The trees that dotted both sides of the river grew closer together just ahead and formed a little forest toward which the three were running. Skruf had seized La-ja by a hand and was dragging her along, while Frug brought up the rear. Although La-ja was running it was evident that she was attempting to break loose from Skruf, and Frug was striking at her with a heavy switch in an effort to goad her to greater speed. It seemed certain that they would reach the forest ahead of the mammoth-men if nothing delayed them, though by a small margin. Perhaps then they might escape, yet La-ja was trying to delay them. Her only reason, as far as von Horst could imagine, was that she would prefer to be the captive of the mammoth-men than to remain a prisoner of the Bastians.

Uppermost in von Horst's mind was the desire to reach the great brute that was striking the girl. Never before in his life had the instinct to kill an enemy so overwhelmingly mastered him. He even forgot the menace of the advancing mammoth-men in the heat of his hate and blood lust.

He came diagonally upon the three from the side and a little to the rear, but so engrossed were they with one another and their flight that they did not see him until he was almost upon them and had shouted a curt command to Frug to stop striking the girl. A new fear was added to the terror already reflected in Skruf's eyes, a new hope leaped to La-ja's, a glad cry to her lips as she voiced the one word, "Von!" What a wealth of relief and hope were expressed in that single monosyllable! Surprise and rage were in Frug's snarled recognition as he vouchsafed his reply and registered his contempt for the man by striking again at La-ja. And then, just at the edge of the wood, von Horst leaped for him, leaped for his throat; and the two went down, rolling on the flower starred turf in what each hoped was a duel to the death.

Both men were powerful; but Frug outweighed his antagonist by thirty pounds, an advantage that, however, was offset by von Horst's agility and skill. All that was in the mind of either was to kill the other—everything else was forgotten. Each fought for a hold upon the other's throat, each struck terrific blows at the other's face. The caveman grunted and cursed; von Horst fought in silence. And thus the mammoth-men came upon them, surrounding them. A dozen leaped from their huge mounts and fell upon the two. These, too, were mighty men. They dragged the combatants apart and made them prisoners.

It was then that von Horst had an opportunity to look around for La-ja. She was nowhere in sight; neither was Skruf. The chief of the mammoth-men was looking for them, too; and when he saw that they were missing he sent a party of his men across the river in search of them. The remainder mounted the mammoths after having two of the great beasts swing von Horst and Frug to their heads in front of their riders; then, without waiting for the party that had gone in search of La-ja and Skruf, they set off again in the direction they had been going at the time the discovery of the three had interrupted their march.

The mammoth-men appeared very sure of themselves, so much so that they did not even bind their prisoners' hands; which was the equivalent of saying that escape was impossible; nor did von Horst doubt but that such was the case. The leader and some of the others questioned him. They asked him his name, from what country he came, where he was going. They were gruff, unfriendly men; and it was easy to see that they hated all strangers. So accustomed was von Horst to this characteristic of Pellucidarians that he made no effort to assure them that he was friendly, reasoning, and rightly, that it would have been a waste of energy and breath.

As they moved on up the river they presently discovered a huge mammoth ahead of them. It was in the open, so that they could not stalk it; but evidently they particularly wished it.

"It is he," said one. "I would know him as far as I could see him."

"The trap did not get him," commented the leader. "He is too wise to be fooled by traps."

"What good would he be if we did catch him?" demanded another. "He is an ugly customer. Already he has killed ten men that we know of who hunted him. He could never be trained now, he is too old."

"Mamth wishes him," said the leader. "That is enough; Mamth is chief. He will use him in the little canyon. He will give us great sport."

The great beast had been moving off across the plain when they first saw him; now he turned and faced them— a huge creature, larger than any of those the mammoth-men rode.

"It's he all right," said the warrior upon whose mount von Horst rode; "it's *Ah Ara, Ma Rahna.*"

It was then that von Horst first noticed the great patch of white hair on the animal's left jowl. "*Ah Ara, Ma Rahna;* Old White, The Killer," he mused. The killer! He realized now how foolhardy he had been in approaching the beast at all. The fact that he had not been killed suggested that the huge creature was not only endowed with great intelligence but with a well developed sense of gratitude. Only thus could he account for his being still alive.

The leader of the band issued some instructions, and the party spread out and started to circle Old White, which remained facing them, making no effort to escape.

"Trog's going to try to drive him," remarked the warrior with von Horst. "If he can bring in *Ah Ara* he will be a great man."

"Can he?" asked von Horst.

The warrior shrugged. "The sun-bleached bones of ten warriors are a better answer than any living tongue can offer."

Slowly the warriors drew around behind *Ah Ara* in a half circle; then they closed and moved forward. In the meantime the quarry had turned again to face them. His little eyes gleamed, his trunk weaved slowly to and fro as he rocked his head from side to side. The warriors commenced to shout and wave their spears. They came closer. It seemed incredible that the animal did not turn and break for freedom; but it did not—*Ah Ara* stood his ground.

Suddenly he raised his trunk and, with a loud scream, charged. Straight for the center of the line he came—a solid line, for the mammoths were touching side to side. He lowered his head; and when he struck, two mammoths were knocked down. As he passed over them he seized one of the riders and hurled him fifty feet; then, as he passed over him, he trampled him. After that he appeared to pay no more attention to the party, but moved on majestically in the direction he had been going before the interruption. It seemed to von Horst that his whole manner screamed contempt for the man-things that had dared to delay him.

Trog shook his head ruefully and turned toward the river. The two felled mammoths came to their feet—one of them was riderless, but he followed on with the others. No one paid any attention to the mangled warrior lying on the plain. Perhaps he was dead, but he may not have been. It was evident to von Horst that these men held human life lightly and that they were without compassion. He wondered if Thorek would recall that he had suggested that they be friends should they meet again, for it was possible that he might meet him now that he was a prisoner of Thorek's fellows. Prompted by this recollection of the man who had escaped from the Bastians with him he turned toward the warrior riding behind him.

"Do you know Thorek?" he asked.

"Yes; what do you know of him?"

"We are friends."

The warrior laughed. "No stranger is friend to a mammoth-man," he said.

"Did Thorek return from Basti?" asked von Horst.

"No," and then suddenly, "What is your name?"

"Von. If Thorek were here he would tell you that we are friends."

"Well, perhaps Thorek was your friend; but no other mammoth-man will be. Friendship for a stranger is weakness in a warrior. Strangers are to be killed; that is why they are strangers. If there were no strangers there would be no one to kill except one another, and that would not be good for the tribe. We would soon kill each other off. Men must fight and kill; it is the life blood of warriors."

Presently they came to the river and crossed it, keeping slightly above the regular ford; then Trog and some of the others dismounted and examined the ground in the trail leading in to the river. Von Horst watched them with amusement, for he recognized the spot well. He saw that the men were surprised and angry at what they discovered.

"*Ah Ara* has been down here," exclaimed Trog. "There is blood here; but where are the stakes? They have all been removed."

"I saw mud and blood on the right side of *Ah Ara* as he passed close to me when he charged through our line," volunteered a warrior.

"Yes; he was down here," growled Trog. "We had him, but how could he have escaped?"

"He is very old and very wise," said one.

"He could never be old enough or wise enough to pick the splinters from his pads and his side, to pick them

141

all out of the ground," remonstrated Trog. "That could only be done by a man."

"Here are the foot-prints of a man," exclaimed a warrior.

"But who would dare approach *Ah Ara* and take the splinters from him? Had a man done that we should find his body close by." Trog shook his head. "I do not understand."

They found the splinters where von Horst had tossed them aside, and they set them out again with great care and well concealed upon the opposite side of the river; then they mounted and rode back toward the hills from which they had been coming when von Horst first sighted them.

"We'll get him yet," remarked von Horst's warrior.

"How?" asked the European.

"When he gets splinters in his feet the pain is so great that he cannot stand; the pads of a tandor are thick, but they are very sensitive. When we come back and find him down we put heavy thongs of mammoth hide about his neck. These are fastened to three mammoths on each side of him, mammoths trained for this work; then we take the splinters from the ground around him and from his pads and let him get up. After that it is easy. The six mammoths drag him until he tires of being choked. After that he will follow quietly."

"Will you ever be able to train *Ah Ara*, provided you get him?" asked von Horst.

The warrior shook his head. "He would never be safe. Mamth will put him in the little canyon, and he will afford us much amusement."

"In what way?"

The warrior looked at von Horst and grinned. "I think you will find out soon enough," he said.

After the party reached the foothills it followed a well worn trail that led up to a wide plateau upon which several mighty canyons debouched from the mountains beyond. The plateau was covered with lush grasses and was crossed by several streams that issued from the mouths of the canyons, into one of which Trog led his savage troop. The grandeur of the scenerey within the canyon was impressive, and to such an extent that for the moment von Horst almost forgot the hopelessness of his situation. Within its narrow mouth the canyon widened into a lovely valley walled by precipitous cliffs that were broken occasionally by the narrow mouths of smaller canyons. A stream flowed through the bed of the canyon, trees and flowering shrubs grew in profusion, fish leaped in the river, and birds of weird, prehistoric shapes and coloration flew from tree to tree.

Von Horst sighed. "What a lovely place," he thought, "if only La-ja and I were here alone."

La-ja! What had become of her? Had she escaped from Skruf, or was she still his captive? She would have been better off here among the mammoth-men, or at least no worse off; for no one could have been more repugnant to her than Skruf. At least, were she here, she would have had one friend whom she might trust even though he were unable to do anything for her.

Von Horst sighed. He had a premonition that he would never again see La-ja, and it suddenly occurred to him that this strange world was going to be a very much more terrible place to live in because of that. He realized that something had gone out of his life that nothing could replace. Perhaps it hurt his pride to admit it even to himself, for the girl had certainly given him sufficient proof on numerous occasions that he meant nothing whatever to her; yet he could not forget the pathetic longing note in her voice when she had recognized him and called to him just before the mammoth-men had separated them forever.

Depressed by this sad reverie, his future fate seemed to mean nothing to him. He did not care what the mammoth-men did to him. The sooner it was over, the better. Without a single companion for whom he cared, he might as well be dead as alive; for there was no chance that he might ever return to the outer world, nor little more that he would find Sari should he escape from his present predicament.

While he was occupied by these unhappy thoughts the troop turned into one of the smaller canyons, and shortly thereafter he saw the caves of the mammoth-men pitting the face of the lofty cliff ahead. A considerable number of men, women, and children were on the ground at the foot of the cliff where a grove of trees offered shelter from the noonday sun. Some of the women busied themselves around cooking fires; others were fashioning sandals or loin cloths. Men chipped laboriously at stone weapons in the making, scraped spear shafts into shape, or merely loafed at ease. At sight of the returning troop, they quit whatever had been occupying them and clustered about to inspect the prisoners and exchange gossip with the arriving warriors.

Trog looked very important. "Where is Mamth?" he demanded.

"He is in his cave, sleeping," said a woman.

"Go and awaken him," commanded Trog.

"Go yourself," replied the woman; "I do not wish to be killed."

Trog, who, with the other warriors of his party, had dismounted, was standing near the woman; and at her refusal he swung his spear quickly and felled her with the haft, knocking her unconscious; then he turned to another woman. "Go and awaken Mamth," he said.

The woman laughed in his face. "Guva has no man," she said, "but I have. You will not knock me down with your spear. You would not have knocked Guva down if she had had one. Go and awaken Mamth yourself."

"I am not afraid of your man," blustered Trog.

"Then why don't you knock me down," taunted the woman, "for I am not going to awaken Mamth."

The crowd gathered about commenced to laugh at Trog, adding to his discomfiture and his rage. He stood there, red in the face, swinging his spear to and fro and looking from one to another of them.

"What are you looking for?" demanded the woman, "—widows and orphans?"

"You will pay for this," growled Trog; then his eyes alighted on von Horst. "Go and awaken Mamth," he commanded.

The European grinned. "Where is he?" he asked.

Trog pointed to a cave entrance part way up the cliff. "He is in there," he growled. "Get along with you!" He swung his spear, striking at von Horst. The prisoner dodged, and seizing the weapon wrenched it from Trog's grasp; then he broke it across his knee and flung it on the ground at the mammoth-man's feet.

"I am neither a woman nor a child," he said; and, turning, started toward the cliff and Mamth's cave, in his ears the shouts and laughter of the tribesmen.

"I kill!" shouted Trog, and started after him, drawing his stone knife.

Von Horst wheeled and waited the mad charge of the mammoth-man. Trog approached him at a run, brandishing his knife above his shoulder. When he struck, von Horst seized his wrist, turned quickly, stooped low and, drawing the man's arm across his shoulder, hurled him over his head and heavily to the ground; then he continued on his way to the foot of the cliff and up the rude ladders that led to Mamth's cave. Glancing back over his shoulder he saw Trog still lying where he had fallen, apparently insensible, while the crowd laughed uproariously, evidencing to von Horst that his act had not prejudiced them against him and, also, that Trog did not appear to be overly popular.

He wondered just how popular he himself would be with Mamth when he awakened him, for he had gathered from what he had just heard that Mamth did not relish being awakened from his sleep; and he had seen just how primitive these people were and how little control they had of their tempers—like primitive people everywhere, even those who were supposed to be civilized and yet had primitive minds. When at last he came to the mouth of the cave he looked in, but he could see nothing, because of the darkness of the interior. He shouted Mamth's name in a loud voice and waited. There was no response. The laughter below had ceased. The watchers were waiting in tense expectancy the result of his temerity.

Von Horst shouted again, this time more loudly; and this time there was a response—a bull-like bellow and the sound of movement within. Then a perfect mountain of a man emerged from the cave, his hair dishevelled, his beard awry, his eyes sleep bleared and bloodshot. When he saw von Horst he stopped in amazement.

"Who are you?" he demanded. "Why did you awaken Mamth? Do you wish to be killed?"

"I am a prisoner," replied von Horst. "Trog sent me to awaken you because he was afraid to do it himself; and as for being killed, that is probably what I was taken prisoner for."

"Trog sent you, did he?" demanded Mamth. "Where is he?"

Von Horst pointed toward the foot of the cliff where Trog still lay. Mamth looked down.

"What is the matter with him?"

"He tried to kill me with a dagger," explained the prisoner.

"And you killed him?"

"I don't think so. He is probably merely stunned."

"What did he wish of me?"

"He wished to show you the two prisoners he brought in. I am one of them."

"He disturbed my sleep for that!" grumbled Mamth. "Now I cannot get to sleep again." He pointed to the ladder. "Go down."

Von Horst did as he was bid, and Mamth followed him. When they reached the ground Trog was regaining consciousness. Mamth went and stood over him.

"So-ho!" he exclaimed. "So you were afraid to come and awaken Mamth, but you sent a prisoner who might have sneaked into the cave and killed Mamth in his sleep. You are a fool. And you let the prisoner knock the wits from your head. You are a fine one to be sub-chief. What happened?"

"He must have hit me over the head with a big rock when I wasn't looking," said Trog.

"He did not," cried a woman. "Trog was going to hit the prisoner with his spear. The prisoner took Trog's spear from him and broke it in two. There it lies. Then Trog tried to kill the prisoner with his knife. The prisoner picked Trog up and threw him over his head."

A number of them commenced to laugh as the woman recalled the events, but they did not laugh so loudly in the presence of Mamth.

The chief looked searchingly at von Horst. "So you

broke Trog's spear and then threw him over your head!" he exclaimed. "Where is the other prisoner?"

"Here," said one of the warriors guarding Frug.

Mamth looked at the Bastian. "He is even bigger than the other," he said. "They should furnish us good sport in the little canyon. Take them away. Gorph, take this one to your cave and see that he does not escape." He jerked a thumb toward von Horst. "Truth, you take charge of the other. Have them ready when Mamth wishes them. Trog, you are no longer a sub-chief. Mamth will appoint a better man."

XIV

"HE DIES!"

GORPH WAS A short, stocky, middle-aged man with a wealth of whiskers and small, close-set eyes. Von Horst judged him a mean customer even before the fellow gave any indication of his true nature, which he was not long in doing; for as soon as Mamth indicated that he was to take over the prisoner he stepped up to von Horst, seized him roughly by the shoulder and gave him a push toward the foot of the cliff and the nearest ladder.

"Get along!" he growled, "and be quick about it." Then, without other reason than pure brutality, he prodded his prisoner in the back with the point of his spear—a vicious jab that brought blood. Resentment and rage flared in the breast of the man from the outer crust, the sudden pain goading him to instant action. He wheeled and crouched. Gorph, sensing attack, jabbed at him again with his spear; but von Horst pushed the weapon aside and leaped close, pinioning the mammoth-man's head beneath his right arm; then he commenced to spin, faster and faster. Gorph's feet left the ground, his body whirled, almost horizontal, in a flattening circle; von Horst released his hold and sent the fellow spinning to the ground.

Mamth broke into a loud guffaw, which was echoed by the other spectators. Gorph staggered dizzily to his feet; but before he was fully erect von Horst clamped the same hold upon him, and once again whirled and threw him. When Gorph arose this time, dizzy and befuddled, the other was standing over him. His fists were clenched, one arm was back ready to deliver a blow to the bewhiskered chin that would have put the mammoth-man out for good; but then his rage left him as suddenly as it had come.

"The next time you try anything like that on me, Gorph, I'll kill you," he said. "Pick up your spear and go along. I'll follow."

He had given no thought as to what the reaction of the other mammoth-men might be to his attack upon one of their fellows; nor had he cared; but their laughter assured him that they had enjoyed the discomfiture of Gorph, as they would probably enjoy the discomfiture of any creature. Gorph stood for a moment, hesitant. He heard the laughter and the taunts of his fellows. He was trembling with rage; but he looked at the man who had bested him, standing there waiting to best him again; and his courage proved unequal to his anger.

He stepped over to retrieve his spear, and as he passed von Horst he spoke in a low tone of voice. "I'll kill you yet," he said.

The European shrugged and followed him. Gorph walked to a ladder and started to ascend. "See that nothing happens to him, Gorph," shouted Mamth. "He'll be a good one for the little canyon."

"You see," remarked von Horst, "that between Mamth and me it'll be best for your health that you treat me well."

Gorph mumbled in his beard as he climbed to the third tier of caves, von Horst following him upward. Here the mammoth-man followed the wide ledge to the right and stopped before a large entrance in which squatted three women. One was middle-aged, the other two much younger. Of these, she who appeared to be the elder was short and squat like Gorph, an unprepossessing girl with a sinister countenance. Their only clothing was scanty loin-cloths.

"Who is that?" demanded the woman.

"Another mouth to feed," grumbled Gorph; "one of the prisoners that Trog brought in. We keep him and guard him, but if he falls off the cliff it will not be my fault."

The elder of the two girls grinned. "He might," she said.

The man walked to the younger girl and kicked her. "Get me food," he growled, "and be quick about it."

The girl winced and scurried into the cave. Gorph squatted beside the other two women. The elder was fashioning a pair of sandals with soles of mammoth-hide; the other just sat staring vacantly at nothing.

Gorph eyed her, scowling. "How much longer shall I have to hunt for you, Grum?" demanded Gorph. "Why don't you get a man? Won't any of them have you?"

"Shut up," growled Grum. "If they won't have me it's because I look like you—because I am like you. If you'd been a woman you'd never have had a mate. I hate you."

Gorph leaned over and struck her in the face. "Get out of here!" he cried; "go get yourself a man."

"Leave her alone," said the older woman wearily.

"Keep out of this," warned Gorph, "or I'll kick your ribs in."

The woman sighed.

"That is all that Mumal does," sneered Grum. "She just sits and sighs—she and that monkey-faced Lotai. Sometimes I could kill them both."

"You are a bad daughter," said Mumal. "The time that I bore you was a bad time indeed."

"Get out!" growled Gorph. "I told you to get out." He pointed a stubby finger at Grum.

"Try to put me out," snapped the girl. "I'd scratch out your eyes. Get me a man. If you were any good you'd get men for both your daughters. You're a coward. You're afraid to fight men for us."

"If I ever made a man marry you he'd sneak up behind me in the woods the first chance he got and kill me."

"I'd help him," said Grum.

"Lotai!" bellowed Gorph. "Where is the food?"

"Coming!" called the girl from the interior of the cave, and a moment later she came with a handful of dried meat. She tossed it on the ground in front of Gorph and backed away to the far corner of the entrance, where she sat in huddled misery.

Gorph attacked the meat like a ravenous wolf, breaking off great hunks between his powerful teeth and swallowing them whole.

"Water!" he snapped, when he had finished.

The girl called Lotai arose and hurried back into the cave. A moment later she returned with a gourd which she handed to Gorph.

"That is all," she said; "there is no more water."

Gorph gulped it down and arose. "I am going to sleep now," he said. "I'll kill anyone who awakens me. Mumal, you and Grum go for water. Lotai, watch the prisoner. If he tries to escape, scream; and I'll come out and—"

"And what?" inquired von Horst.

"Do as I told you," said Gorph to the women, ignoring von Horst's query; then he lumbered into the cave.

The two older women followed him, returning shortly each with a large gourd; then they descended the ladders on their way for water. Von Horst looked at the young girl who had been left to guard him. Now that the others had gone the strained expression that had clouded her face had disappeared, and she was more beautiful than before.

"Happy family," he remarked.

She looked at him questioningly. "Do you think so?" she asked. "Perhaps the others are happy, though they do not seem so. I know that I am not."

Once again von Horst was faced with the literal-mindedness of the stone age. He was reminded of La-ja.

"I was only laughing with words," he explained.

"Oh," she said, "I see. You do not really think that we are happy?"

"Is it always like this?" he demanded.

"Sometimes it is worse; but when Mumal and I are alone, we are happy. Grum hates me because I am pretty and she is not; Gorph hates everyone. I think he even hates himself."

"It is strange that you have no mate," said von Horst; "you are very good-looking."

"No man will take me because he would have to take Grum, too, if Gorph insisted—that is a law of the mammoth-men. You see, she is older than I; and should have a man first."

"What did Grum mean when she said that Gorph was afraid to fight men for you?"

"If we picked out men that we wanted they would have to take us if Gorph fought them and won; but I would not wish a man that way. I would wish my man to want me so much that he would fight to get me."

"And that is the only way that Grum could get a mate?" asked von Horst.

"Yes, because she has no brother to fight for her, nor any friend to do it for her."

"You mean that any man who would fight for her could get her a mate?"

"Why, yes; but who would do it?"

"A friend might," he said; "or any man who wanted you badly enough."

She shook her head. "It is not so easy as that. If a man who was not her father or brother fought for her and lost, he would have to take her. And Grum has made it even worse by choosing Horg as the man she wishes to mate with. No one could defeat Horg. He is the biggest and strongest man in the tribe."

"Rather a precarious method of getting a mate," mused von Horst. "If your man is vanquished, you get him; but you may get a corpse."

"No," she explained. "They fight with bare hands until one of them gives up. Sometimes they are badly hurt, but seldom is any one killed."

They sat in silence for a while, the girl watching the man intently. Von Horst was thinking of La-ja and wondering what fate had befallen her. He was sad in the knowledge that she had passed out of his life forever— the haughty, imperious little slave girl who hated him. He wondered if she really did hate him. There were times when he doubted that she did. He shook his head. Who could ever understand a woman?

Lotai stirred. "What is your name?" she asked.

"Von," he replied.

"I think you are a very nice man," she said.

"Thank you. I think you are a very nice girl."

"You are not like any man I have ever seen before. I

think you are a man that I would trust. You would never beat me. You would always be kind, and you would talk to me as men talk to men. That is something our men never do. At first, maybe, they are nice; but soon they only speak to give orders or to scold.

"Oh, some of them are not so bad as others," she added. "I think that Gorph, my father, is the worst. He is very bad. He never says a pleasant word to any of us, and he is worse with me than with the others. He beats me and kicks me. I think that he hates me. But that is all right, because I hate him.

"There was one very nice man. I liked him, but he went away and never came back. He must be dead. He was a big man and a great warrior; but he was kind to women and children, and he laughed and was pleasant. The women would all have liked him for a mate, but he never would take a mate to live always in his cave. Thorek was different that way."

"Thorek?" exclaimed von Horst. "He did not come back to Ja-ru?"

"You know him?" asked Lotai.

"We were prisoners of the Bastians, and we escaped together. We were friends. He should have been here before this. Since we parted I have travelled far and slept many times. Something must have happened to him."

The girl sighed. "He was such a nice man; but then, what difference does it make? He was not for me. I will get a mate like Gorph and be kicked and beaten the rest of my life."

"The women of Ja-ru have a hard time of it, I should say," remarked von Horst.

"Not all of them. Only those like Mumal and myself. Some of them are big and strong and like to fight. If they are kicked, they kick back. These have a happy time. Mumal and I are different. She is not of Ja-ru.

Gorph stole her from another tribe. I am like her, and Grum is like Gorph. We would run away and go back to my mother's country; but it is very far, and the dangers are great. We would be killed long before we got to Sari."

"Sari," mused von Horst. "That is the country that Dangar came from. That is where I should like to go when I escape from here."

"You will never escape," said Lotai. "You will go into the little canyon, and you will never come out."

"What is this little canyon I have heard so much about?" demanded the man.

"You will find out soon enough. Here come Mumal and Grum with the water. We must not talk together too much in front of Grum and Gorph. If they thought that I was friendly with a prisoner they would kick me and beat me all the more."

The two women came into view up the ladder from below, each balancing a heavy gourd of water on her head. Mumal looked tired and dejected. Grum was hot and irritable, her evil face twisted in a black frown. She paused in the entrance to the cave.

"I am going to sleep," she said. "See that you don't make any noise;" then she entered the cave.

Mumal stooped and stroked Lotai's hair as she passed. "I too am going to sleep, little one," she said.

"I should like to sleep myself," remarked Lotai after the others had entered the cave.

"Why don't you?" asked von Horst.

"I have to watch you."

"I'll promise not to go away while you are guarding me," he assured her. "Go in and sleep. I'd like to myself."

She looked at him intently for a long time before she spoke. "I believe that you would not try to escape if you told me you would not," she said, "but if Gorph found you out here while I was asleep in the cave it would be just as bad for me as though you had escaped. If you will go in though and not come out while I am sleeping it will be safe. We can go into a far corner of the cave and sleep, and then they won't bother us."

Von Horst was very tired, and he must have slept a long time. When he awoke, Lotai was not there. He found her with the others on the ledge before the cave. They were eating jerked venison, washing it down with great draughts of water. Gorph and Grum ate noisily, like beasts.

No one offered von Horst food. It lay in a little pile on a piece of skin in which it had been wrapped, filthy looking and malodorous; but it was food, and von Horst was famished. He walked over to it where it lay close to Gorph, and stooped to take some. As he did so Gorph struck his hand away.

"This fine food is not for slaves," he growled. "Go to the back of the cave and get the scraps and the bones that are there."

From the vile odor that he had noticed in the cave, von Horst could surmise the nature of the food that was intended for him, food that only actual starvation could drive him to eat. He knew that his future life with these people, however short or however long it might be, would depend largely upon the attitude that he took at this time. He reached again for the food; and again Gorph struck at his hand, but this time von Horst seized the fellow's wrist, jerked him to his feet, and struck him a heavy blow on the jaw. Gorph dropped in his tracks. Von Horst gathered up a handful of the venison, picked up a gourd of water and crossed to the opposite side of the entrance where Mumal and Lotai sat wide eyed and trembling. There he sat down and commenced to eat.

Grum had not spoken, and now she sat with her eyes upon von Horst; but what was passing in the dark convolutions of that savage brain none might guess. Was she filled with rage that a stranger had struck down her father? Was she selfishly resentful that he had taken food? Or was she secretly admiring his courage, strength, and skill?

Presently consciousness returned to Gorph. He opened his eyes and raised himself on one elbow. He looked puzzled, and was evidently trying to gather the threads of what had transpired. He stared at von Horst and the venison he was eating. Presently he rubbed his jaw, feeling of it gingerly as though to discover if it were broken; then he fell to eating. During all that had transpired no one had spoken; but von Horst was satisfied—he knew that he would not again be denied food and needed no verbal assurance of the fact.

The endless Pellucidarian day dragged on. Von Horst ate and slept. Gorph hunted, sometimes returning with the carcass of a kill or cuts from those he had hunted with companions, sometimes empty handed. Von Horst saw parties of mammoth-men come and go on their huge mounts. He talked with Lotai and with Mumal. Occasionally Grum joined in the conversations, but more often she sat in silence staring at von Horst.

The man wondered what his fate was to be and when he would know. The timelessness of Pellucidar offered no standard for the measurement of duration. It was this fact, he judged, that made the Pellucidarians seem so often to be dilatory. "Immediately" here might encompass the passage of an hour or a day of the outer crust's solar time or, conceivably, a much longer period. Perhaps Mamth thought that he was handling the fate of the two prisoners with dispatch, but to von Horst it seemed an eternity. He had never seen Frug since they had been separated at the foot of the cliff, and if he never saw him again it would be far too soon.

On one occasion von Horst was sitting on the ledge before the entrance to the cave thinking of La-ja, as he often did, and wondering if she still lived. He was alone, for Gorph was hunting, Mumal and Lotai had gone up the canyon for a potato-like tuber, and Grum was asleep in the cave. He was enjoying the solitude, free from the scolding and cruelty of the family when either Grum or Gorph were present. He was day-dreaming, recalling pleasant memories, conjuring the faces and figures of friends of by-gone days—friends that he would never see again; but the thought did not make him particularly sad. It was good to recall the happier events of the past. His reveries were interrupted by the shuffling of sandaled feet within the cave. Grum was awake. Presently she came out on the ledge. She stood looking at him intently for a moment.

"You would make me a good mate," she said. "I want you."

Von Horst laughed. "What makes you think I would make a good mate?" he asked.

"I saw the way you handled Gorph," she replied. "I was told what you did to Trog. I want you for my mate."

"But I am a stranger and a prisoner. I think I've heard one of you say that your women couldn't mate with the men of other tribes."

"I will see Mamth about that. Perhaps he would consent. You would make a good warrior for Mamth."

Von Horst stretched comfortably and grinned. He felt quite safe. "Mamth would never give his consent," he said.

"Then we will run away," announced Grum. "I am tired of living here. I hate them all."

"You've got it all figured out, haven't you?"

"I have. It is all settled," replied Grum.

"But suppose I don't want you for a mate?" he inquired.

"It will be better than death," she reminded him. "If you stay here you will go to your death in the little canyon."

"We could not escape. If escape had been possible, I would have been gone long since. I have constantly watched for my chance."

"We can escape," said Grum. "I know a way that you do not know of."

"How about Horg?" he asked. "I thought you wanted Horg."

"I do, but I can't get him."

"If I helped you to get Horg, would you help me to escape?" he asked, as an idea suddenly developed in his mind.

"How could you get Horg for me?"

"I have an idea that I could. If we could go to Mamth together, and you asked him to let me be your mate, he would refuse; then I could explain the plan I have that would get Horg for you. I think he would like it."

"Will you do it?" she demanded.

"Will you help me to escape?"

"Yes," she promised.

As they talked, von Horst saw a party of mammoth-men returning to the village on their huge mounts. They came with shouts and laughter, like conquering warriors; and there was one among them riding double behind another warrior, who was surrounded by a great crowd of jabbering, gesticulating natives as soon as he dismounted. The man from the outer crust watched them with but little interest and only casual curiosity. He could not know the cause of their exultation.

Shortly after the return of the warriors, von Horst noticed considerable activity in the grove at the foot of the cliff. Cooking fires were being built on the ground, which was unusual, as most of the cooking was done by individual families on the ledges before their caves.

"There is going to be a *karoo*," said Grum. "We shall all go down and have much to eat and drink."

"What is a *karoo*?" he asked. It was a word he had not heard before.

Grum explained that it was a feast and celebration in honor of some noteworthy event, in which all of the members of the tribe joined. She did not know the reason for this *karoo*, but judged that it was to celebrate something important that the returning party had accomplished.

"We can't go down until Gorph returns or Mamth sends for us," she said, "because my orders are to remain here and watch you; but when Gorph comes he will take you down, as otherwise one of us would have to remain here with you and miss the celebration. You are a nuisance. I wish you were dead."

"Then you wouldn't get Horg," he reminded her.

"I won't get him anyway. There is nothing that you can do to get him for me. I'll have to take you instead, but you're not the man that Horg is. Wait until you see him. Compared with you he is as the *tandor* is to the *thag*; and, besides, he has a mighty beard. His face is not as yours, smooth like a woman's. Always you are scraping off your beard with the strange, shiny knife that you carry."

Presently Lotai and Mumal returned to the cave, to be followed shortly by Gorph. The man carried the carcass of an antelope he had killed; the women, a supply of tubers; and after they had deposited these things in the cave Gorph ordered them all to descend to the ground. Here there was a considerable gathering, several hundred men, women, and children, comprising von Horst concluded, the entire membership of the tribe. There was much talking and laughing—a holiday spirit seemed to possess the gathering, making a strange contrast to their usual demeanor. The strange warrior was still surrounded by such a large crowd that von Horst did not catch a glimpse of him at first. Little attention was paid to the prisoners as Frug squatted disconsolately with his back to the bole of a tree, while von Horst stood watching with interest the largest concourse of really primitive people that he had ever seen.

Presently Mamth discovered him. "Come here!" he shouted; then he turned to the warrior who seemed the center of attraction. "Here's a prisoner such as no man ever saw before. Take a look at him. He has a face as smooth as a woman's and yellow hair. He tossed Trog and Gorph around as though they were babies. Come here you!" he again commanded von Horst.

As the prisoner approached, the warrior pushed his way through the crowd to see him; and a moment later they stood face to face.

"Thorek!" exclaimed von Horst.

"Well! Well!" roared the mammoth-man. "It is Von or I'm a *jalok*. So this is the man who tossed Trog and Gorph around? I am not surprised. I can toss either of them, and he tossed me."

"You know him?" demanded Mamth.

"Know him? We are friends. Together we escaped from Basti, taking the slaves with us."

"Friends!" exclaimed Mamth. "He is a stranger. Mammoth-men do not make friends of strangers."

"I did, and he made a good friend," retorted Thorek. "Because of that he should have the friendship of all mammoth-men. He is a great warrior, and should be allowed to live with us and take a mate from among our women; or he should be permitted to go his way un-molested."

The heavy visage of Mamth was furrowed by a black scowl. "No!" he shouted. "He is a stranger and an enemy, and he dies as should all the enemies of the mammoth-men. Mamth has been saving him for the little canyon. When Mamth is ready, he goes there. Mamth has spoken."

XV

THE BRIDEGROOM

THE SENTENCE of death had been pronounced; but von Horst was not shocked, because he was not surprised. He had known all along that death in some form would end his captivity if he did not escape. When it would come, in this timeless world, could not be even a matter of conjecture. Thorek was angry; but he could do nothing to save his friend, because Mamth was chief and his word law. He sulked and grumbled beneath his breath, but when the feast started he fell to with the rest and soon apparently forgot his grievance in enjoyment of food and drink. Von Horst and Frug were permitted to join in the celebration; and after a taste of the brew that was being served, von Horst concluded that it would not require much of it to cause a man to forget more than a grievance. It was fermented by the women—a mixture of wild maize, several herbs, and honey—and while far from unpalatable it had the kick of an army mule. One taste sufficed for von Horst. Both men and women partook of it freely with varying results. Some became more loquacious and hilarious, others morose

and quarrelsome; so that there was usually a fight pro-
gressing in some part of the grove. There were some who
did not drink at all, and von Horst noticed that Lotai
and Mumal were among these. Grum, on the contrary,
was evidently a two-fisted drinker; and while she carried
it well, it accentuated her distinctive characteristics, so
that she became more bellicose, domineering, and asser-
tive.

Von Horst watched her not without some amusement,
as she approached an enormous man and threw her arms
about his neck, revealing a characteristic that it had
taken several potent droughts to coax to the surface.
Grum evidencing affection bordered upon the ludicrous.
Evidently the large man felt the same way about it, for
he roughly disengaged her arms from about his neck and
gave her a violent push that sent her sprawling on the
ground. She was up in an instant, a veritable fury, her
face distorted with rage. Von Horst thought that she
was going to attack the ungallant one, but instead she
barged down on Mamth.

"I want a mate," she screamed. "I want Horg."

Mamth turned toward the big man. "What does Horg
say?" he demanded.

So that was Horg. Von Horst appraised the fellow and
was glad that he had not elected to fight him for the
sake of the delectable Grum. The man was a giant. He
must have weighed close to three hundred pounds, and
he bulged with muscles.

Horg guffawed loudly. "Take that she-*tarag* as a mate!"
he bellowed. "I'd as soon take a Mahar."

"You heard him," said Mamth. "Go back to the *karoo*
and leave the man alone. He is not for you."

"He is for me," screamed Grum. "I have a warrior who
will fight Horg for me."

Every eye sought Gorph, and a great laugh followed.

"Come on, Gorph," a warrior shouted; "show us how you will best Horg, but don't kill him."

Horg laughed uproariously. "Come on, Gorph," he cried. "If you beat me I'll take Grum off your hands, and I don't blame you for wanting to be rid of her."

"She's drunk too much *tumal*," growled Gorph. "I never promised to fight Horg for her. Horg is my friend; I do not wish to harm him."

This elicited another roar of laughter, and Horg thought that it was so funny that he rolled on the ground bellowing his amusement. Grum said nothing. She just watched Horg and Gorph in silence for a moment; then she turned to Mamth.

"I didn't say that Gorph was going to fight Horg for me. Gorph is a coward. He would fight nothing if he could get out of it. I have a *man* who will fight Horg—and do it now."

"Who is he?" demanded Mamth.

Von Horst experienced a distinct sinking feeling around the pit of his stomach. He knew what was coming.

Grum pointed a stubby, grimy finger at him. "There he is," she cried in a loud voice.

"He's not a mammoth-man," objected Mamth. "How can he fight for you?"

"Because no one else will," admitted Grum.

Mamth shook his head, but he did not have time to voice a definite refusal before Horg spoke up.

"Let him fight me," he said. "This is a *karoo*, and we should have some amusement."

"You will promise not to kill him?" demanded Mamth. "I am saving him for the little canyon."

"I will not kill him," promised Horg.

Von Horst approached the two. "And when I have beaten you," he demanded, "you will make Grum your mate?"

164

"That is the way of the mammoth-men," said Mamth. "He will have to take her, but you will not beat him."

"Beat me!" bellowed Horg. "Let me get hold of him."

"How do we fight?" asked von Horst. "Are there any rules?"

"You fight as the beasts fight," explained Mamth. "You may use no weapon, no stone nor stick. You fight until one of you is unable to fight longer or gives up."

"I am ready," said von Horst.

"Are you ready, Horg?" demanded Mamth.

Horg laughed nonchalantly and contemptuously. "I am ready," he said.

"Then fight!" commanded Mamth.

The spectators formed a circle about the combatants as the two approached one another. Horg was in fine spirits. The *tumal* he had drunk accounted partially for that, and certainty of an easy victory took care of the rest. He cracked jokes with his friends at the expense of both von Horst and Grum. They were rather broad jokes and not at all of the parlor variety, but every one enjoyed them immensely—that is, everyone but Grum. She was furious.

"Wait until I get you," she screamed. "You'll wish you'd never been born."

Von Horst grinned as he featured the life that was in store for Horg should the mammoth-man lose. Death would be sweeter.

Suddenly Horg made a rush at von Horst, the brawny arms, the ham-like hands endeavoring to close upon him; but von Horst stooped and dodged beneath them; then he wheeled and struck Horg on the jaw—a blow that staggered him. Before the mammoth-man could recover, he was struck again; and again his head rocked. Now he was furious. He cracked no more jokes. He bellowed like an angry elephant and charged again. Again von Horst dodged him, and the great hulk went lumbering on a dozen paces before it could stop.

When Horg turned he saw von Horst charging him. This was what he wished. Now he could get hold of the fellow, and once he got hold of him he could crush him, break his bones if he wished unless he gave up.

He stood waiting, his feet spread far apart, his arms open. Von Horst ran swiftly straight toward Horg. Just before he reached him he leaped into the air, flexed his knees, drawing his feet close to his body, and then with all his strength backed by the momentum of his charge he kicked Horg with both feet full in the face. The result was astonishing—especially to Horg. He turned a complete back somersault, landed on his head, and dropped face down in the dirt.

Groggy and only half conscious, he staggered slowly to his feet. Von Horst was waiting for him. "Have you had enough?" he asked. He did not wish to punish the man further in the condition he was in. The crowd was yelling encouragement to him; and with the fickleness and cruelty of crowds was jeering at its fallen champion. Grum, seeing her hopes about to be realized, screamed at the top of her voice as she urged von Horst to finish the almost helpless man; but Horg would not give in. Perhaps he heard Grum and preferred death. He lunged for his lighter antagonist, growling beast-like.

"I kill!" he screamed.

Thus was von Horst compelled to continue, for he knew that Horg had uttered no idle threat. If the fellow could get those great paws on him, get one good hold, he would kill him. In both his hands he seized one of the outstretched wrists, swung quickly around, bent suddenly forward, and hurled the mighty man over his head —a trick of jujitsu far simpler than it appeared to the amazed onlookers. Horg fell heavily and lay still. Von

Horst approached and stood over him. There were cries of "Kill him! Kill him!" for the blood-lust of these primitive savages was aroused, stimulated perhaps by the *tumal* they had drunk.

Von Horst turned to Mamth. "Have I won?" he asked.

The chief nodded. "You have won," he said.

The victor looked at Grum. "Here is your mate," he said. "Come and take him."

The woman ran forward and fell upon the prostrate Horg, beating and kicking him. Von Horst turned away in disgust. The others, laughing, returned to the food and the *tumal*.

Thorek came and slapped von Horst on the back. "I told them you were a great warrior," he exulted.

"You should know," said von Horst with a grin.

"Come and join the *karoo*," said Thorek. "You have had nothing to eat or drink. That is not the way to make *karoo*."

"Why should I make *karoo*?" demanded von Horst. "I do not even know what is being celebrated."

"They have captured Old White, The Killer. That is something to celebrate. There never was such a wise old mammoth, nor one as large. After the next sleep we shall start training him, and when he is trained Mamth will ride him. He is a fit mammoth for a chief."

"I should like to see him trained," remarked von Horst; for he thought it might be an interesting occasion if Old White objected, which he was sure that he would.

"I'll ask Mamth if you can come," said Thorek. "It will probably be after the next sleep. Every one will wish to sleep after the *karoo*."

The two men talked for awhile, exchanging experiences that had befallen them since they had separated; then Thorek wandered away to drink with his fellows, and von Horst sought out Lotai. Together they watched the celebration, which was by this time loud and boisterous. Fights were more numerous, the laughter deafening. Usually dignified old warriors were performing foolish antics and laughing uproariously at themselves. Many of the women were thick tongued and bleary eyed. As von Horst watched them he was struck by the very obvious fact that human nature had undergone little or no change from the stone age to the present time. Except for the difference in language and apparel these might be people from any present-day country of the outer crust. Presently he saw Grum approaching unsteadily. For the moment she had relaxed surveillance over her new mate. Von Horst attracted her attention and beckoned to her.

"What do you want?" she demanded.

"You have not forgotten our bargain?" inquired the man.

"What bargain?" she asked.

"If I got Horg for you, you were to help me escape."

"When they are asleep after the *karoo* I will show you the way, but you cannot go now. The tarags would get you. After the prisoners are taken to the little canyon, the tarags will be gone; then you could go."

"It will be too late then," he said, "for I am to go to the little canyon; and if I have surmised correctly from what I have heard, I shall not return."

"No," she admitted with a shrug, "you will not. But I promised to show you how you might escape. It is the only way I know; if you can't use it, that is not my fault." Then she staggered away in search of Horg, and von Horst returned to Lotai.

The celebration dragged on—interminably, it seemed to von Horst; but at last those who could still walk reeled to their caves to sleep.

Horg had drunk himself into a stupor, and Grum was beating him over the head with a stick in an effort either to punish or arouse him—perhaps to kill him. Von Horst could not guess which.

Lotai, Mumal, and Gorph were climbing to their caves —the last so befuddled that climbing the ladder toward his ledge seemed to von Horst almost to verge upon suicide.

The European passed close to Grum. "They are all going to their caves to sleep," he whispered. "Now is your chance to tell me."

"Go to the ledge before Gorph's cave, and wait there for me."

As he climbed the ladders toward the ledge he could hear Grum berating Horg as she beat him, and he smiled as he speculated on the similarity between the people of the old stone age and those of modern-day civilization. The principal difference seemed to lie in the matter of inhibitions. He had known women of the outer crust who were like Grum—their thoughts were taloned.

He sat down upon the ledge to wait. He was quite alone. The others had gone into the cave to sleep. He though of Lotai and the sad lives that she and Mumal led. He thought too of La-ja, and these thoughts were sad thoughts. It seemed strange that this little savage should have won to such a place in his life that a future without her loomed dull and grey. Could it be that he loved her? He sought to analyze his feelings that he might refute such a theory, but he only arrived at another sigh with the realization that no matter what logic he brought to bear the fact remained that her passing from his life had left an emptiness that hurt.

Presently Grum came. Her little eyes were blood-shot, her frowzy hair at its frowziest. She was the personification of a stench, both morally and physically.

"Well," she said, "I guess Horg knows that he has a mate."

"Why did you beat him?" asked von Horst.

"You've got to start right with them," she explained. "If you give them the least little toe-hold you're lost, just as Mumal is."

He nodded in understanding of her philosophy; for, again, he had known women of the outer crust who were like her. Perhaps their technic was more refined, but their aim was identical. Marriage to them, meant a struggle for supremacy. It was a 50-50 proposition of their own devising—they took fifty and demanded the other fifty.

"Now," he said, "tell me how I may escape."

"There is a hole in the rear of Gorph's cave," explained Grum. "It drops down a few feet into a tunnel. When I was a little girl Gorph was beating me. I broke away and hid in this hole. I knew he would not dare to follow me, because he had always told us that this tunnel led to the Molop Az. Gorph chased me and tried to get hold of me, reaching into the hole to seize me; so I had to move back into the tunnel to escape him. He threatened to kill me when I came out—if I didn't fall into the Molop Az and get burned up.

"I was very much afraid of Gorph then when I was a little girl. When this happened he had been drinking too much *tumal,* and I knew that if I came out he really would kill me; so I determined to stay where I was until I thought he was asleep.

"Then I got to thinking about Molop Az. Perhaps I could go far enough in the tunnel to see it and return safely. After all it didn't make much difference to me if I did fall into it. Gorph was very cruel, and sooner or later he was sure to kill me. Of that I was convinced; so I thought I might as well take a chance with the Molop Az. Being young, I was very curious. The more I thought about it the more I wished to investigate it. I decided to follow the tunnel and see the Molop Az."

"What is the Molop Az?" asked von Horst.

"It is a sea of fire, Pellucidar floats upon it. We know that, because there are places in Pellucidar where the smoke and fire come up through the ground from the Molop Az. There are holes in mountains where melted rock flows up.

"The dead that are buried in the ground are taken down bit by bit by little demons and burned up in Molop Az. There is no doubt about that because when we dig up a body that has been buried we find that some of it has been carried away—perhaps all of it."

"And did you find the Molop Az?"

She shook her head "No. The tunnel does not lead to Molop Az; it leads to the little canyon. From there, except at certain times, you could easily make your escape from Ja-ru; just go up the canyon and climb the cliff at the upper end. Beyond, you can drop down into another canyon that leads out of our country into a country where mammoth-men seldom if ever go."

"Thanks," said von Horst.

"But you can't go now. The tarags would get you. They are in the far end of the tunnel. They will be there until the prisoners are taken to the little canyon."

"What is the little canyon?" he asked.

She looked at him in surprise. "What would a little canyon be but a little canyon?" she demanded.

"What happens there?"

"You will find out soon enough. Now I am going back to Horg. You got him for me, and I have kept my promise. I don't know whether he was worth the trouble, but at least I shall have a cave of my own." She turned then and left him.

'At least I shall have a cave of my own!' von Horst

grinned. Evidently it was an immemorial custom that girls should wed to escape their families.

XVI

OLD WHITE

BELOW HIM the leaves of the trees moved to a gentle breeze as von Horst came from the cave after sleeping. The air was fresh and clear, and the breeze was cool, tempering the heat of the high sun, as though it blew across the snow of far mountains. The man looked about him and saw that life was astir again in the cliff village of the mammoth-men. He heard his name called from below and saw Thorek beckoning to him to come down. Gorph had to yet come from the cave; so von Horst descended and joined Thorek at the foot of the cliff. Many warriors were assembling. Mamth was there, and though he saw von Horst he paid no attention to him.

"We are going to train Old White," said Thorek. "Mamth has said that you may come with us. You may ride with me upon my mammoth."

Presently the herd appeared, driven by herders mounted on their great beasts. These were all well trained mammoths, and they moved quietly and obediently. When all the warriors were mounted Mamth led the way up the main canyon. The gorges that ran into it were mostly narrow with steep, rocky sides. Before the entrance to one of them Mamth halted. The opening into the gorge was very narrow and across it were bars each of which was a good size tree. The top bar was roped securely into place by a large rope that had been made by braiding long grass. Warriors removed the rope; and two of the mammoths, directed by their riders, lifted the bars and removed them; then the party filed into the gorge. Beyond the entrance it widened and the floor was level. They had ridden up it but a short distance when von Horst saw a huge mammoth standing in the shade of a tree. It was swaying to and fro on its great feet, its head and trunk undulating to the cadence of its swaying body. On its left jowl was a patch of white hair. It was Old White, the Killer. Von Horst would have recognized the huge beast among hundreds of its kind.

At sight of the party the animal raised its trunk and screamed. The rocky hills trembled to the giant's warning. It started toward them, and then von Horst saw that one of its feet was secured to a great log. It could move about, but the log prevented it from moving rapidly. Two mammoths were ridden in on either side of Old White. When he attempted to raise his trunk to seize the riders the other mammoths caught and held it with theirs, and it required the combined strength of the two to do it.

Now a third warrior rode close and clambered over the back of one of the tame mammoths to sit astride Old White's neck, and the close contact of the man threw the captive into a fury. Trumpeting and bellowing, he sought to escape from the beasts that pressed close on either side. He fought to raise his trunk and snatch the man-thing from him as he lurched erratically about the floor of the gorge dragging the great log in his wake.

Old White, the Killer, was wise with great age; and when he realized that he could accomplish nothing by force he suddenly became quiet and apparently as docile as a lamb; then commenced his training. The rider struck him a sharp blow with the flat of his hand on his back just behind where the warrior sat, and simultaneously a mammoth in his rear and those on either side of him pushed him forward. A blow on the head in front of the rider was a signal to stop, and the three great training mammoths stopped him. Time and again he was rehearsed in these movements; then he was taught to turn to the right or left by a kick on the opposite jowl. Old White learned quickly. Mamth was delighted. Here, indeed, was a powerful and intelligent beast worthy to be the mount of a chief. The trainers watched Old White carefully, his ears, his tail, his trunk, his eyes, for these were the indices of his temper; and they all proclaimed resignation and docility.

"Never have I seen a wild mammoth subdued so easily or taught so quickly," exclaimed Mamth. "He is already trained. Let him be ridden alone now without the other mammoths. Later we will remove the log."

The riders withdrew the other three mammoths to a short distance from Old White; and the great beast stood gently swinging his trunk to and fro, a picture of contentment and docility. The young warrior riding him struck him sharply on the back, signaling him to move forward. As quickly as a snake strikes, Old White swung his trunk up and seized his rider; and simultaneously he was transformed into a raging devil of hate and fury.

Screaming with rage, he raised the struggling warrior high above his head; then he dashed him heavily to the ground in front of him. The three warriors who had been assisting with his training urged their mounts in, but too late. Old White placed a great foot on the warrior and trampled him into the earth. Then he seized the warrior on the nearest mount and hurled him across the gorge, and all the while he trumpeted and bellowed. As he lunged for another of the warriors the two turned their mammoths and retreated; but Old White pursued them, dragging the heavy log after him. That was the end of the mighty captive's training. Mamth, disappointed and angry, ordered all from the gorge, the bars of the gate were replaced; and they rode back down the canyon toward the village.

Von Horst had been an interested spectator, his interest augmented because of his former remarkable experience with Old White. His sympathies were with the mammoth, and he was secretly pleased by the manner in which the wise old beast had completely deceived his captors and won at least a partial revenge for the sufferings and indignities that he had been subjected to.

Von Horst had also been interested in learning the method used by the mammoth-men in controlling their ponderous mounts; and as they left the gorge he asked Thorek if he might pilot the animal the two were riding; and Thorek, amused, consented. Thus he acquired an accomplishment that appeared quite as useless as anything that he had ever learned in his life.

"Will you ever be able to tame Old White?" he asked.

Thorek shook his head. "Not unless Mamth is crazy," he replied, "will he ever risk another warrior on that brute. He is a natural killer. Such as he are never tamed. He has killed many warriors, and knowing how easy it is to kill us he would never be safe."

"What will become of him?"

"He will be destroyed, but not before he has afforded the tribe some entertainment."

They rode on in silence. Von Horst's thoughts were rummaging in the attic of memory rediscovering many a half forgotten souvenir. Bold and fresh and clear among them was the figure of La-ja. He turned his face a little toward Thorek.

"Lotai is a fine girl," he said.

Thorek looked surprised, and scowled. "What do you know of Lotai?" he demanded.

"I am quartered in Groph's cave."

Thorek grunted.

"Lotai will make some warrior a good mate," ventured von Horst.

"He will have to fight me," said Thorek.

Von Horst smiled. "Grum has a mate," he said. "Whoever takes Lotai will not have to take Grum, too. He will only have to fight you. But I did not know that you cared. Lotai does not know that you care."

"How do you know?"

"She said so."

"Do you want her?" demanded Thorek.

"She is very desirable, but she loves another."

"And you are afraid to fight him?"

"No," replied von Horst. "I am not afraid to fight him. I have already done so and beaten him."

"And you have mated with her?" Thorek's tone sounded like the growl of a beast.

"No. I know that she loves him."

"Who is he? He'll not have her. I'll kill him. Who is he? Tell me."

"You," said von Horst, grinning.

Thorek looked very foolish. "You are sure?" he asked.

"Positive. She has told me."

"Before the next sleep I shall ask Mamth, and I shall take Lotai to my cave."

"Do you have to ask Mamth?"

"Yes; he is chief."

"Ask him now," suggested von Horst.

"As well now as later," agreed Thorek. He urged his mount forward until he rode abreast of Mamth.

"I would take Lotai, the daughter of Gorph, to be my mate," he said to the chief.

Mamth scowled. "No," he said.

"Why?" demanded Thorek. "I am a great warrior. I have no mate. I want Lotai."

"So do I," said Mamth.

Thorek flushed. He was about to make some rejoinder when von Horst put a warning finger to his own lips and slowed the mammoth down until it had again taken its place in the column.

"I have a plan," said von Horst.

"What sort of a plan?" asked Thorek.

"A plan whereby you may get Lotai and at the same time do something that will make her very happy."

"And what is that?"

"She and her mother, Mumal, are very unhappy here. Mumal wishes to return to Sari, the country from which Gorph stole her; and Lotai wishes to go with her."

"Well, what can I do about it?" demanded Thorek.

"You can take them. It is the only way that you can get Lotai."

"I cannot take them," said Thorek. "I could never get them out of the village."

"Would you go to Sari with them if you could?"

"I would only be killed by the men of Sari."

"The Sarians would not kill you. Mumal is a Sarian, and I have a friend named Dangar who would see that you were taken into the tribe. He would do anything that I asked."

"It is useless," insisted Thorek. "I could never leave the village with two women."

"Would you, if you could?" demanded von Horst.

"Yes; if Lotai would go with me I would go anywhere."

"In the back of Gorph's cave there is an opening into a tunnel."

"Yes, I know of it; it leads to Molop Az."

"It leads to the little canyon. When the tarags at the other end are gone you may go out that way with Lotai and Mumal."

"How do you know that it leads to the little canyon?" demanded Thorek.

"I have talked with one who went through it as far as the place where the tarags are."

Thorek rode in silence for a time before he spoke again. The party came to the village and dismounted. The herders drove the mammoths away. Mamth was irritable and glum. He turned on von Horst.

"Get to Gorph's cave," he ordered, "and stay there. Perhaps before the next sleep we shall take you to the little canyon."

"That is the end for you, my friend," said Thorek. "I am sorry. I thought that perhaps we might find a way for you to go with us to Sari; but the way will not be open, the tarags will not be gone until after you have been taken to the little canyon; then it will be too late."

Von Horst shrugged. "There is not very much that one can do about it," he said.

"There is nothing," asserted Thorek.

He walked on beside von Horst toward the ladder that led upward to Gorph's cave. "Perhaps this is the las time that we shall talk together," he said.

"Perhaps," agreed von Horst.

"Will you speak to Lotai for me?"

"Certainly. What shall I say?"

"Ask her if she will go with me to Sari, she and Mumal. If she will, raise your right arm straight toward the sun when next you see me. If she will not, raise your left arm. I shall be watching. If they will go, tell them that when the others go to the little canyon, they must hide. I will do the same, and after all are gone we can enter the tunnel and go as far as the tarags. When the tribe has left the little canyon, we can come out and go away in search of Sari."

"Good-by," said von Horst. They had reached the foot of the ladder. "Good-by and good luck. I will speak to Lotai as soon as possible."

Von Horst found Lotai and Mumal alone in front of the cave, and immediately explained the plan that he and Thorek had discussed. Both women were delighted, and they sat for a long time planning on the future. Presently Gorph came and demanded food. As usual he was surly and brutal. He glowered and growled at von Horst.

"I shall not have to feed you again," he said. "Mamth has spoken, and soon all will be in readiness in the little canyon. You will be taken there with the other prisoners, and you will not come back."

"I shall miss you, Gorph," said von Horst.

The mammoth-man looked at him in stupid amazement. "I shall not miss you," he said.

"I shall miss your pleasant ways and your hospitality."

"You are a fool," said Gorph. He gobbled his food and arose. "I am going into the cave to sleep," he said. "If word is passed that we are going to the little canyon, wake me."

As he crossed to enter the cave he aimed a vicious kick at Lotai, which she dodged by rolling quickly out of the way. "Why don't you get a man?" he demanded. "I am sick of seeing you around; I am tired of feeding you;" then he passed on into the cave.

The three sat in silence. They dared not plan for fear they might be overheard. The thoughts of the women were filled with happiness—thoughts of escape, of Sari, of love, and of happiness. The man thought not of the future but of the past—of the world of his birth, of his friends, and his family, of a beautiful girl who had touched his life briefly and yet had filled it. There was no future for him—only a brief interval of uncertainty and then death. A young man climbed agilely up the ladders to the ledge before Gorph's cave. He halted and surveyed the three, his eyes resting on Lotai.

"You are to go to the cave of Mamth," he said. "He

has chosen you to be his mate."

Lotai turned very white; her wide eyes were horror filled. She tried to speak; but she only gasped, her fingers clutching at her throat.

Von Horst looked at the messenger. "Tell Mamth that Lotai has been ill," he said, "but that she will come presently."

"She had better not be long," warned the man, "if she doesn't want a beating."

After he had departed the three sat whispering together for some time; then Lotai arose and went into the cave. Von Horst and Mumal remained where they were for a short time; then they too, feeling the urge to sleep, went into the cave.

Von Horst was awakened by loud voices outside the cave; then Gorph entered, calling Lotai. There was no reply. Von Horst sat up.

"Lotai is not here," he said. "Don't make so much noise; I want to sleep."

"Where is she?" demanded Gorph. "She has got to be here."

"Perhaps, but she is not. Mamth sent for her to come to his cave. Go and inquire of Mamth where she is."

Two warriors entered the cave. "She did not come to Mamth's cave," said one of them. "He sent us to fetch her."

"Perhaps something happened to her," suggested von Horst.

The two, with Gorph, searched the cave. They questioned Mumal, but she only replied as had von Horst that Mamth had sent for Lotai. At last they departed, and the others followed them to the ledge. Presently von Horst saw a number of warriors commence a search of the village. They searched every cave, but they did not find Lotai. Von Horst could see Mamth standing among the trees at the foot of the cliff, and he guessed from his gestures that he was very angry. Nor was he mistaken. Presently the chief came himself to the cave of Gorph and searched it; and he questioned Gorph, and Mumal, and von Horst. He wanted to blame one or all of them, but he had no evidence to support him. He stopped in front of von Horst, scowling.

"You are bad luck," he said, "but it will not be for long—we go now to the little canyon."

To the little canyon! The end of his adventure in Pellucidar was approaching. Well, what of it? One must die. It is little easier one time than another. Even the very old and hopeless cling tenaciously to life. They may not wish to, but they cannot help it—it is just another of Nature's immutable laws.

He followed the warriors down the ladders to the foot of the cliff. Here the clan was gathering, men, women, and children. A herd of mammoths was being driven into the village; and the great beasts were lifting men, women, and children to their backs. Von Horst looked about in search of Thorek, but he could not find him; then he was ordered to the back of a mammoth, where he sat behind a warrior. He saw Frug on another beast, as well as other prisoners similarly mounted. There were men from Amdar, from Go-hal, from Lo-har. Von Horst had never met any of the other prisoners except Frug; but he had heard them spoken of by Mumal, Grum, and Lotai. He would have been glad to have talked with the man from Lo-har, because that was La-ja's country. Because of that he felt closer to him. His heart might have warmed even to the redoubtable Gaz.

Presently he caught sight of Thorek. He was standing at one side among the trees staring steadily at von Horst; and the instant that the man from the outer crust caught his eye, he raised his right arm aloft toward the sun.

Thorek nodded and turned away. Immediately thereafter Mamth moved off upon his great mount, and the others followed. The hairy warriors with their women and children, the monstrous beasts that bore them, presented a picture of primitive savagery that thrilled von Horst despite its sinister connotation. It was indeed an inspiring prelude to death. He looked about him. Riding beside and almost abreast of him, he discovered Gorph alone upon the back of his mammoth.

"Where is Mumal?" inquired von Horst.

Gorph looked at him and scowled. "She is sick," he said. "I hope she dies; then I could get me a good mate. I will not hunt for two of them and their brats."

Presently the trail wound up the side of the canyon to the summit of a ridge that paralleled a steep-sided canyon. Here the tribe dismounted, turning the mammoths over to the herders; after which the men, women, and children ranged themselves along the edge of the canyon which formed an amphitheater below them.

"This," said the warrior with whom von Horst had ridden, "is the little canyon."

XVII

THE LITTLE CANYON

AT THE EDGE of the canyon was a ledge along which the members of the tribe pressed to obtain a view of the floor of the canyon some thirty feet below. At the upper end of the canyon a massive corral had been built in which were several mammoths, and in the wall opposite the spectators a cave entrance was barred with small timbers. As von Horst stood looking down into the little canyon, Horg came carrying a rope in one end of which was a noose.

"Stick your leg through this," he said to von Horst, "and hold on tight."

Two other warriors approached and took hold of the rope with the first. "Get over the edge," directed Horg. "Your troubles will soon be over. I would almost like to change places with you."

Von Horst grinned. "No thanks," he said. "I know when I'm well off."

"When you reach the bottom, step out of the rope," instructed Horg; then the three lowered him to the floor of the canyon.

As they pulled the rope up again they tossed down a stone knife and a stone tipped spear; then they lowered another prisoner. It was Frug.

The chief of the Basti glowered at von Horst. "You've got me into a nice mess," he growled.

"You are rationalizing, my friend," replied von Horst. "You are also passing the buck, as my American friends so quaintly put it; all of which confirms an opinion I have long held—that styles in whiskers and bowler hats may change, but human nature never."

"I don't know what you are talking about."

"It is quite immaterial. If I am any sort of a judge, nothing that we may or think down here at the bottom of the little canyon will ever be material to any one, not even to ourselves."

From above were dropped weapons for Frug; and then, one by one, the three remaining prisoners were lowered and armed. The five doomed men stood in a little group waiting for death, wondering, perhaps, in what form the grim reaper would present himself. They were stalwart men, all; and each in his own mind had doubtless determined to sell his life as dearly as possible.

The fact that they had been armed must have held out a faint hope that they might be given a chance, however slender, to win life and freedom in combat.

Von Horst was scrutinizing the three he had not previously seen. "Which of you is from Lo-har?" he asked.

"I am from Lo-har," said the youngest of the three. "Why do you ask?"

"I have been long with a girl from Lo-har," replied von Horst. "Together we escaped from Basti, where we were being held in slavery. We were on our way to Lo-har when two men from Basti stole her from me while I slept."

"Who was this girl?" inquired the man from Lo-har.

"La-ja."

The man whistled in surprise. "The daughter of Brun, the Chief," he said. "Well, you are just as well off here as you would have been had you succeeded in reaching Lo-har with her."

"Why?" demanded von Horst. "What do you mean?"

"I mean that you can only be killed here; and if you had reached Lo-har with La-ja, Gaz would have killed you. He has been on the warpath ever since La-ja disappeared. It is a good thing for the Bastians that he did not know who stole her. Gaz is a mighty man. Single handed he might destroy a whole tribe such as the Bastians"

Gaz again! Von Horst was almost sorry that he was never to have the opportunity to see this doughty warrior.

He turned to Frug. "The man from Lo-har doesn't think much of you Bastians," he taunted.

"Is he a Bastian?" demanded the Lo-harian.

"He is the chief," explained von Horst.

"I am Daj of Lo-har," cried the young warrior. "You stole the daughter of my chief, you eater of men. I kill!"

He leaped toward Frug, holding his stone-tipped spear

like a bayonetted rifle. Frug sprang back, parrying the first thrust. A shout of approval rose from the savage audience on the ledge above. Then the two men settled down to a stern, relentless dual. Frug outweighed his opponent by fifty pounds, but the other had the advantage of youth and agility. The former sought to rush Daj and bear him down by sheer physical weight, but Daj was too quick for him. Each time, he leaped aside; and on Frug's third attempt, Daj dodged as he had before; then he wheeled quickly and jabbed his spear into the Bastian's side.

The mammoth-men shouted their approval. "Kill! Kill!" they screamed. Frug roared with pain and rage, wheeled again and lumbered down upon Daj. This time the Loharian stood his ground until Frug was almost upon him; then he crouched suddenly beneath the extended weapon of his adversary and thrust viciously upward into the belly of the Bastian. As Frug writhed, screaming, upon the ground, Daj wrenched his weapon from the other's belly and plunged it through his heart. Thus died the Chief, Frug of Basti; thus was La-ja avenged by one of her own clan.

Amidst the shouts and yells of the mammoth-men, the man from Amdar shouted, "Look! Tarags! There," and pointed toward the opposite side of the canyon.

With the others, von Horst looked. The grating that had been before the entrance to the cave had been raised by warriors from above, and now five great tarags were slinking onto the floor of the canyon—five mighty, saber-toothed tigers.

"Tandors!" exclaimed the man from Go-hal. "They are turning the tandors loose on us. They give us a spear and a knife to fight tarags and tandors."

"They think well of us as fighting men," said von Horst, grinning, as he glanced toward the upper end of the canyon and saw that the mammoths had been released from the corral.

There were five mammoths, bulls that were untamable killers. One of them towered above his fellows, a huge monster, bellowing angrily as it caught the scent of the tarags and the men. The five moved ponderously down toward the center of the canyon, while the great cats crossed directly toward the five men awaiting their doom. Thus the paths of the beasts seemed certain to meet before the tarags reached the men. But one of the latter trotted ahead, so that it seemed apparent that it would cross in front of the mammoths and reach the four prisoners without interruption.

Von Horst was sufficiently familiar with the tempers of both mammoths and tigers to know that, being hereditary enemies, they would attack one another if they came in contact. Just what this would mean to himself and his fellow prisoners he could only guess. Perhaps enough of them might be disabled in the ensuing battle to permit the men to dispatch those that were not killed. Whether or not they would be any better off then, he did not know. It might be that those who survived would be released. He asked Daj of Lo-har about it.

"The mammoth-men never let a prisoner escape if they can help it," replied Daj. "If we are not killed by the beasts, we shall be killed in some other way."

"If we can reach the upper end of the canyon," said von Horst, "we may be able to escape. I see a little trail there running from beside the corral to the summit. I have been told that if we can escape in that way the mammoth-men will not pursue us, as it would take them into a country that, for some reason, they never enter."

"The tarags and the tandors will never permit us to reach the upper end of the canyon," replied Daj.

The tarag that was in the lead was preparing to charge.

He crouched low, now, and crept forward. His sinuous tail twitched nervously. His blazing eyes were fixed upon von Horst who stood a little in advance of his fellows. Behind this tarag the others had met the tandors. The canyon thundered to the roaring and trumpeting and screaming of the challenging beasts.

"Run for the upper end of the canyon," von Horst called back to his companions. "Some of you may escape."

The tarag charged, his lips stretched in a hideous snarl that bared his great saber teeth to the gums, his jaws distended. Roaring, he charged upon the puny man-thing. Once before had von Horst stopped the charge of a tarag with a stone tipped spear. That time he had accorded the palm to luck. It seemed incredible that such luck would hold again. Yet, had it been wholly luck? Skill and strength and iron nerve had been contributing factors in his victory. Would they hold again against this devil-faced demon?

As the tarag rose in its final spring, von Horst dropped to one knee and planted the butt of the spear firmly against the ground. He was very cool and deliberate, though he had to move with lightning speed. He held the point of the spear forward, aiming it at the broad white chest of the sabertooth; then, as the beast struck, the man rolled to one side, leaping quickly to his feet.

The spear sank deep into the chest of the tarag, and with a hideous scream the beast rolled in the dust of the canyon floor. But it was up again in an instant seeking with ferocious growls and terrifying roars the author of its hurt. It turned its terrible eyes upon von Horst and tried to reach him; but the butt of the spear, sticking into the ground, drove the point farther into its body; and it stopped to claw at the offending object. Its roars, now, were deafening; but von Horst saw that it was reduced to nothing more menacing than noise and looked about him to see what chance he had to reach the upper end of the canyon. His companions were moving in that direction. To his right, the tarags and mammoths were engaged in a titanic struggle. Three of the former had centered their attack upon the smallest of the bulls. The other four bulls stood in a little group, tail to tail, while the remaining tarag, the largest of the five, circled them.

Von Horst moved in the direction of the upper end of the canyon. He hoped that he might go unnoticed by the beasts, but the great tarag that was circling the four bulls saw him. It stopped in its tracks, eyeing him; and then it came for him. No longer was there a spear with which to dispute the outcome of the encounter with the fanged and taloned beast—the outcome that now must be a foregone conclusion.

The man gauged the distance to the end of the canyon. Could he reach it before the mighty carnivore overtook him? He doubted it. Then he saw the huge bull that he had noticed before break from the group and start forward as though to intercept the tarag. Von Horst imagined that the tandor thought the great cat was trying to escape him and was thus emboldened to pursue and attack.

Now there might be a chance to escape. If the mammoth overtook the sabertooth before the latter reached von Horst; or if the sabertooth's charge were diverted by a threatened attack by the mammoth; then he might easily reach safety while all of the animals in the canyon were occupied with one another. With this slender hope to speed him on, he started to run. But the tarag was not to be denied this easy prey. It paid no attention to the mammoth as it continued on in pursuit of the man. Von Horst, glancing back across a shoulder, was astounded by the terrific speed of the huge mammoth. Like a thoroughbred, it raced to head off the carnivore. The latter gained rapidly upon von Horst. It was a question which would reach him first, and to the man it seemed only a question as to the manner of his death. Would he die with those terrible talons at his vitals, or would he be tossed high in air and then trampled beneath tons of prehistoric flesh?

Upon the rim of the canyon the savage cave-men were howling their delight and approval of this exciting race with death. Mamth had discovered that three of his prisoners had located the path at the upper end of the canyon and were on their way to freedom. That the path was not guarded was due to the fact that the mammoth-men believed that no one but themselves knew of it, and it was so faintly traced upon the canyon's wall that no one who did not know of its existence could have discovered it.

But now that Mamth saw that the three had reached the end of the canyon and started to ascend, he hurriedly sent warriors to intercept them. Whether they would reach the head of the canyon in time to do so was problematical.

Below, on the floor of the canyon, the tarag leaped to seize von Horst. The savage beast was apparently either indifferent to the close proximity of the mammoth racing now parallel with it, or else it sought to wrest the prey from its competitor. Then a strange thing happened. The mammoth's trunk shot out with lightning speed and circled the body of the tarag, halting its spring in mid-air. Once the mighty Titan swung the screaming, clawing creature to and fro; then, with all its great strength, it hurled it high in the air and to one side.

Whether by intent or chance it hurled it to the rim of the canyon among the spectators, scattering them in all directions. Infuriated, and only slightly injured, the tarag charged among the fleeing tribesmen, striking them down to right and left.

But none of this von Horst witnessed. He was too much engrossed with his own perilous adventure. And perilous it seemed. For no sooner had the mammoth disposed of the tarag than it encircled the man with its powerful trunk and lifted him high in the air. To von Horst it signified the end. He breathed a silent prayer that it might be soon over and without suffering. As the beast wheeled he had a fleeting glimpse of the melee on the ledge above—the mad tarag, a score of spearmen rallying courageously to meet its savage attack; then he saw the three tarags and the four mammoths engaged in a terrific battle to the accompaniment of trumpeting, screams, growls, and roars that were almost deafening.

The bull that was carrying him aloft moved straight down the canyon at a shuffling trot. Von Horst wondered why he had not been tossed or trampled. Was the creature playing with him to prolong his torture? What was in the sagacious brain of the ponderous monster? Now the trunk curled back, and to von Horst's amazement he was lowered gently to the beast's neck. For a moment the trunk held him there until he gained his equilibrium; then it was removed.

Past the madly battling beasts the mammoth bore von Horst toward the lower end of the little canyon. The man settled himself more firmly back of the great ears which he grasped as additional support, and as he did so he chanced to glance down. Upon the mammoth's left jowl grew a path of white hair!

Ah Ara, ma Rahna—Old White, the Killer! Could it be that the great beast recognized him? Was it repaying the man for the service he had rendered it? Von Horst could scarcely believe this; yet why else had it refrained from killing him? What was it doing now other than seeking to save him?

Von Horst was well aware of the great sagacity of these huge beasts and the unusual wisdom ascribed to Old White by the mammoth-men; so it was this knowledge and the hope that springs eternal that tended to convince him against his better judgment that he had found a faithful friend and a mighty ally. But what might it avail him? They were still trapped in the little canyon in which blood-mad beasts battled to the death. If he were at the upper end of the canyon, he might escape by the trail; but he was not—he was being borne toward the lower end across which was a massive gate of logs.

That Old White was seeking escape from the canyon in this direction was soon evident. He was directing his shuffling trot straight for the barrier. Now, as he approached it, he increased his gait; and as he came within fifty feet of it, he lowered his head and charged.

Von Horst was aghast. Ahead, upon the instant of impact with the logs of the barrier, lay death for both of them. He thought of slipping from the back of the charging beast. But why? Death beneath the fangs and talons of the great cats might be far more hideous than that which lay just ahead—the terrific impact and then oblivion. There would be no suffering.

The mammoth seems a slow moving, ungainly animal; but it is far from such. Now, in the full rush of its charge, Old White bore down upon the gate of logs with the speed of an express train—a living battering ram of incalculable power. Von Horst lay flat, his arms hooked beneath the great ears. He waited for the end, and he had faced so many dangers in savage Pellucidar since he disembarked from the O-220 that he was not greatly concerned by the imminence of death. Perhaps, now that he had lost La-ja, it would be a welcome surcease of constant battling for survival. After all, was life worth this unremitting strife?

It was all over in a split second. The mighty skull crashed into the heavy barrier. Logs, splintered like matchwood, flew in all directions. The great beast stumbled to its knees over the lower bars, nearly unseating the man; then caught itself and rushed from the little canyon to freedom.

XVIII

BISON-MEN

That he was free seemed almost incredible to von Horst. A veritable miracle, the reward for his humane treatment of his giant savior, had wrought his salvation in an extremity from which only a miracle might have saved him. But what of the future? He had a mount, but what could he do about it? Where was it taking him? Could he control it? Could he even escape it? And if he did, where was he to go? He knew now that there was practically no hope that he might ever find Sari. Even though he might retrace his steps to The Forest of Death, through which he must pass to pick up Dangar's trail, he knew that it would be suicidal to enter that grim and forbidding wood.

He would have liked to make his way to Lo-har because that was La-ja's country. From the point at which he had left The Forest of Death he knew the general direction of Lo-har, and so he decided that when he was again a free agent he would seek out the land of La-ja. There might always be at least the hope that she found her way there. That she could, though, through this fearsome land of grotesque and terrible dangers appeared such a remote possibility as to verge closely upon the impossible.

And how was he to reach it even though chance might put him on the right trail? He was unarmed except for the crude stone knife the mammoth-men had given him and the now useless belt of cartridges which he had clung to for some reason almost as inexplicable as the fact that his captors had not taken it from him.

It is true that the time he had spent in Pellucidar and his increased knowledge of her ways had given him greater confidence in his ability to take care of himself, but it had also impressed upon him a healthy respect for the dangers that he knew must confront him. So much for the future. How about the present?

Old White had reduced his speed and was ambling down the main canyon away from the village of the mammoth-men and the little canyon. No sign of pursuit had developed, and von Horst thought it probable that the tribesmen had been so occupied with the saber-toothed tiger rampant among them that they had failed to notice the sudden departure of Old White and himself.

Presently the mammoth came out of the foot-hills and set its course down toward the river upon the banks of which von Horst had come upon it and where he had later been captured by the mammoth-men. The gentle slope of the plain ahead was dotted with feeding animals, sight of which raised the question in von Horst's mind as to how he was to procure food with only a stone knife as a weapon. He was also concerned with the destination of Old White. Were the animal to leave him in the open plain he might never pass through these great herds to the trees by the river, and he must reach the sanctuary of trees if he were to have even a chance for survival.

There he could find partial concealment and the materials for the bow and arrows and the spear he must have to wage the eternal battle for life which constitutes the whole existence of man in that savage world.

But now Old White was veering off to the left on a course parallel to the river. Von Horst did not want to go in that direction, for the country lay open and only sparsely treed as far as the eye could reach. Trees, plenty of them, trees beside water he must reach.

He had witnessed the unsuccessful attempt to tame Old White. He had seen him obey the signals of his rider before he killed him, and he wonderd if the great beast remembered what he had learned; or, remembering, if he would obey. Perhaps an attempt to guide him would recall to the mammoth the indignities that had been heaped upon him by his captors and the manner in which he had rid himself of his last rider.

Von Horst hesitated a moment; then he shrugged and kicked Old White with his left foot. Nothing happened. He kicked again several times. Now the beast changed its direction toward the right, and von Horst kept on kicking until it was headed straight for the river. Thereafter he kept the beast on this course by the signals he had learned from the mammoth-men—that they had both learned thus.

When the river was reached von Horst struck Old White a sharp blow on top of the head, and the beast stopped; then the man slipped to the ground. He wondered what the animal would do now, but it did nothing—only stood placidly waving its trunk to and fro. Von Horst stepped in front of its shoulder and stroked its trunk. "Good boy," he said in quiet tones, as a man speaks to his horse. Old White wound his trunk about the man gently; then he released him, and von Horst walked away toward the trees and the river. He lay down on his belly and drank, and the mammoth came and drank beside him.

Von Horst could not know how long he remained there among the trees beside the river. He caught fish and gathered nuts and fruit and ate and slept several times; and he fashioned a bow and arrows and a good, stout spear. He made his spear with a thought to tarags. It was longer than the spears he had had before, but not too long; and it was heavy. The wood of which it was made was long-grained and pliant. It would not break easily.

While he was there he saw Old White often. The great beast fed in a great patch of bamboo that grew beside the river only a short distance from the tree in which von Horst had constructed a rude shelter. Often, when not feeding, it came and stood beneath the tree that housed the man. Upon such occasions von Horst made it a point always to handle the beast and talk to it, for it offered him the only companionship that he had. After awhile he came to look forward to Old White's return, and worry a little if he seemed gone over-long. It was a strange friendship, this between a man and a mammoth; and in it von Horst thought he recognized a parallel to the accidents that had resulted eons before in the beginning of the domestication of animals upon the outer crust.

His weapons completed, von Horst determined to set off upon his search for Lo-har. He did not expect ever to find the country, but he had to have an objective. It was just as likely that he would stumble upon Sari as that he should find Lo-har, but he could not simply remain where he was waiting for death by accident or old age. Furthermore, a sense of humor as well as curiosity impelled him to wish to see the fabulous Gaz.

Old White was standing under a nearby tree, out of the heat of the noon-day sun, swaying gently to and fro;

and von Horst walked over to give him a final good-by caress, for he had grown to be genuinely fond of his gigantic friend and companion.

"I'm going to miss you, old boy," he said. "You and I've been places and done things. Good luck to you!" and he gave the rough trunk a final slap as he turned and walked away into the unknown upon his hopeless quest.

As his eyes scanned the broad, horizonless vista that melted into a soft vignette at the uttermost range of human eye-sight it was difficult to reconcile the complete primitiveness of this untouched world with his knowledge that a bare five-hundred miles beneath his feet might be a city teeming with the traffic and the concerns of countless humans like himself who went their various ways and lived their lives confronted by no greater menace than a reckless driver or a banana peel thrown carelessly upon the pavement.

It amused him to speculate upon what his friends might say could they see him now, the trim, sophisticated Lieutenant Frederich Wilhelm Eric von Mendeldorf und von Horst naked but for a loin-cloth, a man of the Pleistocene if ever there was one. And then his thoughts turned back to Pellucidar and La-ja. He wondered why she disliked him so, and he winced at the insistent realization this reverie conjured. He had sought to deny it and beat it down below the threshold of his consciousness, but it persisted with the insistent determination of a stricken conscience. *He loved her;* he loved this little barbarian who was as unconscious of the existence of an alphabet as of finger-bowls.

He plodded on sunk deep in reverie, which is no way to plod Pellucidar where one must be either very quick or very dead. He did not hear the thing that walked behind him, for it walked on padded feet—he was thinking of La-ja of Lo-har. Then, suddenly, he was startled into consciousness of his surroundings and the need for constant vigilance; but too late. Something seized him around the waist and swept him off his feet. As he was lifted high in air he squirmed and looked down into the rough and hairy face of Old White; then he was lowered gently to the broad neck. He almost laughed aloud in his relief. Instantly he felt new hope for the future—that will companionship do, even the companionship of a dumb beast.

"You old son-of-a-gun!" he exclaimed. "You nearly scared the breech-cloth off me, but I am glad to see you! Guess you get lonesome, too, eh? Neither of us seems to have many friends. Well, we'll stick together as long as you'll stick."

Through dangers that must otherwise have seemed fatal Old White bore the man-thing for whom he had conceived this strange attachment. Even the mighty tarag slunk aside out of the path of the mammoth; no bull of the great herds through which they passed charged. Once a thipdar circled about them, the great Pteranodon of the Lias which could carry off a full grown bull Bos. Beneath the shadow of its twenty foot wing spread they moved, the mammoth unconcerned, the man apprehensive; but it did not dive to the attack.

They stopped at intervals to feed and water and to sleep; but as time meant nothing in this timeless world, von Horst made no effort to compute it. He only knew that they must be a long way from Ja-ru. Often he walked to rest his muscles, and Old White plodded so close to him that his hairy trunk usually touched the naked body of the man.

To occupy his mind, von Horst had taught the beast several things—to raise him to its head upon command and to lower him to the ground, to kneel and to lie down, to walk or trot or charge at the proper signal, to lift and carry objects, to place his head against a tree and push it down, or to encircle one with its trunk and uproot it.

Old White seemed to enjoy learning and to be proud of his accomplishments. That he was highly intelligent, von Horst had long realized; and there was one characteristic of the mighty beast that proved it to the man beyond doubt. That was Old White's sense of humor. It was so well developed that there could be no mistaking it, and there were occasions when von Horst could have sworn that the mammoth grinned in appreciation of his own jokes, one of which was to seize the man by an ankle from behind and swing him into the air; but he never dropped him nor ever hurt him, always lowering him to the ground gently. Again, if he thought von Horst had slept too long, he would place a foot upon his body and pretend to trample him, holding him down; or he would fill his trunk with water and shower him. The man never knew what to expect nor when to expect it, but he soon learned that Old White would never harm him.

Von Horst had no idea how far they had travelled; but he knew it must have been a considerable distance, yet they had passed no village nor seen a human being. He marvelled at the vast expanse of uninhabited country given over entirely to wild animals. Thus had been the outer crust at one time. Yet, as he thought of conditions there now, it seemed incredible.

Whether he was nearer to Lo-har than before he could not guess. Often the excursion seemed hair-brained and hopeless. But what else was there for him to do? He might as well keep moving whether in the right direction or the wrong. Had he had a human companion—had La-ja been with him—he might have been reconciled to settle permanently in one of the many beautiful valleys he had crossed; but to live always alone in one place was unthinkable. And so he pushed on, exploring a new world that no one might ever know about but himself.

Each new rise of ground that he approached aroused his enthusiasm for the unknown. What lay beyond the summit?

What new scenes would be revealed? Thus once, as Old White moved ponderously up a slight acclivity, the man's mind conjectured what might lie beyond the summit they were approaching, his anticipation of new scenes and his enthusiasm seemingly undiminished; then he heard a deep bellow, followed by others. Mingled with them seemed to be the voices of men.

To von Horst men meant enemies, so definitely had he habituated himself to the reactions of the stone age; but he determined to have a look at these people. Perhaps they were Lo-harians. Perhaps he had reached Lo-har! The sounds suggested men driving a herd of cattle in which were many bulls, for the deep tones of the bellows gave color to his belief that there were mostly bulls beyond the ridge.

Slipping from Old White's back, von Horst ordered the great beast to remain where it was; then he crept stealthily forward, hoping to reach the summit of the ridge unobserved. In this he was successful, and a moment later he was looking down upon a scene that might well have made him question the credibility of his eyesight.

He lay upon the edge of a low cliff, and below him were four creatures such as might have materialized only from a bad dream. They had the bodies of men— squat, stocky men. Their faces, their shoulders, and their breasts were covered with long, brown hair. From opposite sides of their foreheads protruded short, heavy horns much like the horns of a bison; and they had tails with a bushy tuft of hair at the end. From their throats issued the bull-like bellows he had heard, as well as the speech of men.

They carried no weapons; and it was evident that they were being held at bay by some creature or creatures that were hidden from the sight of von Horst by the overhanging of the cliff upon which he lay, for every time they started to approach closer to the cliff fragments of stone would fly out and drive them back. This always set them to bellowing angrily; and sometimes one or another of them would stamp the ground or paw up the dust with a foot, for all the world like a mad bull; so that von Horst thought of them then and always as the bison-men.

From the fact that missiles were being hurled at these creatures by their prey, von Horst assumed that the latter might be human beings; though, of course, in Pellucidar they might be any strange variety of man or beast. That they were bison-men, he doubted; as he noticed that none of the four threw rocks in return, as he was reasonably certain they would have done had they been sufficiently intelligent.

Occasionally he caught a word or two as the four spoke to one another, and he discovered that they spoke the common language of the human beings of Pellucidar. Presently one of them raised his voice and shouted to whatever it was they had brought to bay at the foot of the cliff.

"Stop throwing rocks, gilak," he said. "It will only go worse with you when we get you, and we shall get you —be sure of that. You have neither food nor water; so you must come out or starve."

"What do you want of us?" demanded a voice from the bottom of the cliff.

"We want the woman," replied the bison-man who had previously spoken.

"You don't want me?" demanded the voice.

"Only to kill you; but if you give us the woman, we will spare you."

"How do I know you'll keep your word?"

"We do not lie," replied the bison-man. "Bring her here and we will let you go."

"I bring her," announced the voice from below.

"The son of a pig!" ejaculated von Horst beneath his breath.

A moment later he saw a man emerge from below the overhang of the cliff, dragging a woman by the hair. Instantly he was upon his feet, charged with horror and with rage; for at the first glance he had recognized them —Skruf and La-ja.

A sheer drop of thirty or forty feet to the ground below left him temporarily helpless, and for a moment he could only stand and look down upon the tragedy; then he fitted an arrow to his bow, but Skruf was partially shielded by the body of the girl. Von Horst could not shoot without endangering her.

"La-ja!" he cried. The girl tried to turn her head back in the direction of his voice. Skruf and the bison-men looked up at the figure standing upon the top of the cliff. "One side, La-ja!" he called. "Go to one side!"

Instantly she swung to the right, turning Skruf sideways so that he was fully exposed to the archer whose bow was already drawn. The bow-string twanged. Skruf screamed and went down clutching at the feathered shaft sunk deep in his body, and as he fell he released his hold upon La-ja's hair.

"Run!" commanded von Horst. "Run parallel to the cliff and I will follow until I find a way down."

Already, recovered from their first surprise, the bison-men were running toward the girl; but she had a little start, and with luck she might outdistance them. Their heavy, squat figures did not seem designed for speed.

Von Horst turned and called to Old White to follow; then he ran along the cliff-top a little behind La-ja. Almost at once he realized that the appearance of the bison-men belied their agility—they were overhauling the girl. Again he fitted an arrow to his bow. Just for an instant he paused—long enough to take aim at the leading bison-man and release the shaft; then he sprang forward, but he had lost ground that he could not regain. However, he had temporarily widened the gap between La-ja and her pursuers; for the leading bison-man lay groveling on the ground, an arrow through his back.

The others were closing up, and again von Horst was forced to stop and shoot. As before, the girl's closest pursuer pitched to the ground. The fellow rolled over and over, but when he stopped he lay very still. Now there were only two, but again von Horst had lost distance. He tried to gain on them but he could not. At last he halted and sent two more arrows after the remaining bison-men. The nearer fell, but he missed the other. Twice after that he loosed his shafts; but the last one fell short, and he knew that the man was out of range—out of range and rapidly gaining on his quarry. Just ahead of the fleeing girl loomed a forest of giant trees. If she could reach these she might elude her pursuer, and she was fleet of foot.

In silence the three raced on, von Horst on the cliff-top barely maintaining his ground; then the girl disappeared among the boles of the great trees; and a moment later the bison-man followed her. Von Horst was frantic. The interminable cliff offered no avenue of descent. There was nothing to do but continue on until he found such a place, but in the meantime what would become of La-ja?

To have found her so unexpectedly, to have been so close to her, and then to have lost her left him heart-sick and hopeless. Still, he knew now that she lived; and that was something. And now, close behind him, he heard the familiar trumpeting of Old White; and a moment later a hairy trunk encircled him and swung him to the now familiar seat in the hollow back of the massive skull.

Just beyond the edge of the forest they came upon a rift in the escarpment; and here the mammoth, finding precarious foot-hold, picked his way carefully down. Von Horst turned him back to the point at which La-ja had disappeared; but here he was forced to dismount, as the trees grew too closely to permit the great beast to enter the forest, and he could neither uproot nor push over the giant boles.

As von Horst left Old White to enter the forest he had a premonition that this was the last time that he would ever see his faithful friend and ally; and it was with a heavy heart that he passed into the grim, forbidding wood.

Only for an instant was his mind occupied with thoughts of Old White, for at a distance he heard a faint scream; and then a voice called his name twice—"Von! Von!"—the voice of the woman he loved.

XIX

KRU

GUIDED ONLY BY the memory of that faint cry in the distance, von Horst pushed on into the forest. Never had he seen trees of such size growing in such close proximity, often so near to one another that there was just room for him to pass between. There was no trail, and because of the zig-zag course he was forced to pursue he soon lost all sense of direction. Twice he had called La-ja's name aloud, hoping that she would reply and thus give him a new clue to her whereabouts, but there had been no answer. He realized that about all he had accomplished had been to apprize her captor that he was being pursued and thus put him on his guard; so, though he moved as rapidly as he could, he was most watchful.

As he hurried on he became more and more imbued with a sense of frustration and the futility of his search, feeling that he was quite probably moving in circles and getting nowhere. He was even impressed by the probability that he might never even find his way out of this labyrinthine maze of gloomy trees, to say nothing of reaching La-ja in time to be of any service to her. And thus his mind was occupied by gloomy thoughts when he came suddenly to the end of the forest. Before him lay the mouth of a canyon leading into low but rugged hills, and here at last was a trail. It wound, well marked, into the canyon.

With renewed hope von Horst stepped confidently out to follow wherever the way might lead; for a brief examination told his now practiced eyes that someone had recently entered the canyon at this point, and faintly in the dust of the trail he saw the imprint of a tiny foot. The canyon was little more than a narrow, rocky gorge winding snake-like into the hills; and as he proceeded he passed the mouths of other similar gorges that entered it at intervals; but the main trail was plain, and he continued upon it, certain now that he must soon overtake La-ja and her captor.

He had been for some little time in the gorge and was becoming impatient with each fresh disappointment when he rounded a bend and did not see those he sought ahead of him, when he heard a noise behind. He turned quickly and saw a bison-man creeping stealthily upon him. The instant that the fellow realized he had been discovered he voiced a bellow that might have issued from the throat of an angry bull. It was answered from down the gorge and from up, and then others came rapidly into view both in front and behind.

Von Horst was trapped. Upon either side the walls of the canyon, while not high, were unscalable; and behind him were bison-men cutting off retreat, and in front were bison-men effectually blocking his advance. Now they were all bellowing. The rocky walls of the gorge reverberated the angry, bestial chorus of challenge and of menace. They had been waiting for him. Von Horst knew it now. They had heard him call to La-ja. They had known he was following, and they had waited in the concealment of one of the gorges he had passed. How easily they had trapped him. But what might he have done to prevent it? How else might he search for La-ja without following where she went?

What was he to do now? The bison-men were coming toward him very slowly. They seemed to hold him in great respect. He wondered if the abductor of La-ja had had either the time or opportunity to tell his fellows of the havoc this strange gilak had played with the four that had first met him. That was one of the tantalizing characteristics of the inner world—that one might never know the measure of elapsed time, which might easily gauge the difference between life and death.

"What are you doing here in our country?" demanded the nearest of the bison-men.

"I have come for the woman," replied von Horst. "She is mine. Where is she?"

"Who are you? We never saw a gilak like you before, or one who could send death from a long way off on little sticks."

"Get me the woman," demanded von Horst, "or I'll send death to you all." He withdrew an arrow from his quiver and fitted it to his bow.

"You cannot kill us all," said the creature. "You have not as many sticks as there are Ganaks."

"What are Ganaks?" asked von Horst.

"We are Ganaks. We will take you to Drovan. If he says not to kill you, we will not kill you."

"Is the woman there?"

"Yes."

"Then I will go. Where is she?"

"Follow the Ganaks in front of you up the gorge."

They all moved on then in the direction that von Horst had been going, and presently they came to a large, open valley in which there were many trees dotted picturesquely over gently rolling ground. Out upon the plain a short distance lay what appeared to be a circular, palisaded village; and toward this the bison-men led the way.

As he came nearer, von Horst saw that there were fields of growing crops outside the village and that in these fields men and women were working—human beings like himself, not Ganaks; but there were many Ganak bulls loitering around. These performed no labor.

A single small gateway led into the village which consisted of a complete circle of mud huts, one adjoining the other except in this one spot where the gateway lay. Trees grew all around the circle in front of the huts, spreading shade trees. In the center of the large compound was a cluster of huts, and here too there were shade trees.

To these central huts his guides led von Horst, and here he saw a large bison-man standing in the shade switching the flies from his legs with his tufted tail. Facing him stood La-ja with her captor, and half surrounding them was a curious throng of Ganaks.

As the new party approached, the big bull looked in

their direction. He had massive horns, and the hair upon his face and shoulders and chest was heavy. His small, round eyes, set wide apart, were red-rimmed and fierce as they glowered menacingly at von Horst. His head was lowered, much after the manner of a beast's.

"What is this?" he demanded, indicating von Horst.

"This is the gilak that killed the three who were with me," said La-ja's captor.

"Tell me again how he killed them," directed the big bull.

"He sent little sticks to kill them," said the other.

"Little sticks do not kill, Trun. You are a fool or a liar."

"Little sticks did kill the three that were with me and another that was there, a gilak. I saw them kill, Drovan. See them? They are in that thing upon his back."

"Fetch a slave," commanded Drovan, "an old one that is not much good."

Von Horst stood there gazing at La-ja. He scarcely saw or heard what was going on about him. La-ja was looking at him. Her face was almost expressionless.

"So you are not dead yet," she said.

"I heard you call me, La-ja," he said. "I came as soon as I could."

She raised her chin. "I did not call you," she said haughtily.

Von Horst was dumbfounded. He had heard her call, plainly, twice. Suddenly he became angry. His face flushed. "You are a little fool," he said. "You are absolutely without appreciation or gratitude. You are not worth saving." Then he turned his back on her.

Instantly he regretted his words; but he was hurt—hurt as he never had been in his life before. And he was too proud to retract what he had said.

A bison-man approached bringing an old slave woman

with him. He led her to Drovan. The chief gave her a rough push.

"Go over there and stand," he ordered.

The old woman moved slowly away—a bent and helpless old creature.

"That's far enough," shouted Drovan. "Stand there, where you are."

"You!" he bellowed, pointing at von Horst. "What is your name?"

The man eyed the half-beast insolently. He was mad all the way through—mad at himself and the world. "When you speak to me, don't bellow," he said.

Drovan lashed his legs angrily with his tail and lowered his head like a mad bull about to charge. He took a few slow steps toward von Horst; and then he stopped and pawed the ground with one foot and bellowed, but the man did not retreat, nor did he show fear.

Suddenly the chief espied the old slave woman standing out in the compound as he had directed her; then he turned again to von Horst. He pointed at the old woman.

"If your sticks will kill," he said, "kill her. But I do not believe that they will kill."

"My sticks will kill," said von Horst. "The Ganaks will see that they will kill."

He took a few steps out into the compound toward the old slave woman and fitted an arrow to his bow; then he turned toward Drovan and pointed at La-ja.

"Will you set that girl and myself free if I show you that my little sticks will kill?" he demanded.

"No," growled the chief.

Von Horst shrugged. "Let it be on your own shoulders," he said; and with that he drew back the feathered shaft, and before anyone could guess his intention or interfere he drove it through Drovan's heart.

Instantly the compound was a riot of bellowing bulls.

They fell upon von Horst before he could fit another arrow to his bow and by weight of numbers bore him to the ground, striking him with their fists and trying to gore him with their horns; but there were so many of them that they interfered with one another.

The man was pretty nearly done for when the attention of his attackers was attracted by a voice of authority. "Do not kill," it commanded. "Let him up. It is I, Kru the Chief, who speaks."

Instantly the bulls abandoned von Horst and turned on the speaker.

"Who says Kru is chief?" demanded one. "It is I, Tant, who will be chief now that Drovan is dead."

During the argument von Horst had dragged himself to his feet. He was half stunned for a moment, but he soon gathered his wits. Quickly he hunted for his bow and found it. Some of the arrows that had dropped from his quiver during the melee he found and retrieved. Now his mind was alert. He looked about him. All the bulls were watching the two claimants for the chieftainship, but some of them were ranging themselves closer to Kru than to Tant. A few went hesitantly to Tant's side. It looked like Kru to von Horst. He stepped over near those who were assembling around Kru.

Surreptitiously he fitted an arrow to his bow. He knew that he was taking a wild chance; and his better judgment told him to mind his own business, but he was still angry and indifferent as to whether he lived or not. Suddenly he straightened up. "Kru is chief!" he cried. Simultaneously he drove an arrow into Tant's chest. "Are there any others who will not accept Kru as chief?" he demanded.

Some of them who had gathered around Tant ran to strike him down; they charged with lowered horns like bulls. But those about Kru charged to meet them; and as they fought, von Horst moved backward slowly until he stood with his back against the chief's hut. Close to him stood La-ja. He paid no attention to her, although it was plain to her that he was aware of her presence.

The man was engrossed in the strange tactics of these half-beasts. When they did not clinch they dove with lowered heads for the belly of an antagonist, seeking to disembowel him with their heavy horns. Oftentimes they met head on with such terrific force that both were knocked down. When they clinched, each antagonist seized another by the shoulders; and, straining and tugging, they sought to gore each other in the face or neck or chest.

It was a scene of savage fury made more terrifying by the bellowing and snorting of the combatants; but it was soon over, for those who opposed Kru were few in numbers and without a leader. One by one, those who survived broke away and retreated, leaving the field to Kru.

The new chief, overcome by his importance, strutted about pompously. He sent immediately for the women of Drovan and Tant, of which there were about thirty; and after selecting half of them for himself turned the others over to his followers to be divided by lot.

In the meantime von Horst and La-ja remained in the background practically unnoticed by the bison-men, nor did they call attention to themselves, as it was obvious that the bulls were worked up to a frenzy of hysterical excitement by all that had so recently transpired and by the sight and smell of blood. Presently, however, the eyes of an old bull fell upon them; and he commenced to bellow deep in his chest and paw the ground. He approached them, lowering his head as though about to charge. Von Horst fitted an arrow to his bow. The bull hesitated; then he turned toward Kru.

"The gilaks," he said. "When do we kill the gilaks or set them to work?"

Kru looked in the direction of the speaker. Von Horst waited for the chief's answer. It had been upon the hope of his gratitude that he had based his hopes for liberty for himself and La-ja, for he was still thinking of the girl's welfare. He found that he could not do otherwise, no matter how ungrateful she might be. He wondered how much gratitude, then, he might expect from this brutal bison-man if La-ja accorded him none.

"Well," said the old bull, "do we kill the gilaks or do we put them to work in the fields?"

"Kill the she!" cried one of the women.

"No," growled Kru, "the she shall not be killed. Take them away and put them in a hut and guard them. Later Kru will decide what to do with the man."

Von Horst and La-ja were taken to a filthy hut. They were not bound. The man's weapons were not taken away from him, and he could only assume that their captors were too stupid and unimaginative to sense the necessity for such precautions. La-ja went to one side of the hut and sat down, von Horst to the other. They did not speak. The man did not even look at the woman, but her eyes were often upon him.

He was unhappy and almost without hope. If she had been kind to him, even civil, he might have envisioned a future worth fighting for with enthusiasm; but now, without hope of her love, there seemed nothing. The knowledge that he loved her aroused in him only self-contempt, while it should have been a source of pride. He felt only a dull sense of duty to her because she was a woman. He knew that he would try to save her. He knew that he would fight for her, but he felt no elation.

Presently he lay down and slept. He dreamed that he slept in a clean bed between cool sheets, and that when he awoke he put on fresh linen and well pressed clothes and went down to a sumptuous dinner at a perfectly appointed table. A waiter, bringing a salver of food, bumped against his shoulder.

He awoke to see a woman standing beside him. She had kicked his shoulder. "Wake up," she said. "Here is your fodder."

She dumped an armful of fresh-cut grass and some vegetables on the filthy floor beside him. "It is for the woman, too," she said.

Von Horst sat up and looked at the woman. She was not a Ganak, but a human being like himself. "What is the grass for?" he asked.

"To eat," she replied.

"We do not eat grass," he said, "and there are not enough vegetables here to make a meal for one."

"You will eat grass here or you will starve," said the woman. "We slaves are not allowed many vegetables."

"How about meat?" inquired von Horst.

"The Ganaks do not eat meat; so there is no meat to eat. I have been here for more sleeps than I can remember, and I have never seen anyone eat meat. You'll get used to the grass after awhile."

"Do they put all their prisoners to work in the fields?" asked von Horst.

"You never can tell what they will do. As a rule they keep the women and work them in the fields until they get too old; then they kill them. If they are short of slaves they keep the men for awhile; otherwise they kill them immediately. They have kept me for many sleeps. I belong to Splay. They will give this woman to some one, because she is young. They will probably kill you, as they have plenty of slaves now—more than they care to feed."

When the woman had gone, von Horst gathered up

the vegetables and placed them beside La-ja. The girl looked up at him. Her eyes flashed.

"Why do you do such things?" she demanded. "I do not want you to do anything for me. I do not want to like you."

Von Horst shrugged. "You are succeeding very well," he said, drily.

She mumbled something that he could not catch and commenced to divide the vegetables into two parts. "You eat your share and I shall eat mine," she said.

"There are not enough for one, let alone two. You'd better keep them all," he insisted. "Anyway, I don't care much for raw vegetables."

"Then you can leave them. I'll not eat them. If you don't like the vegetables, eat the grass."

Von Horst relapsed into silence and commenced to gnaw on a tuber. It was better than nothing—that was about all he could say for it. As the girl ate she occasionally glanced at the man furtively. Once he glanced up and caught her eyes on him, and she looked away quickly.

"Why do you dislike me, La-ja?" he asked. "What have I done."

"I don't wish to talk about it. I don't wish to talk to you at all."

"You're not fair," he remonstrated. "If I knew what I'd done, I might correct it. It would be much pleasanter if we were friends, for we may have to see a lot of each other before we get to Lo-har."

"We'll never get to Lo-har."

"Don't give up hope. These people are stupid. We ought to be able to out-wit them and escape."

"We won't; but if we did, you wouldn't be going to Lo-har."

"I'm going wherever you go," he replied doggedly.

"Why do you want to go to Lo-har? You'd only be killed. Gaz would break you in two. But why do you want to go at all?"

"Because you are going," he said. He spoke scarcely above a whisper, as though to himself.

She looked at him intently, questioningly. Her expression underwent a barely perceptible change, which he did not note because he was not looking at her. It seemed a little less uncompromising. There was the difference between granite and ice—ice is very cold and hard, but it does thaw.

"If you would only tell me what I have done," he insisted—"why you do not like me."

"That, I could not say to you," she replied. "If you were not a fool, you'd know."

He shook his head. "I'm sorry," he said, "but I guess I am; so please tell me because I am such a fool."

"No," she replied emphatically.

"Couldn't you give me a clue?—just a little hint?"

She thought for a moment. "Perhaps I could do that," she said. "You remember that you struck me and carried me away from Basti by force?"

"I did it for your own good, and I apologized," he reminded her.

"But you did it."

"Yes."

"And you didn't do anything about it," she insisted.

"I don't know what you mean," he said hopelessly.

"If I believed that, I might forgive you; but I don't believe anyone can be such a fool."

He sought to find some explanation of the riddle; but though he racked his brains, he could think of none. What *could* he have done about it?

"Perhaps," said La-ja presently, "neither one of us understands the other. Tell me just exactly why you insist on going to Lo-har with me; and if your reason is what I am begin ing to suspect it is, I'll tell you why I have not liked y u."

"That's a bet," exclaimed the man. "I want to go to Lo-har because—"

Two bison-men burst into the hut, cutting him short. "Come!" they commanded. "Now Kru is going to have you killed."

XX

THE BELLOWING HERD

THE TWO Ganaks motioned La-ja to accompany them. "Kru has sent for you, too," they said; "but he is not going to kill you," they added, grinning.

As they passed through the village toward the hut of the chief, many of the Ganaks were lying in the shade of the numerous trees that grew within the compound. Some were eating the grass that had been cut by the slaves; others were placidly chewing their cuds, drowsing with half-closed eyes. Some of the children played sporadically and briefly, but the adults neither played nor laughed nor conversed. They were typical ruminants, seemingly as stupid. They wore neither ornaments nor clothing, nor had they any weapons.

To their lack of weapons, coupled with their stupidity, von Horst attributed the fact that they had not relieved him of his. He still had his bow and arrows and a knife, though he had not recovered his spear which he had dropped during the fight following his slaying of Drovan.

The prisoners were led before Kru who lay in the shade of the great tree that overspread his hut, the hut that had been Drovan's so recently. He looked at them through his red-rimmed eyes, but mostly he looked at La-ja. "You belong to me," he said to her; "you belong to the chief. Pretty soon you go in hut; now you stay outside, watch gilak man die. You will see how you die if you make Kru mad." Then he turned to a bull lying beside him. "Splay, go tell the slaves to bring the dancing-water and the death-tree."

"What's the idea?" demanded von Horst. "Why should you kill me? If it hadn't been for me you wouldn't be chief."

"Too many men slaves," grunted Kru. "They eat too much. Dancing water good; death-tree fun."

"Fun for whom—me?"

"No, fun for Ganaks; no fun for gilak."

Presently Splay returned with a number of slaves. Several of the men carried a small tree that had been stripped of its branches; other men and the women bore quantities of small sticks and rude jars and gourds filled with a liquid.

At sight of them the bison-men commenced to gather from all parts of the village; their women came too, but the young were chased away. They sat down forming a great circle about the tree before the chief's hut. A slave passed a jar to one in the circle. He took a long draught and passed it to the next in line. Thus it started around the circle. The slaves bearing the other gourds and jars followed it around just outside the circle. When it had been emptied another was started at that point.

The men slaves who bore the small tree trunk dug a hole in the ground in an open space between the chief's hut and the village gate. When the hole was sufficiently deep they set the tree upright in it and tamped dirt around it. It protruded about six feet above the surface of the ground. And while this was going on many gourds and jars had been passed around the circle. Now men and women were bellowing, and presently a woman arose and began to leap and skip in clumsy, awkward simulation of a dance. Soon others joined her, both men and women, until all the adults of the village were leaping and staggering and lurching about the compound.

"Dancing-water," said von Horst to La-ja, with a grin.

"Yes, it is the water that takes men's brains away. Sometimes it makes brave men of cowards and beasts of brave men and always fools of all men. Gaz drinks much of it before he kills."

"That must be the tree of death over there." Von Horst nodded in the direction of the sapling the slaves had finished setting up. Now they were piling dry grass and leaves and sticks all around it.

"The death tree!" whispered La-ja. "What is it for?"

"For me," said the man.

"But how? I do not understand. It can't be that they are going to—. Oh, no; they can't be."

"But they are, La-ja. Odd, isn't it?"

"What is odd?"

"That these creatures that are so near the beasts couldn't think of such a thing by themselves nor accomplish it. That only man of all the animals has the faculty of devising torture for amusement."

"I had never thought of that," she said; "but it is true, and it is also true that only man makes the drink that steals away his brains and makes him like the beasts."

"Not like the beasts, La-ja—only more human; for it removes his inhibitions and permits him to be himself."

She did not reply, but stood staring at the stake in the center of the compound, fascinated. Von Horst watched her lovely profile, wondering what was passing in that half savage little brain. He knew that the end must be nearing rapidly, but he had made no move to escape the horrible death the slaves were preparing for him. If there had been only himself to consider, he could have made a break for liberty and died fighting; but there was the girl. He wanted to save her far more than he wanted to save himself.

All about them the bison-men were dancing and bellowing. He heard Kru shout, "Fire! Fire! Give us a fire to dance around. More dance-water! Bring more dance-water, slaves!"

As the slaves refilled the jars and gourds, others built a large fire near the stake; and the bellowing herd immediately commenced to circle it. With the lighting of the fire the demeanor of the bison-men became more uncontrolled, more boisterous, and more bestial; and with the added stimulus of the new supply of drink they threw aside all discretion.

To right and left they were falling to the ground—those remaining on their feet so drunk that they could scarcely stagger. Then some one raised the cry, "The gilak! To the death-tree with him!"

It was taken up on all sides by those who could still speak, and then Kru came staggering toward von Horst.

"To the death tree with him!" he bellowed. "The girl!" he exclaimed. It was as though he had forgotten her until his eyes fell on her on that minute. "Come with me! You are Kru's." He reached out a dirty paw to seize her.

"Not so fast!" said von Horst, stepping between them; then he struck Kru in the face, knocking him down, seized La-ja by the hand and started to run for the village gate, which the slaves had left open when they brought in the tree and the fire-wood. Behind them was the whole herd of bison-men, bellowing with rage as they commenced to get it through their befuddled minds that the prisoners were making a break for escape. In front of them were the slaves. Would they try to stop them? Von Horst dropped La-ja's hand and removed his now

useless cartridge belt. Useless? Not quite. A slave tried
to stop him, and he swung the loaded belt to the side of
his head, knocking him down.

That and one look at von Horst's face sent the other
slaves scurrying out of his way, but now some of the
bison-men were taking up the pursuit. However, a single
backward glance assured von Horst that either he or
La-ja could out-distance them at the moment; as they had
difficulty in remaining on their feet at all, while those
that did moved about so erratically as to make the idea of
pursuit by them appear ridiculous. Nevertheless, they
were coming, and the gate was a long way off. To von
Horst's disgust, he saw that a few of the bison-men were
steadying. But their vile drink held most of them in a
state of helplessness. A few, however, had rallied and
formed a definitely menacing group as they followed the
two fugitives.

"I'll give 'em something to think about besides us,"
said von Horst, and as they passed the roaring fire he
threw his cartridge belt into it.

As they neared the gate he spoke again to La-ja.
"Run," he said. "I'll try to hold them for a moment or
two"; then he wheeled and faced the oncoming bison-
men. There were only about a dozen of them sober
enough to control their actions or hold to a fixed purpose.
The majority of the others were milling about the fire or
lying helpless on the ground, and even the dozen were
erratic in their movements.

Von Horst loosed an arrow at the nearest of the pursuers. It caught him in the belly, and he went down
shrieking and bellowing. A second arrow bowled over
another. The remainder were quite close now, too close
for comfort. He sent another arrow into a third; and that
stopped them, momentarily at least. Then the cartridges
in the fire began to explode. At the first detonation those

who were pursuing the fugitives turned to see what had caused this startling sound, and simultaneously von Horst wheeled and started for the gate.

He found La-ja standing directly behind him, but she too turned and ran the instant that she saw that he was leaving.

"I thought I told you to run," he said.

"What good would it have done, if you had been re-captured or killed?" she demanded. "They would only have caught me again. But it would have done them no good. Kru would not have had me."

He saw then that she carried her stone knife in her hand, and a lump rose in his throat from pity for her. He wanted to take her in his arms from sympathy, but when one is running from imminent death one cannot very well take a woman who hates one into one's arms.

"But you might have escaped and reached Lo-har," he protested.

"There are other things in the world beside reaching Lo-har," she replied enigmatically.

They were past the gates now. Behind them rose the din of exploding cartridges and the mad bellowing of the bison-men. Before them stretched an open, rolling, tree-dotted valley. To their left was the great forest, to their right a fringe of trees at the base of low, wooded cliffs.

Von Horst bore to the right.

"The forest is closer," suggested La-ja.

"It is in the wrong direction," he replied. "Lo-har should lie in the direction we are going. It does, doesn't it?"

"Yes, in this general direction."

"But more important is the fact that if we got into the great forest we'd lose ourselves in no time—and no telling where we'd come out."

La-ja glanced back. "I think they're gaining on us,"

she said. "They are very fast."

Von Horst realized that they'd never reach the cliffs ahead of their pursuers, that their break for liberty had only delayed the inevitable.

"I have a few more arrows left," he said. "We can keep on until they overtake us. Something may happen—a miracle, and it will have to be a miracle. If nothing does, we can make a stand for it. I may be able to kill off enough of them to frighten the others away while we make a fresh start for the cliffs."

"Not a chance," said La-ja. "Look back there near the village."

Von Horst whistled. More warriors were emerging from the gateway. Evidently Kru was sending all who could stand on their feet to join in the pursuit.

"It looks like a hard winter," he remarked.

"Winter?" queried La-ja. "I see nothing but Ganaks. Where is the winter?" She was panting from exertion, and her words came in little gasps.

"Well, let it pass. We'd better save our breath for running."

Thereafter they bent all their energies to the task of out-distancing the bison-men, but without hope. Constantly they lost ground; yet they were nearing the cliffs and the little fringe of wood that half hid them.

Von Horst did not know why he felt so certain that they might be safe if they reached the cliffs; yet he did feel it, and his judgment seemed justified by the fact that the bison-men appeared so anxious to overtake them as quickly as possible. If they had known that the fugitives could not escape even after reaching the cliffs, it seemed reasonable to assume that they would have shown less haste and excitement and would have trailed more slowly and with far less exertion.

Presently La-ja stumbled and fell. Von Horst wheeled

and was at her side instantly. She seemed very weak as he helped her to her feet.

"It's no use," she said. "I cannot go on. I have been running away from Skruf for a long time, always without sufficient food or rest. It has made me weak. Go on without me. You might easily save yourself. There is nothing more that you can do for me."

"Don't worry," he said. "We'll make our stand here. We'd have had to made it pretty soon anyway."

He turned to glance at the oncoming half-beasts. In a moment they'd be within arrow range. There were nine of them, and he had six arrows left. If he got six of the pursuers he might bluff off the other three, but how about the swarm that was now pouring up the valley from the village?

He was thinking how futile was his foolish little stand against such odds, when something impelled him to turn suddenly and look at La-ja. It was one of those strange, psychic phenomena which most of us have experienced, and which many trained researchers ridicule; yet the force which caused von Horst to turn about seemed almost physical, so powerfully did it affect him and so peremptorily. And as he turned he voiced a cry of alarm and leaped forward, seizing La-ja's right wrist.

"La-ja!" he cried. "Thank the Lord I saw you."

He wrenched her stone knife from her fingers, and then dropped her hand. He had broken out into a cold sweat and was trembling.

"How could you? La-ja, how could you?"

"It is best," she said. "If I were dead you might escape. Soon they will take us; and then we shall both die; for they will kill you, and I will kill myself. I will not let Kru have me."

"No," he said, "that is right; but wait until all hope is gone."

"It is gone. You have already done too much for me. The least I can do is to make you free to save yourself. Give me back my knife."

He shook his head.

"But if they get me, and I have no knife, how can I escape Kru?"

"I'll let you have it," he said, "if you'll promise not to do that until after I am dead. As long as I live there is hope."

"I promise," she said. "I do not want to die. I just wanted to save you."

"Because you hate me?" he asked with a half-smile.

"Perhaps," she replied unsmilingly. "Perhaps I do not want to be under such obligations to one I don't like—or perhaps—"

He handed the knife back to her. "You have promised me," he reminded her.

"I shall keep my promise. Look; they are very close."

He turned then and saw that the bison-men were almost within bow-shot. He fitted an arrow and waited. They saw, and came more slowly. Now they spread out to afford him a poorer target. He had not given them credit for that much sense.

"I'll get some of them," he called back to La-ja. "I wish you would run for the cliffs. I think you could make it. I am sure I can hold them for a while."

The girl did not reply and he could not take his eyes from the bison-men long enough even to glance back at her. His bow twanged. A bison-man screamed and fell.

"I'm getting pretty hot at this archery stuff," he commented aloud. This evidence of childish pride upon the very threshold of death amused him, and he smiled. He thought that if he were home he could give exhibitions at town fairs. Perhaps he could even learn to shoot backward through a mirror as he had seen rifle experts do. It was all very amusing. He pictured the embarrassment of his fellow officers and other friends when they saw large colored lithographs announcing the coming of "Lieutenant Frederich Wilhelm Eric von Mendeldorf und von Horst, Champion Archer of the World. Admission 25 pfennings."

He loosed another arrow, still smiling. "I think I shall charge more admission," he mused as another bison-man dropped, "I'm pretty good."

La-ja interrupted his amusing train of thought with an exclamation of despair. "A tandor is coming, Von," she cried. "It is coming for us. Its tail is up, and it is coming straight for us. It must be an old bull that has gone mad. They are terrible."

Von Horst glanced back. Yes, a mammoth was coming; and it was coming straight as an arrow in their direction. There could be no doubt but that it had seen them and was trotting up to charge. When it got closer it would trumpet, its tail and trunk and ears would all go up; and it would barge down on them like a runaway locomotive. There would be no escaping it. Bison-men in front, a mad mammoth in the rear!

"This doesn't seem to be our lucky day," he said.

"Day?" inquired La-ja. "What is day?"

The bison-men were watching the mammoth. Behind them their fellows were approaching rapidly. Soon there would be fully a hundred of them. Von Horst wondered if they would stand the charge of a mammoth. They bore no arms. How could they defend themselves. Then he glanced back at the mammoth, and his heart leaped. It was quite close now, and it was about to charge. He could see the patch of white hair on its left jowl quite plainly. He voiced the call with which the great beast had been so familiar. Simultaneously the great trunk went up, a thunderous trumpeting shook the earth, and Old White charged.

Von Horst swept La-ja into his arms and stood there in the path of the gigantic monster. Could it be that Old White did not know him, or had he really gone mad and bent on killing, no matter whom, just for the sake of killing?

The girl clung to the man. He felt her arms about his neck, her firm young breasts pressed against his body, and he was resigned. If it were death, he could not have chosen a happier end—in the arms of the woman he loved.

With a squeal of rage, Old White brushed past them so close that he almost bowled them over and bore down upon the bison-men. These scattered, but they did not run. Then it was that von Horst saw how they fought the mighty tandor.

Leaping aside, they sprang in again, goring at the great beast's side and belly as he raced past. They were thrown down by the impact, but they were on their feet again instantly. As a group lured Old White in one direction, fifty Ganaks rushed in upon his sides and rear seeking to reach and tear him with their stout horns.

Perhaps they had overcome other mammoths in this way, for it was evident that they were but following an accustomed routine; but Old White was not as other mammoths. When he had felt a few horns tear his tough sides he ceased charging. He did not let any of them get behind him again. He moved slowly toward them, reminding von Horst of a huge cat stalking a bird. The bison-men waited for the charge, ready to leap aside and then in to gore him; but he did not charge. He came close and then made a short, quick rush, seized a bison-man, raised him high above his head and hurled him with terrific force among his fellows, downing a dozen of them. Before they could collect themselves,

Old White was among them, trampling and tossing, until those who managed to elude him were glad to run for their village as fast as they could go.

The mammoth pursued them for a short distance picking up a few stragglers and hurling them far ahead among the frightened, bellowing herd; then he turned about and came at his slow, swinging pace toward von Horst and the girl.

"Now he will kill us!" she cried. "Why didn't we run away while we had the chance?"

XXI

DESERTED

"HE WON'T hurt us," von Horst assured her.

"How do you know he won't?" she demanded. "You saw what he did to the Ganaks."

"We are friends, Old White and I."

"This is no time to laugh with words," she said. "It is very brave but it isn't good sense."

The mammoth was nearing them. La-ja involuntarily pressed close to von Horst. He threw a protective arm about her and held her still closer. He was aware that her attitude seemingly belied her repeated assurances of dislike and wondered if fear could so quickly overcome her pride. That did not seem at all like La-ja. He was puzzled, but he was not too insistent upon questioning any circumstance that brought her into his arms. The fact was enough. All that he could do was acknowledge another debt of gratitude to Old White.

The mammoth stopped in front of them. He seemed to be questioning the presence of the girl. Von Horst's only fear was that the great, savage beast might not accept her. He had known but one human friend. All others had been enemies to be killed. The man spoke to him and stroked the trunk that was reaching tentatively toward the girl. Then he gave the command to lift them to his back. There was a moment's hesitation as the sensitive tip moved slowly over La-ja. The girl did not shrink. For that von Horst was thankful. How very brave she was! The trunk encircled them, and again the girl's arms went around the man's neck. Old White tightened his grip. Von Horst repeated the command to lift them, and they were swung from the ground and deposited just behind the great head. At the man's signal, the mammoth moved off in the direction of Lo-har.

La-ja breathed a little sigh that was half gasp. "I do not understand," she said. "How can you make a wild tandor do what you tell him to do?"

Von Horst told her then of his first encounter with Old White and of all that had occurred since—his captivity among the mammoth-men, of the little canyon, and of his eventual escape.

"I saw you attack Frug," she said; "and then Skruf dragged me across the river, and I never knew whether you were killed by Frug or by the mammoth-men, or if they captured you.

"Skruf hid with me in a cave beside the river. He put a gag in my mouth so that I couldn't cry out and attract the attention of the mammoth-men. We heard them hunting us. I would rather have been captured by them than taken back to Basti, and Skruf knew it. I thought you might be a prisoner among them, too."

She caught herself quickly, as though she had spoken without thought. "Of course I didn't care. It was only that the country of the mammoth-men is much nearer Lo-har than Basti is. I did not want to be taken all the way back to Basti.

"We hid for a long time; then we started out again, but at the first sleep I escaped. The thongs he tied me with were so loose that I slipped my hands from them.

"I ran away toward Lo-har. I went a long way and thought that I was safe. I slept many times; so I know I must have come far. I was very lucky. I met only a few of the flesh-eaters and these always when there was a place to hide—a tree or a cave with a very small entrance. I saw no man until once I looked behind me from the top of a low hill and saw Skruf following me. He was a long way off, but I knew him at once. He saw me. It was very plain that he saw me, for he stopped suddenly and stood still for a moment; then he started after me at a trot. I turned and ran. I tried every way that I knew to throw him off my track, and after a long time I thought that I had succeeded. But I had not. He came upon me while I was sleeping, and started to drag me back to Basti. It was then that the bison-men discovered us. You know the rest."

"You have had a hard time of it, La-ja," said von Horst. "I can't understand how you have come through alive."

"I think I have had a very easy time of it," she replied. "Very few girls who are stolen from the tribe ever escape their captors. Many of them are killed; the others have to mate with men they do not like. That I would not do. I would kill myself first. I think I am a very lucky girl."

"But think of all the dangers and hardships you have had to face," he insisted.

"Oh, yes," she admitted, "it is not easy to be alone always with enemies. It is not pleasant, but I have not had so many dangers. The Gorbuses were the worst. I did not like them."

Von Horst was amazed. It seemed incredible that a girl could pass through what she had without being a nervous wreck, yet La-ja appeared to take it all as a matter of course. It was difficult for him not to compare her with girls of his own world and forget how different her environment had been. Where they walked with assurance, she might be as terrified as would they in Pellucidar—though it was not easy to visualize La-ja as terrified under any circumstances.

It often pleased him to dream of taking her back to the outer world with him. There were so many things, commonplace to him, that would astonish her—her first ride on a train, in an automobile, in an airplane; the sight of the great buildings, the giant liners, huge cities. He tried to imagine what the reaction would be of one who had never seen any of these things, nor dreamed of their existence, nor of the civilization that had produced them.

She would find many things foolish and impractical— the wearing of high-heeled shoes that pinched her feet; she would think it foolish to wear furs when it was not cold, to dress warmly in the daytime and go half naked at night. All clothes would hamper her; she would not like them. But with the beauty of her face and figure, her pride, and her femininity she would soon learn to like them, of that he was quite certain.

Poor little La-ja! What a crime it would be to let civilization spoil her. However, that was nothing for him to worry about. She would not have him even in Pellucidar, nor was there much likelihood that he would ever himself see the outer world again, much less take her or anyone else back with him.

With reveries such as these and desultory conversation with La-ja he whiled the time while Old White bore them in the direction of Lo-har. Even the larger beasts of prey they encountered on the way turned aside from the path of the great bull mammoth, so that their journey was one of ease, free from the constant menace of these fierce flesh-eaters which would have constantly harassed them had they been on foot.

They had slept three times and eaten not a few when La-ja announced that they were approaching Lo-har. They had halted to rest and sleep—it would be the last sleep before they reached Lo-har, and La-ja seemed preoccupied and dejected. During this last journey together she had been friendly and companionable, so that von Horst's hopes had risen; though he had had to admit to himself that she still gave him no reason to believe that side which they were camped and upon which great very happy—happier than he had been since he had entered this strange world; perhaps happier than he had ever been, for he had never been in love before.

They had made camp and he had gone out on the plain and brought down a small antelope with an arrow from his bow. Now they were grilling cuts over a small fire. Old White had moved ponderously to a clump of young trees which he was rapidly denuding of foliage. The noon-day sun beat down upon the open plain beside which they were camped and upon which great herds grazed peacefully, for the moment undisturbed by any prowling carnivore.

Von Horst felt the peace and contentment that hung over the scene like a white cloud above a summer sea, and his mood was in harmony with his environment. His eyes rested upon La-ja, devouring her; and almost upon his lips was an avowal of the passion that filled his whole being.

She chanced to turn and catch his eyes upon her; for a moment they held; then she looked off across the plain. She pointed.

"When we set out again," she said, "I go in that direction—alone."

"What do you mean?" he demanded. "That is not the

direction of Lo-har—it is straight ahead, in the direction we have been travelling."

"A great lake lies to our left," she explained. "We have had to make a detour to pass around it. You cannot see it from here because it lies in a deep basin rimmed by cliffs."

"You are not going alone," he said. "I am going with you."

"Haven't I made it clear to you many times that I do not want you to come with me? How many times must I tell you that I do not like you? Go away and leave me. Let me go back to my own people in peace."

Von Horst flushed. Bitter words were in his throat, but he choked them. All he said was, "I am going with you, because I—because—well, because you can't go on alone."

She rose. "I do not need you, and I do not want you," she said; then she went and lay down in the shade of a tree to sleep.

Von Horst sat brooding disconsolately. Old White, his meal finished, drank from the stream beside the camp and came and stood beneath a nearby tree, dozing. Von Horst knew that he would remain there and constitute a better guard than any man; so he stretched himself upon the ground and was soon asleep.

When he awoke, Old White was still standing in the shade, his great shaggy body rocking gently to and fro; the herds still grazed over the broad plain; the eternal noon-day sun still shone down serenely upon the peaceful scene. He might have slept for no more than a minute; or, he realized, he might have been sleeping for a week of outer-earthly time. He looked for La-ja. She was not where he had last seen her. A sudden presentiment of evil brought him to his feet. He looked quickly in all directions. The girl was nowhere in sight. He called her name aloud again and again, but there was no response.

Then he went quickly to where she had been sleeping and searched the ground in the vicinity of the camp. There was no sign that either man or beast had been there other than themselves; but this was not entirely strange, as the grass, close cropped by the grazing herds, would have registered no sign of an ordinary passing.

Presently he dismissed the possibility that La-ja had been taken forcibly by either beast or man. Had such an attempt been made she would have called to him for help, and surely Old White would have protected the camp from any intruder. There was but one explanation —La-ja had gone on alone, eluding him. She had told him that she did not want him to come with her. His insistence that he would come anyway had left her no alternative other than the thing she had done—she had simply run away from him.

His pride was hurt, but that hurt was as nothing to the ache in his heart. The bottom had dropped out of his world. There seemed nothing in life to look forward to. What was he to do? Where might he go? He had no idea where Sari lay, and only in Sari might he hope to find a friend in all this vast, savage world. But only for a moment was he undecided; then he called to Old White, and at his command the beast swung him to its back. As the mammoth moved off, von Horst guided it in the new direction La-ja had pointed out before they had slept. His mind was made up. He was going to Lo-har. While life remained in him he would not give up hope of winning the girl he loved.

He urged Old White on in the hope of overtaking the girl. Not knowing how long he had slept he had no idea how far ahead of him she might be. She had told him that Lo-har lay but a single march from their last camp site, yet on and on they went until he was half dead with fatigue; and at last Old White refused to go farther without rest, yet there was neither sign of La-ja nor of any village nor even of the great lake that she had told him they must skirt.

He wondered if he were searching in the right direction, for it was easily possible that the village might lie either to the right or left of his line of march; but it seemed strange that he should have passed close to any village without seeing some sign of man. Hunting parties were always abroad, and the sight of a stranger would have brought them to investigate and probably to have ki_ed. He banked on his acquaintance with La-ja, however, to get him a peaceable hearing from her father, Brun, the chief, when it was his intention to ask to be taken into the tribe.

At last he was forced to halt that Old White might feed and rest; but it was not until they finally did so beside a stream that he realized how much he, too, was in need of both food and sleep. He had brought with him, wrapped in its own hide, some of the antelope he had killed at his last camp; and upon this and some fruit he broke his long fast; then he slept.

He must have slept for a long time, for he was very tired; but with his safety assured by the watchful presence of Old White he slept soundly. When he awoke, something was touching his breast. He did not immediately open his eyes, for he recognized the feel of the moist tip of Old White's trunk upon his naked flesh. He just lay there luxuriating in the sensuous delight of the brief, lazy moments that lie between awakening and full consciousness. But as consciousness returned, bringing command of all the senses, he gradually became aware of an odor that was not the odor of Old White. It was a strong, acrid scent; and slowly he raised his lids.

A sudden numbness seized him as he recognized the creature that stood over him sniffing at his body with its

233

moist muzzle moving over his bare flesh. It was that most gigantic and feared of all Pellucidarian beasts of prey, the ryth, a colossal cave bear long extinct upon the outer crust.

He closed his eyes again and feigned death, for he had heard that a bear will not maul a dead body unless it is its own kill. He had little belief in the truth of the statement, but it was the proverbial straw and the only one. All that he could do was lie still and hope for the best.

The nose left his body. There was no sound but the breathing of the beast. What was it doing? The suspense was maddening, and at last he could endure it no longer. The bear was standing over him with its head turned to one side, looking away, sniffing, listening. Von Horst lay in a gentle depression beneath a wide-spreading tree. He could see but a short distance in the direction the bear was looking. Nor could the bear see farther than the summit of the gentle slope that ran down to the bank of the stream beside which von Horst lay, but it must have scented or heard something approaching.

Von Horst thought that it must be Old White returning. He must have wandered much farther from camp than usual. There would be a battle royal when he returned and saw the ryth menacing his friend. The man knew that Old White was afraid of nothing, and he knew the reputation of the mighty cave bear for fearlessness and bellicosity. He had been told that one of these great beasts could kill a mammoth with a single blow of its mighty paw; but Old White was not just *a* mammoth; he was *the* mammoth. The mammoth-men had said there was never one like him for size and ferocity and cunning. And then a man topped the rise and walked in full view of the bear and von Horst. He was quartering down the slope so that he was not facing them directly; and he had not yet seen them, for they were in the dense shade of the tree.

He was half way down the slope, and von Horst thought the bear was going to let him pass, when he saw them. Simultaneously von Horst recognized him. It was Daj, the young warrior from Lo-har whom he had met in the little canyon in Ja-ru, the land of the mammoth-men.

When Daj saw the bear he looked for the nearest tree. It was man's only defense against such a creature. As he started to run, the bear voiced a deafening roar and started for him. Von Horst sprang to his feet. He was saved, for he could clamber into the tree above now before the bear could turn and reach him. But what of Daj? The tree nearest him was evidently a little too far away to be reached before the bear overtook him, yet Daj was straining very muscle to reach it.

As von Horst had risen he had gathered up his bow and arrows that had lain on the ground beside him. In them he saw a possibility of saving Daj. Fitting an arrow to his bow he took aim and let drive. The missile sank deep in the bear's rump eliciting a roar of rage and pain and bringing it around with an alacrity and agility that belied its great bulk as it sought the temerarious creature that dared assault it; and upon the instant, without a pause, it charged von Horst.

He had saved Daj; but perhaps he had underestimated the safety of his own position, for he had not reckoned with the surprising agility and speed of the enormous ryth.

The instant that he had loosed the first arrow he had fitted another to his bow which he bent now until the point of the arrow rested upon his thumb, and when he loosed it he drooped his weapon and sprang for a tree branch directly above him.

He did not know if he had scored a hit or not. The

bear did not pause, but came thundering down upon him. He felt the wind of its raking talons against his legs as he drew them to the safety of the tree. A deep sigh of relief registered acknowledgement of his escape from a seemingly hopeless situation.

When he looked down he saw the bear standing beneath him pawing at the feathered shaft that protruded from the left side of its chest. It was roaring, but not so strongly now; and blood was flowing from its mouth. Von Horst saw that his last shot had delivered a serious wound, though perhaps not fatal. Those mighty, prehistoric creatures were most tenacious of life.

The bear pawed viciously at the shaft and then sprawled forward, struggled spasmodically, and lay still. Von Horst guessed that it had driven or twisted the arrow into its own heart, but he did not venture down at once. He looked for Daj but could not see him, as much foliage intervened; then he called his name aloud.

"Who are you?" came the answer.

"The mammoth-men called me Von; we met in the little canyon. Now do you recall me?"

"Yes. Because of you I escaped death that day. I could not very well forget you. What has happened to the bear? It is lying down. It looks as though it were dead, but what could have killed it?"

"Wait until I make sure that it's dead," cautioned von Horst. "If it is, we'll come down."

With his stone knife he hacked a branch from the tree and threw it down upon the bear. As the beast gave no sign that it had felt it, von Horst was satisfied that it was dead, and slipped down to the ground.

As he was retrieving his weapons Daj approached him, a friendly smile upon his face. "Now you have saved my life again," he said. "I do not know why, because we are not of the same tribe."

"We are of the same race," said von Horst; "we are both gilaks."

The Pellucidarian shrugged. "If everyone felt that way there would be too many gilaks in Pellucidar and all the game would soon be killed off."

Von Horst smiled as he thought of the vast area of the inner world with its handful of inhabitants and of the teeming city slums of the outer crust.

"For the good of the gilaks of Pellucidar," he said, "may you never be persuaded to the brotherhood of man."

"I do not know what you are talking about," admitted Daj; "but what I would like to know is what made the ryth die."

Von Horst showed him the bloody arrows that he had withdrawn from the carcass. "The one in his chest killed him," he said. "It punctured his heart."

"Those little slivers of wood killed a ryth!" exclaimed Daj.

"There was a lot of luck mixed in with them," admitted von Horst; "but if you get one of them into the heart of anything, it will kill."

"Yes, but how did you get it in? You couldn't go close enough to a ryth to stick it in without being killed, and they're too light to throw in as you might a spear."

Von Horst showed Daj his bow and explained its use, and the Pellucidarian was much interested. After he had examined it for a moment he handed it back.

"We'd better move away from here," he said. "That ryth was down here on the plain hunting. His mate may be around somewhere. If he doesn't show up she'll follow his scent until she finds him. This will not be a good place to be."

"Where are you going?" asked von Horst.

"To Lo-har," replied Daj. "I have been many sleeps on

the way from Ja-ru, but now I shall be there in three or four more sleeps."

"Three or four?" demanded von Horst. "I thought I was very close to Lo-har."

"No," said Daj, "but where are you going?"

"To Lo-har," replied von Horst.

"Why?"

"I have no other place to go. I am from another world to which I cannot possibly return. I know one person in Sari who would be my friend, but I cannot find my way to Sari. In Lo-har I know two people who should not dislike me. I am going there to ask Brun to make me a member of the tribe."

"Whom do you know in Lo-har?" asked Daj.

"You and La-ja," replied von Horst.

Daj scratched his head. "Brun will probably have you killed," he said. "If he doesn't, Gaz will kill you; but if you want to go to Lo-har, I will take you. You might as well die there as anywhere."

XXII

GAZ

THREE LONG MARCHES in the direction from which he had just come brought von Horst and Daj to the camp site at which La-ja had deserted the former and convinced him that the girl had deliberately set him upon the wrong trail. The realization of this fact, coupled with the desertion of Old White, disheartened him to such an extent that he seriously considered abandoning his evidently futile pursuit of La-ja; but when Daj was ready to set out after they had slept, von Horst accompanied him; though it only added to his depression when he found that the route toward Lo-har was that which he and La-ja had been following up until the moment that she had sent him off in the wrong direction.

One long march brought them to a sandstone canyon and the cliff-dwellings of Lo-har, where Daj was received with more show of enthusiasm and affection than von Horst had previously seen exhibited by the humans of Pellucidar. But of von Horst they were wary and suspicious, appraising him with hostile eyes while Daj explained innumerable times that the stranger was a friend who had liberated him from captivity and twice saved his life.

"What does he want in Lo-har?" demanded the sentry who had first halted them at a safe distance from the village, and the question was constantly repeated by others as they advanced.

In reply Daj explained that von Horst was a great warrior from another world who wished to come and live in Lo-har, joining the tribe; and all the while, paying no attention to the muttering and grumbling about him, von Horst searched for La-ja with eager eyes.

"Where is Brun?" demanded Daj. "He will decide whether or not the stranger remains."

"Brun is not here," replied a warrior.

"Where is he?"

"Perhaps he is dead. Many sleeps have passed since he went away to search for La-ja, his daughter."

"Then who is acting chief now?" asked Daj.

"Gaz," replied the other.

Daj appeared puzzled. "He was chosen by the warriors?" he asked.

The other shook his head. "No; he took the power, threatening to kill any who interfered. Gaz is a mighty man. No one has as yet disputed his right, though many would do so if they were not afraid, for we are not happy under Gaz."

"Where is he?" Daj's eyes were wandering about the village.

"He was gone after La-ja."

Von Horst was instantly alert and attentive. "Where has she gone?" he asked.

Both the warrior and Daj looked at him questioning, for Daj knew nothing of von Horst's love for La-ja. "Why do you want to know, stranger?" demanded the warrior suspiciously.

"If I know where the woman has gone, I shall be able to find the man."

Daj and the warrior nodded. "That is right," said the former, and then he asked a question that von Horst had wished to ask but had not dared. "Why has Gaz gone after La-ja? She has been missing for many sleeps, and her father has already gone after her. If Gaz were going after her, why didn't he go before this?"

"You do not understand," said the warrior. "La-ja returned a few sleeps ago, and Gaz claimed her as his mate; but she would have nothing to do with him. When he would have taken her to his cave by force, she eluded him and ran away."

"And Gaz?" asked von Horst.

"He followed her. Doubtless before this he has caught her and she is his mate. It is well for a girl, especially a chief's daughter, to show spirit. Gaz will like her better for it. Those who are too easy to get are not liked for so long a time as the others. Perhaps La-ja only ran away out of sight of the village and then waited for Gaz. Many a girl has done this."

"Which way did she go?" demanded von Horst again. His voice was hoarse and dead in his throat.

"If you know what is well for you you will not interfere

with Gaz now but wait until he returns. He will be bad enough then. If I were you, stranger, I'd get as far away from Lo-har as I could before Gaz comes back."

"Which way did he go?" repeated von Horst.

The warrior shook his head. "That way," he said, pointing up the canyon. "Beyond the divide at the head of the canyon is a beautiful valley. It is such a place as a man might take his woman—or a woman lure her man."

Von Horst shuddered; then without a word he set off toward the head of the canyon and the beautiful valley to which a woman might lure her man.

The warrior and Daj stood looking after him. The latter shook his head. "It is too bad," he said; "he is a great warrior and a good friend."

The warrior shrugged. "What difference does it make?" he asked. "Gaz will only kill him a little sooner; that is all."

As von Horst clambered the steep ascent at the head of the canyon his mind was a turmoil of hopes and fears and passion—of love and hate. The last vestige of centuries of civilization had fallen away, leaving him a stark cave man of the stone age. As some primitive ancestor of the outer crust may have done eons before, he sought his rival with murder in his heart. As for the woman he desired, he would take her now whether she wished it or not.

Beyond the summit he looked down into the most beautiful valley he had ever seen, but he gave it scarcely a glance. What his eyes sought was something far more beautiful. He sought for some sign of the direction in which the two had gone as he dropped down toward the floor of the valley, and at last he found it in a well marked game trail that wound beside a little stream that meandered down toward a larger river that he could faintly distinguish in the haze of the distance. Here was an occasional print of a tiny sandalled foot and often overlapping them those of a large foot that could have belonged only to a huge man.

Von Horst started along the trail at a trot. He wanted to call the girl's name aloud; but he knew that she would not reply even though she heard him, for had she not made it plain that a love such as his could arouse no corresponding emotion. He wondered vaguely what had become of his pride, that he could pursue a woman who hated him and have it in his heart to take her by force against her will. He thought that he should be ashamed of himself, but he was not. For a while he was puzzled; and then he realized that he had changed—that he was not the same man who had entered the inner world God only knew how long ago. Environment had metamorphosed him—savage Pellucidar had claimed him as her own.

The very thought of Gaz raised him to a fury. He realized that he had been hating the man for longer than he knew. He had no fear of him, as he had no fear of death. Perhaps it was the latter that kept him from fearing Gaz, for from all that he had heard of the man Gaz spelled death.

At a steady trot he pushed on. How far ahead they were he had no way of knowing. How much of truth or falsity there was in the insinuations of the warrior who had set him on the trail he could not even guess—the very thought of them made him frantic, the thought that he might be too late; but what was even worse was the haunting fear that La-ja had come willing and waited. She had told him that it was her duty to mate with a mighty warrior, and why not Gaz? Von Horst groaned aloud and quickened his pace. If ever a man suffered the tortures of the damned, it was he.

He came upon a place where the trail branched, a

smaller, less worn trail running off at right angles toward the stream that lay to his right. After a moment's careful inspection he determined that the two he sought had taken the smaller trail, and in the mud of both river banks at the crossing he again found the spoor, this time well defined. From there the trail ran directly into the mouth of a small side canyon, and afterward he had only to follow the floor of the canyon upward. Presently he heard a commotion ahead and the hoarse voice of a man shouting. He could not distinguish the words. The voice came from beyond a bend in the canyon which hid the speaker from his sight.

From now on he should have gone cautiously, but he did not. Instead he pushed on even faster, taking no precautions; and thus he came suddenly upon Gaz and La-ja. The latter was clinging precariously to a tiny ledge upon the face of a lofty escarpment. Her feet rested upon this narrow support, her body was flattened against the face of the cliff, her arms were outspread, her palms pressed tightly against the hard stone. Gaz, unable to scale the cliff, stood on the ground below shouting orders for La-ja to descend to him. At sight of the two and their positions that so eloquently told a story, von Horst breathed a sigh of relief—he had not been too late!

Suddenly Gaz picked up a rock and hurled it at La-ja. "Come down!" he roared, "or I'll knock you down." The rock struck the face of the cliff close beside La-ja's head. Gaz stooped to take up another.

Von Horst shouted at him, and the man wheeled in surprise. The man from the outer crust reached over his shoulder for an arrow to fit to his bow. He had no compunctions whatsoever about shooting down a man armed only with a crude spear and a stone knife. To his astonishment, he found that his quiver was empty.

Where could his arrows have gone? He was sure he had had them when he entered the village. Then he recalled how the natives had pulled and hauled him around, milling and pressing against him. It must have been then that someone had taken his arrows.

Gaz was coming toward him belligerently. "Who are you?" he demanded. "What do you want here?"

"I have come for you, Gaz," replied von Horst. "I have come to kill you and take the girl for myself."

Gaz roared and came on. He thought it a huge joke that any warrior should challenge his supremacy. La-ja turned her head far enough so that she could look down. What were her feelings when she recognized von Horst, as she must have done immediately? Who may know? As a matter of fact she gave no indication that she even saw him; but once, a moment later, when he glanced away from Gaz momentarily, von Horst saw that the girl was descending. What her intentions he could not even guess. She might be going to help the man of her choice in the impending battle, or she might be going to take advantage of the preoccupation of the two men to run away again.

"Who are you?" demanded Gaz. "I never saw you before."

"I am von Horst, and La-ja is my woman," growled the other.

"Do you know who I am?"

"You're the man I've crossed a world to kill," replied von Horst. "You're Gaz."

"Go away!" shouted La-ja. "Go away before Gaz kills you. I won't have you—not if you killed a thousand Gazes would I have you. Run! Run while you can."

Von Horst looked at Gaz. He was a monster-man, an enormous, bearded fellow who might have weighed well over three hundred pounds; and he was as gross and repulsive and brutal in appearance as he was large. His snaggle teeth were bared in a snarl as he charged von Horst. The latter had no fear. He had met warriors of the stone age before. They had no skill; and the hairy, massive bodies of some of them suggested strength far greater than they possessed. Von Horst had discovered that he was stronger than any he had met. They had had only an advantage in weight, nor was that always an advantage, as it lessened their agility.

Von Horst's patience with La-ja was at an end. He wanted to be done with Gaz as quickly as possible so that he could take the girl in hand. He even contemplated giving her a sound beating. He thought that she deserved it. He was thinking in terms of the stone age.

As Gaz charged down upon him, von Horst struck him a heavy blow in the face, as he stepped aside out of the path of the huge body. Gaz staggered and let out a bellow of rage, and as he turned to rush von Horst again he drew his stone knife from his G string. He, too, wished to end the duel at once; for he was crazed with chagrin that this smaller man had defied him and had done the first damage in the fight—all in the presence of the woman he had chosen to be his mate. Much more of the same and he would be the laughing stock of the village.

Von Horst saw the weapon in Gaz's hand and drew his own. This time he waited, and Gaz came in more slowly. When he was quite near von Horst, he leaped in, swinging a terrific knife blow at his antagonist's chest. Von Horst parried with his left arm, plunged his blade into Gaz's side, and leaped away; but as he did so his foot struck a stone protruding above the ground, and he went down. Instantly Gaz was on top of him, hurling his great carcass full upon the body of his fallen antagonist. One great paw reached for von Horst's throat, the other drove the stone blade down toward his heart.

The European caught the other's wrist, stopping the descending knife; but with his other hand Gaz was choking the life from him, and at the same time he was trying to wrench his knife hand free and plunge the weapon into von Horst's heart. As von Horst had fallen he had dropped his own knife. Now, while he held Gaz's weapon from him he groped for his own on the ground about him. Occasionally he relinquished his search to strike Gaz a heavy blow in the face, which always caused him to loosen his hold upon the other's throat, giving von Horst an opportunity to gulp in a mouthful of fresh air; but the man from the outer world realized that he was weakening rapidly and that unless he found his knife the end would come quickly.

He had struck Gaz again heavily, and when he reached down again to grope for his weapon his hand contacted it immediately, as though someone had placed it in his grasp. He did not pause then to seek an explanation; in fact the only thing that mattered was that he possessed the knife.

He saw Gaz glance back and heard him curse; then he drove his blade deep into the left side of the cave-man. Gaz screamed and, releasing his hold on von Horst's throat, sought to seize his knife arm; but the other eluded him, and again and again the stone knife was driven into his bleeding side.

Then Gaz tried to get up and away from von Horst, but the latter seized his beard and held him. Relentlessly he struck again and again. Gaz's roars and screams diminished. His body commenced to slump; then, with a final shudder, it collapsed upon the victor.

Von Horst pushed it aside and rose. Panting, blood-covered, he looked about for the woman—his woman now. He saw her standing there nearby wide-eyed, incredulous. She came slowly toward him. "You have killed Gaz!" she said in an awed whisper.

"And what of it?" he demanded.

"I didn't think you could do it. I thought that he would kill you."

"I'm sorry to disappoint you," he snapped. "I wonder if you realize what it means."

"I am not disappointed," she said. "And what does it mean?"

"It means that I am going to take you. You are mine. Do you understand? You are mine!"

A slow smile broke like sunlight through the clouds of doubt.

"I have been yours almost from the first," she said, "but you were too stupid to realize it."

"What?" he ejaculated. "What do you mean? You have done nothing but repulse me and try to drive me away from you. When I slept, you ran off and left me after directing me on the wrong trail."

"Yes," she answered, "I did all those things. I did them because I loved you. I knew that if I told you I returned your love you would follow me to Lo-har, and I thought that if you came here you would be killed. How could I guess that you could kill Gaz, whom no man has ever before been able to kill?"

"La-ja!" he whispered, and took her in his arms.

Together they returned to the village of Lo-har. The warriors and the women clustered about them. "Where is Gaz?" they asked.

"Gaz is dead," said La-ja.

"Then we have no chief."

"Here is your chief," replied the girl, laying a hand upon von Horst's shoulder.

Some of the warriors laughed, others grumbled. "He is a stranger. What has he done that he should be chief?"

"When Brun went away, you let Gaz be chief because you were afraid of him. You hated him; and he was a poor chief, but none of you was brave enough to try to kill him. Von killed Gaz in a fair fight with knives, and he has taken the daughter of your chief as mate. Until Brun returns what warrior among you is better qualified to be chief than Von? If any thinks differently let him step forward and fight Von with his bare hands."

And so Lieutenant Frederich Wilhelm Eric von Mendeldorf und von Horst became chief of the cliff-dwellers of Lo-har. He was a wise chief, for he combined with the psychology of the cave man, that he had acquired, all the valuable knowledge of another environment. He became almost a god to them, so that they no longer regretted the loss of Brun.

And then, after a while, came rumors of a strange people that were reported to have come up out of the south. They had weapons against which neither man nor beast could stand—weapons that made a great noise and vomited smoke and killed at a distance.

When von Horst heard these rumors he thrilled with excitement. Such men could only be members of the company that had come from the outer crust in the giant dirigible O-220—his friends. Doubtless they were searching for him. He called his warriors to him. "I am going out to meet these strangers of whom we have heard rumors. I think they are my friends. But if they are not my friends, they will be able to kill many of us with the weapons they have before we can get near enough to kill them. How many of you wish to go with me?"

They all volunteered, but he took only about fifty warriors. La-ja accompanied them, and when they set out they had only the vaguest of rumors to guide them. But as they went south and talked with men of other tribes, whom they captured along the way, the reports became more definite; and then at last von Horst's scouts came back from the front and reported that they had seen a body of men camped by a river a short distance away.

Led by von Horst, the cave-men of Lo-har crept close to the camp of the strangers. Here von Horst saw armed men who bore rifles and bandoleers of cartridges. The arrangement and discipline of the camp, the sentries, the military air assured him that these people had had contact with civilization. But he was still too far away to recognize faces if there were any there that he knew. But of one thing he was confident—this was no party from the O-220.

He whispered to his warriors for a moment; then he rose alone and walked slowly down toward the camp. He had taken but a few steps in the open before a sentry discovered him and gave the alarm. Von Horst saw men rise all about the camp and look toward him. He raised both hands above his head as a sign that he came in peace. No one spoke as he crossed the open ground to the very edge of the camp; then a man ran forward with glad cry.

"Von!"

It was a moment before von Horst recognized who it was that spoke his name. It was Dangar, and behind Dangar were Thorek, Lotai, and Mumal. Von Horst was astounded. How had these come together? Who were the armed men?

Presently a tall, fine looking man came forward. "You are Lieutenant von Horst?" he asked.

"Yes; and you?"

"David Innes. When the O-220 returned to the outer crust and Jason Gridley decided to go back with it, he made me promise that I would equip an expedition and make a thorough search for you. I did so immediately I returned to Sari. I had no luck until some of my men met Dangar returning to Sari after a long absence. He guided us to The Forest of Death. Once we had passed through that we had no idea in what direction to search until we came upon Thorek, Lotai, and Mumal escaping from the land of the mammoth-men.

"They told us that they believed that you had escaped, and they thought you might be searching for Lo-har. We had never heard of Lo-har, but we succeeded in taking a prisoner who knew the direction in which the country lay. Later we came upon a man named Skruf whom you had wounded with an arrow. We promised him protection and he directed us to the village of the bison-men. Now we were nearing Lo-har, but still it was difficult to find. These people only knew the general direction in which it lay. Our one hope was to capture a Lo-harian. This we did before the last sleep. He is with us now and guiding us much against his will toward his own country, for he thinks we will turn upon him and his people."

"Who is he?" asked von Horst.

"Brun, the chief of the Lo-harians," replied Innes.

Von Horst signalled for his tribesmen to come in to the camp, and asked that Brun be brought. Innes sent for him, telling him that some of his own people had come to meet him. But when Brun came and saw von Horst he drew himself up very proudly and turned his back.

"I do not know this man," he said. "He is not of Lo-har."

"Look at those who are coming, Brun," suggested von Horst. "You will know them all, especially La-ja."

"La-ja!" exclaimed the chief. "I had given her up for dead. I have searched a world for her."

The men of Lo-har camped with the men of Sari in friendship, and there was much palaver, and a great deal of food was eaten, and they slept twice in that one camp before they spoke of breaking it.

"You will come back to Sari with us, Lieutenant?" asked Innes. "Gridley may come back on another expedition at any time now; it may be your only chance to return to the outer crust."

Von Horst glanced at a little, yellow haired cave-girl gnawing on a bone.

"I am not at all sure that I care to return to the outer crust," he said.

FAFHRD AND THE
GRAY MOUSER
SAGA